The Woman
with the Fan

by

Robert Hichens

Double 9
BOOKS

The Woman with the Fan
by Robert Hichens

Copyright © 2024

All Rights reserved.

ISBN: 978-93-65784-50-3

Published by

DOUBLE 9 BOOKS
2/13-B, Ansari Road
Daryaganj, New Delhi – 110002
info@double9books.com
www.double9books.com
Tel. 011-40042856

ABOUT THE AUTHOR

Robert Hichens (1864–1950) was a versatile British author and journalist, best known for his work in the Gothic and supernatural fiction genres. Born in Speldhurst, Kent, Hichens initially studied music before turning to writing, a field where he would leave a lasting mark. He gained early fame with his novel "The Green Carnation" (1894), a satire that drew attention for its thinly veiled portrayal of prominent figures in British society. Hichens's literary career spanned several decades, during which he explored a variety of themes, but he is particularly remembered for his contributions to supernatural and horror fiction. His works often delve into psychological drama, blending the eerie and the mysterious with profound character studies. "The Return of the Soul," one of his notable works, exemplifies his skill in creating atmospheric and suspenseful narratives that engage readers on multiple levels. Aside from his fiction, Hichens was also a successful journalist, traveling extensively and drawing upon his experiences in his writing. His ability to capture the uncanny and the supernatural, while also providing deep psychological insight, has secured his place as a significant figure in British literature, particularly within the Gothic and horror traditions.

CONTENTS

CHAPTER I 7

CHAPTER II 18

CHAPTER III 29

CHAPTER IV 37

CHAPTER V 42

CHAPTER VI 60

CHAPTER VII 72

CHAPTER VIII 87

CHAPTER IX 111

CHAPTER X 121

CHAPTER XI 132

CHAPTER XII 144

CHAPTER XIII 162

CHAPTER XIV 170

CHAPTER XV 178

CHAPTER XVI 198

CHAPTER XVII 199

CHAPTER XVIII 204

CHAPTER XIX 210

CHAPTER XX 221

CHAPTER XXI 235

EPILOGUE 242

CHAPTER I

IN a large and cool drawing-room of London a few people were scattered about, listening to a soprano voice that was singing to the accompaniment of a piano. The sound of the voice came from an inner room, towards which most of these people were looking earnestly. Only one or two seemed indifferent to the fascination of the singer.

A little woman, with oily black hair and enormous dark eyes, leaned back on a sofa, playing with a scarlet fan and glancing sideways at a thin, elderly man, who gazed into the distance from which the voice came. His mouth worked slightly under his stiff white moustache, and his eyes, in colour a faded blue, were fixed and stern. Upon his knees his thin and lemon-coloured hands twitched nervously, as if they longed to grasp something and hold it fast. The little dark woman glanced down at these hands, and then sharply up at the elderly man's face. A faint and malicious smile curved her full lips, which were artificially reddened, and she turned her shoulder to him with deliberation and looked about the room.

On all the faces in it, except one, she perceived intent expressions. A sleek and plump man, with hanging cheeks, a hooked nose, and hair slightly tinged with grey and parted in the middle, was the exception. He sat in a low chair, pouting his lips, playing with his single eyeglass, and looking as sulky as an ill-conditioned school-boy. Once or twice he crossed and uncrossed his short legs with a sort of abrupt violence, laid his fat, white hands on the arms of the chair, lifted them, glanced at his rosy and shining nails, and frowned. Then he shut his little eyes so tightly that the skin round them became wrinkled, and, stretching out his feet, seemed almost angrily endeavouring to fall asleep.

A tall young man, who was sitting alone not far off, cast a glance of contempt at him, and then, as if vexed at having bestowed upon him even this slight attention, leaned forward, listening with eagerness to the soprano voice. The little dark woman observed him carefully above the scarlet feathers of her fan, which she now held quite still. His face was lean and brown. His eyes were long and black, heavy-lidded, and shaded by big lashes which curled upward. His features were good. The nose and chin were short and decided, but the mouth was melancholy, almost weak. On his upper lip grew a short moustache, turned up at the ends. His body was slim and muscular.

After watching him for a little while the dark woman looked again at the elderly man beside her, and then quickly back to the young fellow. She seemed to be comparing the two attentions, of age and of youth. Perhaps she found something horrible in the process for she suddenly lost her expression of sparkling and birdlike sarcasm, and bending her arm, as if overcome with lassitude, she let her fan drop on her knees, and stared moodily at the carpet.

A very tall woman, with snow-white hair and a face in which nobility and weariness were mated, let fall two tears, and a huge man, with short, bronze-coloured hair and a protruding lower jaw, who was sitting opposite to her, noticed them and suddenly looked proud.

The light soprano voice went on singing an Italian song about a summer night in Venice, about stars, dark waters and dark palaces, heat, and the sound of music, and of gondoliers calling over the lagoons to their comrades. It was an exquisite voice; not large, but flexible and very warm. The pianoforte accompaniment was rather uneasy and faltering. Now and then, when it became blurred and wavering, the voice was abruptly hard and decisive, once even piercing and almost shrewish. Then the pianist, as if attacked by fear, played louder and hurried the tempo, the little dark woman smiled mischievously, the white-haired woman put her handkerchief to her eyes, and the young man looked as if he wished to commit murder. But the huge man with the bronze hair went on looking equably proud.

When the voice died away there was distinct, though slight, applause, which partially drowned the accompanist's muddled conclusion. Then a woman walked in from the second drawing-room with an angry expression on her face.

She was tall and slight. Her hair and eyes were light yellow-brown, and the former had a natural wave in it. Her shoulders and bust were superb, and her small head was beautifully set on a lovely, rather long, neck. She had an oval face, with straight, delicate features, now slightly distorted by temper. But the most remarkable thing about her was her complexion. Her skin was exquisite, delicately smooth and white, warmly white like a white rose. She did nothing to add to its natural beauty, though nearly every woman in London declared that she had a special preparation and always slept in a mask coated thickly with it. The Bond Street oracles never received a visit from her. She had been born with an enchanting complexion, a marvellous skin. She was young, just twenty-four. She let herself alone because she knew improvement—in that direction—was not possible. The mask coated with

Juliet paste, or Aphrodite ivorine, existed only in the radiant imaginations of her carefully-arranged acquaintances.

In appearance she was a siren. By nature she was a siren too. But she had a temper and sometimes showed it. She showed it now.

As she walked in slowly all the scattered people leaned forward, murmuring their thanks, and the men stood up and gathered round her.

"Beautiful! Beautiful!" muttered the thin, elderly man in a hoarse voice, striking his fingers repeatedly against the palms of his withered hands.

The young man looked at the singer and said nothing; but the anger in her face was reflected in his, and mingled with a flaming of sympathy that made his appearance almost startling. The white-haired woman clasped the singer's hands and said, "Thank you, dearest!" in a thrilling voice, and the little dark woman with the red fan cried out, "Viola, you simply pack up Venice, carry it over the Continent and set it down here in London!"

Lady Holme frowned slightly.

"Thank you, thank you, you good-natured dears," she said with an attempt at lightness. Then, hearing the thin rustle of a dress, she turned sharply and cast an unfriendly glance at a mild young woman with a very pointed nose, on which a pair of eyeglasses sat astride, who came meekly forward, looking self-conscious, and smiling with one side of her mouth. The man with the protruding jaw, who was Lord Holme, said to her, in a loud bass voice:

"Thanks, Miss Filberte, thanks."

"Oh, not at all, Lord Holme," replied the accompanist with a sudden air of rather foolish delight. "I consider it an honour to accompany an amateur who sings like Lady Holme."

She laid a slight emphasis on the word "amateur."

Lady Holme suddenly walked forward to an empty part of the drawing-room. The elderly man, whose name was Sir Donald Ulford, made a movement as if to follow her, then cleared his throat and stood still looking after her. Lord Holme stuck out his under jaw. But Lady Cardington, the white-haired woman spoke to him softly, and he leaned over to her and replied. The sleek man, whose name was Mr. Bry, began to talk about Tschaikowsky to Mrs. Henry Wolfstein, the woman with the red fan. He uttered his remarks authoritatively in a slow and languid voice, looking at the pointed toes of his shoes. Conversation became general.

Robin Pierce, the tall young man, stood alone for a few minutes. Two or three times he glanced towards Lady Holme, who had sat down on a sofa, and was opening and shutting a small silver box which she had picked up from a table near her. Then he walked quietly up the room and sat down beside her.

"Why on earth didn't you accompany yourself?" he asked in a low voice. "You knew what a muddler that girl was, I suppose."

"Yes. She plays like a distracted black beetle—horrid creature!"

"Then—why?"

"I look ridiculous sitting at the piano."

"Ridiculous—you—"

"Well, I hold them far more when I stand up. They can't get away from me then."

"And you'd rather have your singing ruined than part for a moment with a scrap of your physical influence, of the influence that comes from your beauty, not your talent—your face, not your soul. Viola, you're just the same."

"Lady Holme," she said.

"P'sh! Why?"

"My little husband's fussy."

"And much you care if he is."

"Oh, yes, I do. He sprawls when he fusses and knocks things over, and then, when I've soothed him, he always goes and does Sandow exercises and gets bigger. And he's big enough as it is. I must keep him quiet."

"But you can't keep the other men quiet. With your face and your voice—"

"Oh, it isn't the voice," she said with contempt.

He looked at her rather sadly.

"Why will you put such an exaggerated value on your appearance? Why will you never allow that three-quarters at least of your attraction comes from something else?"

"What?"

"Your personality—your self."

"My soul!" she said, suddenly putting on a farcically rapt and yearning expression and speaking in a hollow, hungry voice. "Are we in the prehistoric Eighties?"

"We are in the unchanging world."

"Unchanging! My dear boy!"

"Yes, unchanging," he repeated obstinately.

He pressed his lips together and looked away. Miss Filberte was cackling and smiling on a settee, with a man whose figure presented a succession of curves, and who kept on softly patting his hands together and swaying gently backwards and forwards.

"Well, Mr. Pierce, what's the matter?"

"Mr. Pierce!" he said, almost savagely.

"Yes, of the English Embassy in Rome, rising young diplomat and full of early Eighty yearns—"

"How the deuce can you be as you are and yet sing as you do?" he exclaimed, turning on her. "You say you care for nothing but the outside of things—the husk, the shell, the surface. You think men care for nothing else. Yet when you sing you—you—"

"What do I do?"

"It's as if another woman than you were singing in you—a woman totally unlike you, a woman who believes in, and loves, the real beauty which you care nothing about."

"The real beauty that rules the world is lodged in the epidermis," she said, opening her fan and smiling slowly. "If this"—she touched her face—"were to be changed into—shall we say a Filberte countenance?"

"Oh!" he exclaimed.

"There! You see, directly I put the matter before you, you have to agree with me!"

"No one could sing like you and have a face like a silly sheep."

"Poor Miss Filberte! Well, then, suppose me disfigured and singing better than ever—what man would listen to me?"

"I should."

"For half a minute. Then you'd say, 'Poor wretch, she's lost her voice!' No, no, it's my face that sings to the world, my face the world loves to listen to, my face that makes me friends and—enemies."

She looked into his eyes with impertinent directness.

"It's my face that's made Mr. Robin Pierce deceive himself into the belief that he only worships women for their souls, their lovely natures, their—"

"Do you know that in a way you are a singularly modest woman?" he suddenly interrupted.

"Am I? How?"

"In thinking that you hold people only by your appearance, that your personality has nothing to say in the matter."

"I am modest, but not so modest as that."

"Well, then?"

"Personality is a crutch, a pretty good crutch; but so long as men are men they will put crutches second and—something else first. Yes, I know I'm a little bit vulgar, but everybody in London is."

"I wish you lived in Rome."

"I've seen people being vulgar there too. Besides, there may be reasons why it would not be good for me to live in Rome."

She glanced at him again less impertinently, and suddenly her whole body looked softer and kinder.

"You must put up with my face, Robin," she added. "It's no good wishing me to be ugly. It's no use. I can't be."

She laughed. Her ill-humour had entirely vanished.

"If you were—" he said. "If you were—!"

"What then?"

"Do you think no one would stick to you—stick to you for yourself?"

"Oh, yes."

"Who, then?"

"Quite several old ladies. It's very strange, but old ladies of a certain class—the almost obsolete class that wears caps and connects piety with black brocade—like me. They think me 'a bright young thing.' And so I am."

"I don't know what you are. Sometimes I seem to divine what you are, and then—then your face is like a cloud which obscures you—except when you are singing."

She laughed frankly.

"Poor Robin! It was always your great fault—trying to plumb shallows and to take high dives into water half a foot deep."

He was silent for a minute. At last he said:

"And your husband?"

"Fritz!"

His forehead contracted.

"Fritz—yes. What does he do? Try to walk in ocean depths?"

"You needn't sneer at Fritz," she said sharply.

"I beg your pardon."

"Fritz doesn't bother about shallows and depths. He loves me absurdly, and that's quite enough for him."

"And for you."

She nodded gravely.

"And what would Fritz do if you were to lose your beauty? Would he be like all the other men? Would he cease to care?"

For the first time Lady Holme looked really thoughtful—almost painfully thoughtful.

"One's husband," she said slowly. "Perhaps he's different. He—he ought to be different."

A faint suggestion of terror came into her large brown eyes.

"There's a strong tie, you know, whatever people may say, a very strong tie in marriage," she murmured, as if she were thinking out something for herself. "Fritz ought to love me, even if—if—"

She broke off and looked about the room. Robin Pierce glanced round too over the chattering guests sitting or standing in easy or lazy postures, smiling vaguely, or looking grave and indifferent. Mrs. Wolfstein was laughing, and yawned suddenly in the midst of her mirth. Lady Cardington said something apparently tragic, to Mr. Bry, who was polishing his eyeglass and pouting out his dewy lips. Sir Donald Ulford, wandering round the walls, was examining the pictures upon them. Lady Manby, a woman with a pyramid of brown hair and an aggressively flat back, was telling a story. Evidently it was a comic history of disaster. Her gestures were full of deliberate exaggeration, and she appeared to be impersonating by turns two or three different people, each of whom had a perfectly ridiculous personality. Lord Holme burst into a roar of laughter. His big bass voice vibrated through the room. Suddenly Lady Holme laughed too.

"Why are you laughing?" Robin Pierce asked rather harshly. "You didn't hear what Lady Manby said."

"No, but Fritz is so infectious. I believe there are laughter microbes. What a noise he makes! It's really a scandal."

And she laughed again joyously.

"You don't know much about women if you think any story of Lady Manby's is necessary, to prompt my mirth. Poor dear old Fritz is quite enough. There he goes again!"

Robin Pierce began to look stiff with constraint, and just then Sir Donald Ulford, in his progress round the walls, reached the sofa where they were sitting.

"You are very fortunate to possess this Cuyp, Lady Holme," he said in a voice from which all resonance had long ago departed.

"Alas, Sir Donald, cows distress me! They call up sad memories. I was chased by one in the park at Grantoun when I was a child. A fly had stung it, so it tried to kill me. This struck me as unreason run riot, and ever since then I have wished the Spaniards would go a step farther and make cow-fights the national pastime. I hate cows frankly."

Sir Donald sat down in an armchair and looked, with his faded blue eyes, into the eyes of his hostess. His drawn yellow face was melancholy, like the face of one who had long been an invalid. People who knew him well, however, said there was nothing the matter with him, and that his appearance had not altered during the last twenty years.

"You can hate nothing beautiful," he said with a sort of hollow assurance.

"I think cows hideous."

"Cuyp's?"

"All cows. You've never had one running after you."

She took up her gloves, which she had laid down on the table beside her, and began to pull them gently through her fingers. Both Sir Donald and Robin looked at her hands, which were not only beautiful in shape but extraordinarily intelligent in their movements. Whatever they did they did well, without hesitation or bungling. Nobody had ever seen them tremble.

"Do you consider that anything that can be dangerous for a moment must be hideous for ever?" asked Sir Donald, after a slight pause.

"I'm sure I don't know. But I truly think cows hideous—I truly do."

"Don't put on your gloves," exclaimed Robin at this moment.

Sir Donald glanced at him and said:

"Thank you."

"Why not?" said Lady Holme.

It was obvious to both men that there was no need to answer her question. She laid the gloves in her lap, smoothed them with her small fingers, and kept silence. Silence was characteristic of her. When she was in society she sometimes sat quite calmly and composedly without uttering a word. After watching her for a minute or two, Sir Donald said:

"You must know Venice very well and understand it completely."

"Oh, I've been there, of course."

"Recently?"

"Not so very long ago. After my marriage Fritz took me all over Europe."

"And you loved Venice."

Sir Donald did not ask a question, he made a statement.

"No. It didn't agree with me. It depressed me. We were there in the mosquito season."

"What has that to do with it?"

"My dear Sir Donald, if you'd ever had a hole in your net you'd know. I made Fritz take me away after two days, and I've never been back. I don't want to have my one beauty ruined."

Sir Donald did not pay the reasonable compliment. He only stretched out his lean hands over his knees, and said:

"Venice is the only ideal city in Europe."

"You forget Paris."

"Paris!" said Sir Donald. "Paris is a suburb of London and New York. Paris is no longer the city of light, but the city of pornography and dressmakers."

"Well, I don't know exactly what pornography is—unless it's some new process for taking snapshots. But I do know what gowns are, and I love Paris. The Venice shops are failures and the Venice mosquitoes are successes, and I hate Venice."

An expression of lemon-coloured amazement appeared upon Sir Donald's face, and he glanced at Robin Pierce as if requesting the answer to a riddle. Robin looked rather as if he were enjoying himself, but the puzzled melancholy grew deeper on Sir Donald's face. With the air of a man determined to reassure his mind upon some matter, however, he spoke again.

"You visited the European capitals?" he said.

"Yes, all of them."

"Constantinople?"

"Terrible place! Dogs, dogs, nothing but dogs."

"Did you like Petersburg?"

"No, I couldn't bear it. I caught cold there."

"And that was why you hated it?"

"Yes. I went out one night with Fritz on the Neva to hear a woman in a boat singing—a peasant girl with high cheek-bones—and I caught a frightful chill."

"Ah!" said Sir Donald. "What was the song? I know a good many of the Northern peasant songs."

Suddenly Lady Holme got up, letting her gloves fall to the ground.

"I'll sing it to you," she said.

Robin Pierce touched her arm.

"For Heaven's sake not to Miss Filberte's accompaniment!"

"Very well. But come and sit where you can see me."

"I won't," he said with brusque obstinacy.

"Madman!" she answered. "Anyhow, you come, Sir Donald."

And she walked lightly away towards the piano, followed by Sir Donald, who walked lightly too, but uncertainly, on his thin, stick-like legs.

"What are you up to, Vi?" said Lord Holme, as she came near to him.

"I'm going to sing something for Sir Donald."

"Capital! Where's Miss Filberte?"

"Here I am!" piped a thin alto voice.

There was a rustle of skirts as the accompanist rose hastily from her chair.

"Sit down, please, Miss Filberte," said Lady Holme in a voice of ice.

Miss Filberte sat down like one who has been knocked on the head with a hammer, and Lady Holme went alone to the piano, turned the button that raised the music-stool, sat down too, holding herself very upright, and played some notes. For a moment, while she played, her face was so determined and pitiless that Mr. Bry, unaware that she was still thinking about Miss Filberte, murmured to Lady Cardington:

"Evidently we are in for a song about Jael with the butter in the lordly dish omitted."

Then an expression of sorrowful youth stole into Lady Holme's eyes, changed her mouth to softness and her cheeks to curving innocence. She leaned a little way from the piano towards her audience and sang, looking up into vacancy as if her world were hidden there. The song had the clear melancholy and the passion of a Northern night. It brought the stars out within that room and set purple distances before the eyes. Water swayed in it, but languidly, as water sways at night in calm weather, when the black spars of ships at anchor in sheltered harbours are motionless as fingers of skeletons pointing towards the moon. Mysterious lights lay round a silent shore. And in the wide air, on the wide waters, one woman was singing to herself of a sorrow that was deep as the grave, and that no one upon the earth knew of save she who sang. The song was very short. It had only two little verses. When it was over, Sir Donald, who had been watching the singer, returned to the sofa, where Robin Pierce was sitting with his eyes shut and, again striking his fingers against the palms of his hands, said: "I have heard that song at night on the Neva, and yet I never heard it before."

People began getting up to go away. It was past eleven o'clock. Sir Donald and Robin Pierce stood together, saying good-bye to Lady Holme. As she held out her hand to the former, she said:

"Oh, Sir Donald, you know Russia, don't you?"

"I do."

"Then I want you to tell me the name of that stuff they carry down the Neva in boats—the stuff that has such a horrible smell. That song always reminds me of it, and Fritz can't remember the name."

"Nor can I," said Sir Donald, rather abruptly. "Good-night, Lady Holme."

He walked out of the room, followed by Robin.

CHAPTER II

LORD HOLME'S house was in Cadogan Square. When Sir Donald had put on his coat in the hall he turned to Robin Pierce and said:

"Which way do you go?"

"To Half Moon Street," said Robin.

"We might walk, if you like. I am going the same way.

"Certainly."

They set out slowly. It was early in the year. Showers of rain had fallen during the day. The night was warm, and the damp earth in the Square garden steamed as if it were oppressed and were breathing wearily. The sky was dark and cloudy, and the air was impregnated with a scent to which many things had contributed, each yielding a fragment of the odour peculiar to it. Rain, smoke, various trees and plants, the wet paint on a railing, the damp straw laid before the house of an invalid, the hothouse flowers carried by a woman in a passing carriage—these and other things were represented in the heavy atmosphere which was full of the sensation of life. Sir Donald expanded his nostrils.

"London, London!" he said. "I should know it if I were blind."

"Yes. The London smell is not to be confused with the smell of any other place. You have been back a good while, I believe?"

"Three years. I am laid on the London shelf now."

"You have had a long life of work—interesting work."

"Yes. Diplomacy has interesting moments. I have seen many countries. I have been transferred from Copenhagen to Teheran, visited the Sultan of Morocco at Fez, and—" he stopped. After a pause he added: "And now I sit in London clubs and look out of bay windows."

They walked on slowly.

"Have you known our hostess of to-night long?" Sir Donald asked presently.

"A good while—quite a good while. But I'm very much away at Rome now. Since I have been there she has married."

"I have only met her to speak to once before to-night, though I have seen her about very often and heard her sing."

"Ah!"

"To me she is an enigma," Sir Donald continued with some hesitation. "I cannot make her out at all."

Robin Pierce smiled in the dark and thrust his hands deep down in the pockets of his overcoat.

"I don't know," Sir Donald resumed, after a slight pause, "I don't know what is your—whether you care much for beauty in its innumerable forms. Many young men don't, I believe."

"I do," said Robin. "My mother is an Italian, you know, and not an Italian Philistine."

"Then you can help me, perhaps. Does Lady Holme care for beauty? But she must. It is impossible that she does not."

"Do you think so? Why?"

"I really cannot reconcile myself to the idea that such performances as hers are matters of chance."

"They are not. Lady Holme is not a woman who chances things before the cruel world in which she, you and I live, Sir Donald."

"Exactly. I felt sure of that. Then we come to calculation of effects, to consideration of that very interesting question—self-consciousness in art."

"Do you feel that Lady Holme is self-conscious when she is singing?"

"No. And that is just the point. She must, I suppose, have studied till she has reached that last stage of accomplishment in which the self-consciousness present is so perfectly concealed that it seems to be eliminated."

"Exactly. She has an absolute command over her means."

"One cannot deny it. No musician could contest it. But the question that interests me lies behind all this. There is more than accomplishment in her performance. There is temperament, there is mind, there is emotion and complete understanding. I am scarcely speaking strongly enough in saying complete—perhaps infinitely subtle would be nearer the mark. What do you say?"

"I don't think if you said that there appears to be an infinitely subtle understanding at work in Lady Holme's singing you would be going at all too far."

"Appears to be?"

Sir Donald stopped for a moment on the pavement under a gas-lamp. As the light fell on him he looked like a weary old ghost longing to fade away into the dark shadows of the London night.

"You say 'appears to be,'" he repeated.

"Yes."

"May I ask why?"

"Well, would you undertake to vouch for Lady Holme's understanding—I mean for the infinite subtlety of it?"

Sir Donald began to walk on once more.

"I cannot find it in her conversation," he said.

"Nor can I, nor can anyone."

"She is full of personal fascination, of course."

"You mean because of her personal beauty?"

"No, it's more than that, I think. It's the woman herself. She is suggestive somehow. She makes one's imagination work. Of course she is beautiful."

"And she thinks that is everything. She would part with her voice, her intelligence—she is very intelligent in the quick, frivolous fashion that is necessary for London—that personal fascination you speak of, everything rather than her white-rose complexion and the wave in her hair."

"Really, really?"

"Yes. She thinks the outside everything. She believes the world is governed, love is won and held, happiness is gained and kept by the husk of things. She told me only to-night that it is her face which sings to us all, not her voice; that were she to sing as well and be an ugly woman we should not care to listen to her."

"H'm! H'm!"

"Absurd, isn't it?"

"What will be the approach of old age to her?"

There was a suspicion of bitterness in his voice.

"The coming of the King of Terrors," said Pierce. "But she cannot hear his footsteps yet."

"They are loud enough in some ears. Ah, we, are at your door already?"

"Will you be good-natured and come in for a little while?"

"I'm afraid—isn't it rather late?"

"Only half-past eleven."

"Well, thank you."

They stepped into the little hall. As they did so a valet appeared at the head of the stairs leading to the servants' quarters.

"If you please, sir," he said to Pierce, "this note has just come. I was to ask if you would read it directly you returned."

"Will you excuse me?" said Pierce to Sir Donald, tearing open the envelope.

He glanced at the note.

"Is it to ask you to go somewhere to-night?" Sir Donald said.

"Yes, but—"

"I will go."

"Please don't. It is only from a friend who is just round the corner in Stratton Street. If you will not mind his joining us here I will send him a message."

He said a few words to his man.

"That will be all right. Do come upstairs."

"You are sure I am not in the way?"

"I hope you will not find my friend in the way; that's all. He's an odd fellow at the best of times, and to-night he's got an attack of what he calls the blacks—his form of blues. But he's very talented. Carey is his name—Rupert Carey. You don't happen to know him?"

"No. If I may say so, your room is charming."

They were on the first floor now, in a chamber rather barely furnished and hung with blue-grey linen, against which were fastened several old Italian pictures in black frames. On the floor were some Eastern rugs in which faded and originally pale colours mingled. A log fire was burning on an open hearth, at right angles to which stood an immense sofa with a square back. This sofa was covered with dull blue stuff. Opposite to it was a large and low armchair, also covered in blue. A Steinway grand piano stood out in the middle of the room. It was open and there were no ornaments or photographs upon it. Its shining dark case reflected the flames which sprang up from the logs. Several dwarf bookcases of black wood were filled with volumes, some in exquisite bindings, some paper covered. On the top of the bookcases stood four dragon china vases filled with carnations of various colours. Electric lights burned just under the ceiling, but they were hidden from sight. In an angle of the wall, on a black ebony pedestal, stood an extremely beautiful marble statuette of a nude girl holding a fan. Under this, on a plaque, was written, "*Une Danseuse de Tunisie.*"

Sir Donald went up to it, and stood before it for two or three minutes in silence.

"I see indeed you do care for beauty," he said at length. "But—forgive me—that fan makes that statuette wicked."

"Yes, but a thousand times more charming. Carey said just the same thing when he saw it. I wonder I wonder what Lady Holme would say."

They sat down on the sofa by the wood fire.

"Carey could probably tell us!" Pierce added.

"Oh, then your friend knows Lady Holme?"

"He did once. I believe he isn't allowed to now. Ah, here is Carey!"

A quick step was audible on the stairs, the door was opened, and a broad, middle-sized young man, with red hair, a huge red moustache and fierce red-brown eyes, entered swiftly with an air of ruthless determination.

"I came, but I shall be devilish bad company to-night," he said at once, looking at Sir Donald.

"We'll cheer you up. Let me introduce you to Sir Donald Ulford—Mr. Rupert Carey."

Carey shook Sir Donald by the hand.

"Glad to meet you," he said abruptly. "I've carried your Persian poems round the world with me. They lay in my trunk cheek by jowl with God-forsaken, glorious old Omar."

A dusky red flush appeared in Sir Donald's hollow cheeks.

"Really," he said, with obvious embarrassment, "I—they were a great failure. 'Obviously the poems of a man likely to be successful in dealing with finance,' as *The Times* said in reviewing them."

"Well, in the course of your career you've done some good things for England financially, haven't you?—not very publicly, perhaps, but as a minister abroad."

"Yes. To come forward as a poet was certainly a mistake."

"Any fool could see the faults in your book. True Persia all the same though. I saw all the faults and read 'em twenty times."

He flung himself down in the big armchair. Sir Donald could see now that there was a shining of misery in his big, rather ugly, eyes.

"Where have you two been?" he continued, with a directness that was almost rude.

"Dining with the Holmes," answered Pierce.

"That ruffian! Did she sing?"

"Yes, twice."

"Wish I'd heard her. Here am I playing Saul without a David. Many people there?"

"Several. Lady Cardington—"

"That white-haired enchantress! There's a Niobe—weeping not for her children, she never had any, but for her youth. She is the religion of half Mayfair, though I don't know whether she's got a religion. Men who wouldn't look at her when she was sixteen, twenty-six, thirty-six, worship her now she's sixty. And she weeps for her youth! Who else?"

"Mrs. Wolfstein."

"A daughter of Israel; coarse, intelligent, brutal to her reddened finger-tips. I'd trust her to judge a singer, actor, painter, writer. But I wouldn't trust her with my heart or half a crown."

"Lady Manby."

"Humour in petticoats. She's so infernally full of humour that there's no room in her for anything else. I doubt if she's got lungs. I'm sure she hasn't got a heart or a brain."

"But if she is so full of humour," said Sir Donald mildly, "how does she—?"

"How does a great writer fail over an addition sum? How does a man who speaks eight languages talk imbecility in them all? How is it that a bird isn't an angel? I wish to Heaven we knew. Well, Robin?"

"Of course, Mr. Bry."

Carey's violent face expressed disgust in every line.

"One of the most finished of London types," he exclaimed. "No other city supplies quite the same sort of man to take the colour out of things. He's enormously clever, enormously abominable, and should have been strangled at birth merely because of his feet. Why he's not Chinese I can't conceive; why he dines out every night I can. He's a human cruet-stand without the oil. He's so monstrously intelligent that he knows what a beast he is, and doesn't mind. Not a bad set of people to talk with, unless Lady Holme was in a temper and you were next to her, or you were left stranded with Holme when the women went out of the dining-room."

The Woman with the Fan | 23

"You think Holme a poor talker?" asked Sir Donald.

"Precious poor. His brain is muscle-bound, I believe. Robin, you know I'm miserable to-night you offer me nothing to drink."

"I beg your pardon. Help yourself. And, Sir Donald, what will you—?"

"Nothing, thank you."

"Try one of those cigars."

Sir Donald took one and lit it quietly, looking at Carey, who seemed to interest him a good deal.

"Why are you miserable, Carey?" said Pierce, as the former buried his moustache in a tall whisky-and-soda.

"Because I'm alive and don't want to be dead. Reason enough."

"Because you're an unmitigated egoist," rejoined Pierce.

"Yes, I am an egoist. Introduce me to a man who is not, will you?"

"And what about women?"

"Many women are not egoists. But you have been dining with one of the most finished egoists in London to-night."

"Lady Holme?" said Sir Donald, shifting into the left-hand corner of the sofa.

"Yes, Viola Holme, once Lady Viola Grantoun; whom I mustn't know any more."

"I'm not sure that you are right, Carey," said Pierce, rather coldly.

"What!"

"Can a true and perfect egoist be in love?"

"Certainly. Is not even an egoist an animal?"

Pierce's lips tightened for a second, and his right hand strained itself round his knee, on which it was lying.

"And how much can she be in love?"

"Very much."

"Do you mean with her body?"

"Yes, I do; and with the spirit that lives in it. I don't believe there's any life but this. A church is more fantastic to me than the room in which Punch belabours Judy. But I say that there is spirit in lust, in hunger, in everything. When I want a drink my spirit wants it. Viola Holme's spirit—a flame that will be blown out at death—takes part in her love for that great brute Holme. And yet she's one of the most pronounced egoists in London."

"Do you care to tell us any reason you may have for saying so?" said Sir Donald.

As he spoke, his voice, brought into sharp contrast with the changeful and animated voice of Carey, sounded almost preposterously thin and worn out.

"She is always conscious of herself in every situation, in every relation of life. While she loves even she thinks to herself, 'How beautifully I am loving!' And she never forgets for a single moment that she is a fascinating woman. If she were being murdered she would be saying silently, while the knife went in, 'What an attractive creature, what an unreplaceable personage they are putting an end to!'"

"Rupert, you are really too absurd!" exclaimed Pierce, laughing reluctantly.

"I'm not absurd. I see straight. Lady Holme is an egoist—a magnificent, an adorable egoist, fine enough in her brilliant selfishness to stand quite alone."

"And you mean to tell us that any woman can do that?" exclaimed Pierce.

"Who am I that I should pronounce a verdict upon the great mystery? What do I know of women?"

"Far too much, I'm afraid," said Pierce.

"Nothing, I have never been married, and only the married man knows anything of women. The Frenchmen are wrong. It is not the mistress who informs, it is the loving wife. For me the sex remains mysterious, like the heroine of my realm of dreams."

"You are talking great nonsense, Rupert."

"I always do when I am depressed, and I am very specially depressed to-night."

"But why? There must be some very special reason."

"There is. I, too, dined out and met at dinner a young man whose one desire in life appears to be to deprive living creatures of life."

Sir Donald moved slightly.

"You're not a sportsman, then, Mr. Carey?" he said.

"Indeed, I am. I've shot big game, the Lord forgive me, and found big pleasure in doing it. Yet this young man depressed me. He was so robust, so perfectly happy, so supremely self-satisfied, and, according to his own account, so enormously destructive, that he made me feel very sick. He is married. He married a widow who has an ear-trumpet and a big shooting in Scotland. If she could be induced to crawl in underwood, or stand on a cairn against a skyline, I'm sure he'd pot at her for the fun of the thing."

"What is his name?" asked Sir Donald.

"I didn't catch it. My host called him Leo. He has—"

"Ah! He is my only son."

Pierce looked very uncomfortable, but Carey replied calmly:

"Really. I wonder he hasn't shot you long ago."

Sir Donald smiled.

"Doesn't he depress you?" added Carey.

"He does, I'm sorry to say, but scarcely so much as I depress him."

"I think Lady Holme would like him."

For once Sir Donald looked really expressive, of surprise and disgust.

"Oh, I can't think so!" he said.

"Yes, yes, she would. She doesn't care honestly for art-loving men. Her idea of a real man, the sort of man a woman marries, or bolts with, or goes off her head for, is a huge mass of bones and muscles and thews and sinews that knows not beauty. And your son would adore her, Sir Donald. Better not let him, though. Holme's a jealous devil."

"Totally without reason," said Pierce, with a touch of bitterness.

"No doubt. It's part of his Grand Turk nature. He ought to possess a Yildiz. He's out of place in London where marital jealousy is more unfashionable than pegtop trousers."

He buried himself in his glass. Sir Donald rose to go.

"I hope I may see you again," he said rather tentatively at parting. "I am to be found in the Albany."

They both said they would call, and he slipped away gently.

"There's a sensitive man," said Carey when he had gone. "A sort of male Lady Cardington. Both of them are morbidly conscious of their age and carry it about with them as if it were a crime. Yet they're both worth knowing. People with that temperament who don't use hair-dye must have grit. His son's awful."

"And his poems?"

"Very crude, very faulty, very shy, but the real thing. But he'll never publish anything again. It must have been torture to him to reveal as much as he did in that book. He must find others to express him, and such as him, to the world."

"Lady Holmes?"

"*Par exemple.* Deuced odd that while the dumb understand the whole show the person who's describing it quite accurately to them often knows nothing about it. Paradox, irony, blasted eternal cussedness of life! Did you ever know Lady Ulford?"

"No."

"She was a horse-dealer's daughter."

"Rupert!"

"On my honour! One of those women who are all shirt and collar and nattiness, with a gold fox for a tie-pin and a hunting-crop under the arm. She was killed schooling a horse in Mexico after making Ulford shy and uncomfortable for fifteen years. Lady Cardington and a Texas cowboy would have been as well suited to one another. Ulford's been like a wistful ghost, they tell me, ever since her death. I should like to see him and his son together."

A hard and almost vicious gleam shone for as instant in his eyes.

"You're as cruel as a Spaniard at a bull-fight."

"My boy, I've been gored by the bull."

Pierce was silent for a minute. He thought of Lady Holme's white-rose complexion and of the cessation of Carey's acquaintance with the Holmes. No one seemed to know exactly why Carey went to the house in Cadogan Square no more.

"For God's sake give me another drink, Robin, and make it a stiff one."

Pierce poured out the whisky and thought:

"Could it have been that?"

Carey emptied the tumbler and heaved a long sigh.

"When d'you go back to Rome?"

"Beginning of July."

"You'll be there in the dead season."

"I like Rome then. The heat doesn't hurt me and I love the peace. Antiquity seems to descend upon the city in August, returning to its own when America is far away."

Carey stared at him hard.

"A rising diplomatist oughtn't to live in the past," he said bluntly.

"I like ruins."

"Unless they're women."

"If I loved a woman I could love her when she became what is called a ruin."

"If you were an old man who had crumbled gradually with her."

"As a young man, too. I was discussing—or rather flitting about, dinner-party fashion—that very subject to-night."

"With whom?"

"Viola."

"The deuce! What line did you take?"

"That one loves—if one loves—the kernel, not the shell."

"And she?"

"You know her—the opposite."

"Ah!"

"And you, Carey?"

"I! I think if the shell is a beautiful shell and becomes suddenly broken it makes a devil of a lot of difference in what most people think of the kernel."

"It wouldn't to me."

"I think it would."

"You take Viola's side then?"

"And when did I ever do anything else? I'm off."

He got up, nodded good-night, and was gone in a moment. Pierce heard him singing in a deep voice as he went down the stairs, and smiled with a faint contempt.

"How odd it is that nobody will believe a man if he's fool enough to hint at the truth of his true self," he thought. "And Carey—who's so clever about people!"

CHAPTER III

WHEN the last guest had grimaced at her and left the drawing-room, Lady Holme stood with her hand on the mantelpiece, facing a tall mirror. She was alone for the moment. Her husband had accompanied Mrs. Wolfstein downstairs, and Lady Holme could hear his big, booming voice below, interrupted now and then by her impudent soprano. She spoke English with a slight foreign accent which men generally liked and women loathed. Lady Holme loathed it. But she was not fond of her own sex. She believed that all women were untrustworthy. She often said that she had never met a woman who was not a liar, and when she said it she had no doubt that, for once, a woman was speaking the truth. Now, as she heard Mrs. Wolfstein's curiously improper laugh, she frowned. The face in the mirror changed and looked almost old.

This struck her unpleasantly. She kept the frown in its place and stared from under it, examining her features closely, fancying herself really an old woman, her whimsical fascination dead in its decaying home, her powers faded if not fled for ever. She might do what she liked then. It would all be of no use. Even the voice would be cracked and thin, unresponsive, unwieldy. The will would be phlegmatic. If it were not, the limbs and features would not easily obey its messages. The figure, now beautiful, would perhaps be marred by the ungracious thickness, the piteous fleshiness that Time often adds assiduously to ageing bodies, as if with an ironic pretence of generously giving in one direction while taking away in another. Decay would be setting in, life becoming perpetual loss. The precious years would be gone irrevocably.

She let the frown go and looked again on her beauty and smiled. The momentary bitterness passed. For there were many precious years to come for her, many years of power. She was young. Her health was superb. Her looks were of the kind that lasts. She thought of a famous actress whom she resembled closely. This actress was already forty-three, and was still a lovely woman, still toured about the world winning the hearts of men, was still renowned for her personal charm, worshipped not only for her talent but for her delicious skin, her great romantic eyes, her thick, waving hair.

Lady Holme laughed. In twenty years what Robin Pierce called her "husk" would still be an exquisite thing, and she would be going about without hearing the horrible tap, tap of the crutch in whose sustaining power she really believed so little. She knew men, and she said to herself, as she had said to Robin, that for them beauty lies in the epidermis.

"Hullo, Vi, lookin' in the glass! 'Pon my soul, your vanity's disgustin'. A plain woman like you ought to keep away from such things—leave 'em to the Mrs. Wolfsteins—what?"

Lady Holme turned round in time to see her husband's blunt, brown features twisted in the grimace which invariably preceded his portentous laugh.

"I admire Mrs. Wolfstein," she said.

The laugh burst like a bomb.

"You admire another woman! Why, you're incapable of it. The Lord defend me from hypocrisy, and there's no greater hypocrisy than one woman takin' Heaven to witness that she thinks another a stunnin' beauty."

"You know nothing about it, Fritz. Mrs. Wolfstein's eyes would be lovely if they hadn't that pawnbroking expression."

"Good, good! Now we're goin' to hear the voice of truth. Think it went well, eh?"

He threw himself down on a sofa and began to light a cigarette.

"The evening? No, I don't."

"Why not?"

He crossed his long legs and leaned back, resting his head on a cushion, and puffing the smoke towards the ceiling.

"They all seemed cheery—what? Even Lady Cardington only cried when you were squallin'."

It was Lord Holme's habit to speak irreverently of anything he happened to admire.

"She had reason to cry. Miss Filberte's accompaniment was a tragedy. She never comes here again."

"What's the row with her? I thought her fingers got about over the piano awful quick."

"They did—on the wrong notes."

She came and sat down beside him.

"You don't understand music, Fritz, thank goodness."

"I know I don't. But why thank what's-his-name?"

"Because the men that do are usually such anaemic, dolly things, such shaved poodles with their Sunday bows on."

"What about that chap Pierce? He's up to all the scales and thingumies, isn't he?"

"Robin—"

"Pierce I said."

"And I said Robin."

Lord Holme frowned and stuck out his under jaw. When he was irritated he always made haste to look like a prize-fighter. His prominent cheek-bones, and the abnormal development of bone in the lower part of his face, helped the illusion whose creation was begun by his expression.

"Look here, Vi," he said gruffly. "If you get up to any nonsense there'll be another Carey business. I give you the tip, and you can just take it in time. Don't you make any mistake. I'm not a Brenford, or a Godley-Halstoun, or a Pennisford, to sit by and—"

"What a pity it is that your body's so big and your intelligence so small!" she interrupted gently. "Why aren't there Sandow exercises for increasing the brain?"

"I've quite enough brain to rub along with very well. If I'd chosen to take it I could have been undersecretary—-"

"You've told me that so many times, old darling, and I really can't believe it. The Premier's very silly. Everybody knows that. But he's still got just a faint idea of the few things the country won't stand. And you are one of them, you truly are. You don't go down even with the Primrose League, and they simply worship at the shrine of the great Ar-rar."

"Fool or not, I'd kick out Pierce as I kicked out Carey if I thought—"

"And suppose I wouldn't let you?"

Her voice had suddenly changed. There was in it the sharp sound which had so overwhelmed Miss Filberte.

Lord Holme sat straight up and looked at his wife.

"Suppose—what?"

"Suppose I declined to let you behave ridiculously a second time."

"Ridiculously! I like that! Do you stick out that Carey didn't love you?"

"Half London loves me. I'm one of the most attractive women in it. That's why you married me, blessed boy."

"Carey's a violent ass. Red-headed men always are. There's a chap at White's—"

"I know, I know. You told me about him when you forbade poor Mr. Carey the house. But Robin's hair is black and he's the gentlest creature in diplomacy."

"I wouldn't trust him a yard."

"Believe me, he doesn't wish you to. He's far too clever to desire the impossible."

"Then he can stop desirin' you."

"Don't be insulting, Fritz. Remember that by birth you are a gentleman."

Lord Holme bit through his cigarette.

"Sometimes I wish you were an ugly woman," he muttered.

"And if I were?"

She leaned forward quite eagerly on the sofa and her whimsical, spoilt-child manner dropped away from her.

"You ain't."

"Don't be silly. I know I'm not, of course. But if I were to become one?"

"What?"

"Really, Fritz, there's no sort of continuity in your mental processes. If I were to become an ugly woman, what would you feel about me then?"

"How the deuce could you become ugly?"

"Oh, in a hundred ways. I might have smallpox and be pitted for life, or be scalded in the face as poor people's babies often are, or have vitriol thrown over me as lots of women do in Paris, or any number of things."

"What rot! Who'd throw vitriol over you, I should like to know?"

He lit a fresh cigarette with tender solicitude. Lady Holme began to look irritated.

"Do use your imagination!" she cried.

"Haven't got one, thank God!" he returned philosophically.

"I insist upon your imagining me ugly. Do you hear, I insist upon it."

She laid one soft hand on his knee and squeezed his leg with all her might.

"Now you're to imagine me ugly and just the same as I am now."

"You wouldn't be the same."

"Yes, I should. I should be the same woman, with the same heart and feelings and desires and things as I have now. Only the face would be altered."

"Well, go ahead, but don't pinch so, old girl."

"I pinch you to make you exert your mind. Now tell me truly—truly; would you love me as you do now, would you be jealous of me, would you—"

"I say, wait a bit! Don't drive on at such a rate. How ugly are you?"

"Very ugly; worse than Miss Filberte."

"Miss Filberte's not so bad."

"Yes, she is, Fritz, you know she is. But I mean ever so much worse; with a purple complexion, perhaps, like Mrs. Armington, whose husband insisted on a judicial separation; or a broken nose, or something wrong with my mouth—"

"What wrong?"

"Oh, dear, anything! What *l'homme qui vir* had—or a frightful scar across my cheek. Could you love me as you do now? I should be the same woman, remember."

"Then it'd be all the same to me, I s'pose. Let's turn in."

He got up, went over to the hearth, on which a small wood fire was burning, straddled his legs, bent his knees and straightened them several times, thrusting his hands into the pockets of his trousers, which were rather tight and horsey and defined his immense limbs. An expression of profound self-satisfaction illumined his face as he looked at his wife, giving it a slightly leery expression, as of a shrewd rustic. His large blunt features seemed to broaden, his big brown eyes twinkled, and his lips, which were thick and very red and had a cleft down their middle, parted under his short bronze moustache, exposing two level rows of square white teeth.

"It's jolly difficult to imagine you an ugly woman," he said, with a deep chuckle.

"I do wish you'd keep your legs still," said Lady Holme. "What earthly pleasure can it give you to go on like that? Would you love me as you do now?"

"You'd be jolly sick if I didn't, wouldn't you, Vi, eh?"

The Woman with the Fan | 33

"I wonder if it ever occurs to you that you're hideously conceited, Fritz?"

She spoke with a touch of real anger, real exasperation.

"No more than any other Englishman that's worth his salt and ever does any good in the world. I ain't a timid molly-coddle, if that's what you mean."

He took one large hand out of his pocket, scratched his cheek and yawned. As he did so he looked as unconcerned, as free from self-consciousness, as much a slave to every impulse born of passing physical sensation as a wild animal in a wood or out on a prairie.

"Otherwise life ain't worth tuppence," he added through his yawn.

Lady Holme sat looking at him for a moment in silence. She was really irritated by his total lack of interest in what she wanted to interest in him, irritated, too, because her curiosity remained unsatisfied. But that abrupt look and action of absolutely unconscious animalism, chasing the leeriness of the contented man's conceit, turned her to softness if not to cheerfulness. She adored Fritz like that. His open-mouthed, gaping yawn moved something in her to tenderness. She would have liked to kiss him while he was yawning and to pass her hands over his short hair, which was like a mat and grew as strongly as the hair which he shaved every morning from his brown cheeks.

"Well, what about bed, old girl?" he said, stretching himself.

Lady Holme did not reply. Some part of him, some joint, creaked as he forced his clasped hands downward and backward. She was listening eagerly for a repetition of the little sound.

"What! Is mum the word?" he said, bending forward to stare into her face.

At this moment the door opened, and a footman came in to extinguish the lights and close the piano. By mistake he let the lid of the latter drop with a bang. Lady Holme, who had just got up to go to bed, started violently. She said nothing but stared at him for an instant with an expression of cold rebuke on her face. The man reddened. Lord Holme was already on the stairs. He yawned again noisily, and turned the sound eventually into a sort of roaring chant up and down the scale as he mounted towards the next floor. Lady Holme came slowly after him. She had a very individual walk, moving from the hips and nearly always taking small, slow steps. Her sapphire-blue gown trailed behind her with a pretty noise over the carpet.

When her French maid had locked up her jewels and helped her to undress, she dismissed her, and called out to Lord Holme, who was in the next room, the door of which was slightly open.

"Fritz!"

"Girlie?"

His mighty form, attired in pale blue pyjamas, stood in the doorway. In his hand he grasped a toothbrush, and there were dabs of white tooth-powder on his cheeks and chin.

"Finish your toilet and make haste."

He disappeared. There was a prolonged noise of brushing and the gurgling and splashing of water. Lady Holme sat down on the white couch at the foot of the great bed. She was wrapped in a soft white gown made like a burnous, a veritable Arab garment, with a white silk hood at the back, and now she put up her hands and, with great precision, drew the hood up over her head. The burnous, thus adjusted, made her look very young. She had thrust her bare feet into white slippers without heels, and now she drew up her legs lightly and easily and crossed them under her, assuming an Eastern attitude and the expression of supreme impassivity which suits it. A long mirror was just opposite to her. She swayed to and fro, looking into it.

"Allah-Akbar!" she murmured. "Allah-Akbar! I am a fatalist. Everything is ordained, so why should I bother? I will live for the day. I will live for the night. Allah-Akbar, Allah-Akbar!"

The sound of water gushing from a reversed tumbler into a full basin was followed by the reappearance of Lord Holme, looking very clean and very sleepy.

Lady Holme stopped swaying.

"You look like a kid of twelve years old in that thing, Vi," he observed, surveying her with his hands on his hips.

"I am a woman with a philosophy," she returned with dignity.

"A philosophy! What the deuce is that?"

"You didn't learn much at Eton and Christchurch."

"I learnt to use my fists and to make love to the women."

"You're a brute!" she exclaimed with most unphilosophic vehemence.

"And that's why you worship the ground I tread on," he rejoined equably. "And that's why I've always had a good time with the women ever since I stood six foot in my stockin's when I was sixteen."

Lady Holme looked really indignant. Her face was contorted by a spasm. She was one of those unfortunate women who are capable of retrospective jealousy.

"I won't—how dare you speak to me of those women?" she said bitterly. "You insult me."

"Hang it, there's no one since you, Vi. You know that. And what would you have thought of a great, hulkin' chap like me who'd never—well, all right. I'll dry up. But you know well enough you wouldn't have looked at me."

"I wonder why I ever did."

"No, you don't. I'm just the chap to suit you. You're full of whimsies and need a sledge-hammer fellow to keep you quiet. It you'd married that ass, Carey, or that—"

"Fritz, once for all, I won't have my friends abused. I allowed you to have your own way about Rupert Carey, but I will not have Robin Pierce or anyone else insulted. Please understand that. I married to be more free, not more—"

"You married because you'd fallen jolly well in love with me, that's why you married, and that's why you're a damned lucky woman. Come to bed. You won't, eh?"

He made a stride, snatched Lady Holme up as if she were a bundle, and carried her off to bed.

She was on the point of bursting into angry tears, but when she found herself snatched up, her slippers tumbling off, the hood of the burnous falling over her eyes, her face crushed anyhow against her husband's sinewy chest, she suddenly felt oddly contented, disinclined to protest or to struggle.

Lord Holme did not trouble himself to ask what she was feeling or why she was feeling it.

He thought of himself—the surest way to fasten upon a man the thoughts of others.

CHAPTER IV

ROBIN PIERCE and Carey were old acquaintances, if not exactly old friends. They had been for a time at Harrow together. Pierce had six thousand a year and worked hard for a few hundreds. Carey had a thousand and did nothing. He had never done anything definite, anything to earn a living. Yet his talents were notorious. He played the piano well for an amateur, was an extraordinarily clever mimic, acted better than most people who were not on the stage, and could write very entertaining verse with a pungent, sub-acid flavour. But he had no creative power and no perseverance. As a critic of the performances of others he was cruel but discerning, giving no quarter, but giving credit where it was due. He loathed a bad workman more than a criminal, and would rather have crushed an incompetent human being than a worm. Secretly he despised himself. His own laziness was as disgusting to him as a disease, and was as incurable as are certain diseases. He was now thirty-four and realised that he was never going to do anything with his life. Already he had travelled over the world, seen a hundred, done a hundred things. He had an enormous acquaintance in Society and among artists; writers, actors, painters—all the people who did things and did them well. As a rule they liked him, despite his bizarre bluntness of speech and manner, and they invariably spoke of him as a man of great talent; he said because he was so seldom fool enough to do anything that could reveal incompetence. His mother, who was a widow, lived in the north, in an old family mansion, half house, half castle, near the sea coast of Cumberland. He had one sister, who was married to an American.

Carey always declared that he was that *rara avis* an atheist, and that he had been born an atheist. He affirmed that even when a child he had never, for a moment, felt that there could be any other life than this earth-life. Few people believed him. There are few people who can believe in a child atheist.

Pierce had a totally different character. He seemed to be more dreamy and was more energetic, talked much less and accomplished much more. It had always been his ambition to be a successful diplomat, and in many respects he was well fitted for a diplomatic career. He had a talent for languages, great ease of manner, self-possession, patience and cunning. He loved foreign life. Directly he set foot in a country which was not his own he felt stimulated. He felt that he woke up, that his mind became more alert, his imagination more lively. He delighted in change, in being brought into contact with a society which required study to be understood. His present fate contented him well enough. He liked Rome and was liked there. As his mother was a Roman he had many Italian connections, and he was far more at ease with Romans than with the average London man. His father and mother lived almost perpetually in large hotels. The former, who was enormously rich, was a *malade imaginaire*. He invariably spoke of his quite normal health as if it were some deadly disease, and always treated himself, and insisted on being treated, as if he were an exceptionally distinguished invalid. In the course of years his friends had learned to take his view of the matter, and he was at this time almost universally spoken of as "that poor Sir Henry Pierce whose life has been one long martyrdom." Poor Sir Henry was fortunate in the possession of a wife who really was a martyr— to him. Nobody had ever discovered whether Lady Pierce knew, or did not know, that her husband was quite as well as most people. There are many women with such secrets. Robin's parents were at present taking baths and drinking waters in Germany. They were later going for an "after cure" to Switzerland, and then to Italy to "keep warm" during the autumn. As they never lived in London, Robin had no home there except his little house in Half Moon Street. He had one brother, renowned as a polo player, and one sister, who was married to a rising politician, Lord Evelyn Clowes, a young man with a voluble talent, a peculiar power of irritating Chancellors of the Exchequer, and hair so thick that he was adored by the caricaturists.

Robin Pierce and Carey saw little of each other now, being generally separated by a good many leagues of land and sea, but when they met they were still fairly intimate. They had some real regard for each other. Carey felt at ease in giving his violence to the quiet and self-possessed young secretary, who was three years his junior, but who sometimes seemed to him the elder of the two, perhaps because calm is essentially the senior of storm. He had even allowed Robin to guess at the truth of his feeling for Lady Holme, though he had never been explicit, on the subject to him or to anyone. There were moments when Robin wished he had not been permitted to guess, for Lady Holme attracted him far more than any other woman he had seen, and he had proposed to her before she had been carried off by her husband. He admired her beauty, but he did not believe that it was her beauty which had led him into love. He was sure that he loved the woman in her, the hidden woman whom Lord Holme and the world at large—including Carey—knew nothing about. He thought that Lady Holme herself did not understand this hidden woman, did not realise, as he did, that she existed. She spoke to him sometimes in Lady Holme's singing, sometimes in an expression in her eyes when she was serious, sometimes even in a bodily attitude. For Robin, half fantastically, put faith in the eloquence of line as a revealer of character, of soul. But she did not speak to him in Lady Holme's conversation. He really thought this hidden woman was obscured by the lovely window — he conceived it as a window of exquisite stained glass, jewelled but concealing — through which she was condemned to look for ever, through which, too, all men must look at her. He really wished sometimes, as he had said, that Lady Holme were ugly, for he had a fancy that perhaps then, and only then, would the hidden woman arise and be seen as a person may be seen through unstained, clear glass. He really felt that what he loved would be there to love if the face that ruled was ruined; would not only still be there to love, but would become more powerful, more true to itself, more understanding of itself, more reliant, purer, braver. And he had learnt to cherish this fancy till it had become a little monomania. Robin thought that the world misunderstood him, but he knew the world too well to say so. He never risked being laughed at. He felt sure that he was passionate, that he was capable of romantic deeds, of Quixotic self-sacrifice, of a devotion that might well be sung by poets, and that would certainly be worshipped by ardent women. And he said to himself that Lady Holme was the one woman who could set free, if the occasion came, this passionate, unusual and surely admirable captive at present chained within him, doomed to inactivity and the creeping weakness that comes from enforced repose.

Carey's passion for Lady Holme had come into being shortly before her marriage. No one knew much about it, or about the rupture of all relations between him and the Holmes which had eventually taken place. But the fact that Carey had lost his head about Lady Holme was known to half London. For Carey, when carried away, was singularly reckless; singularly careless of consequences and of what people thought. It was difficult to influence him, but when influenced he was almost painfully open in his acknowledgment of the power that had reached him. As a rule, however, despite his apparent definiteness, his decisive violence, there seemed to be something fluid in his character, something that divided and flowed away from anything which sought to grasp and hold it. He had impetus but not balance; swiftness, but a swiftness that was uncontrolled. He resembled a machine without a brake.

It was soon after his rupture with the Holmes that his intimates began to notice that he was becoming inclined to drink too much. When Pierce returned to London from Rome he was immediately conscious of the slight alteration in his friend. Once he remonstrated with Carey about it. Carey was silent for a moment. Then he said abruptly:

"My heart wants to be drowned."

Lord Holme hated Carey. Yet Lady Holme had not loved him; though she had not objected to him more than to other men because he loved her. She had been brought up in a society which is singularly free from prejudices, which has no time to study carefully questions of so-called honour, which has little real religious feeling, and a desire for gaiety which perhaps takes the place of a desire for morals. Intrigues are one of the chief amusements of this society, which oscillates from London to Paris as the pendulum of a clock oscillates from right to left. Lady Holme, however, happened to be protected doubly against the dangers—or joys by the way—to which so many of her companions fell cheerful, and even chattering, victims. She had a husband who though extremely stupid was extremely masterful, and, for the time at any rate, she sincerely loved him. She was a faithful wife and had no desire to be anything else, though she liked to be, and usually was, in the fashion. But though faithful to Lord Holme she had, as has been said, both the appearance and the temperament of a siren. She enjoyed governing men, and those who were governed by her, who submitted obviously to the power of her beauty and the charm of manner that seemed to emanate from it, and to be one with it, were more attractive to her than those who were not. She was inclined to admire a man for loving her, as a serious and solemn-thinking woman, with bandeaux and convictions, admires a clergyman for doing his duty. Carey had done his duty with such fiery ardour that, though she did not prevent her husband from kicking him out of the house, she could not refrain from thinking well of him.

Her thoughts of Robin Pierce were perhaps a little more confused.

She had not accepted him. Carey would have said that he was not "her type." Although strong and active he was not the huge mass of bones and muscles and thews and sinews, ignorant of beauty and devoid of the love of art, which Carey had described as her ideal. There was melancholy and there was subtlety in him. When Lady Holme was a girl this melancholy and subtlety had not appealed to her sufficiently to induce her to become Lady Viola Pierce. Nevertheless, Robin's affection for her, and the peculiar form it took—of idealising her secret nature and wishing her obvious beauty away—had won upon the egoism of her. Although she laughed at his absurdity, as she called it, and honestly held to her Pagan belief that physical beauty was all in all to the world she wished to influence, it pleased her sometimes to fancy that perhaps he was right, that perhaps her greatest loveliness was hidden and dwelt apart. The thought was flattering, and though her knowledge of men rejected the idea that such a loveliness alone could ever command an empire worth the ruling, she could have no real objection to being credited with a double share of charm—the charm of face and manner which everyone, including herself, was aware that she possessed, and that other stranger, more dim and mysterious charm at whose altar Robin burnt an agreeably perfumed incense.

She had a peculiar power of awakening in others that which she usually seemed not to possess herself—imagination, passion, not only physical but ethereal and of the mind; a tenderness for old sorrows, desire for distant, fleeting, misty glories not surely of this earth. She was a brilliant suggestionist, but not in conversation. Her face and her voice, when she sang, were luring to the lovers of beauty. When she sang she often expressed for them the under-thoughts and under-feelings of secretly romantic, secretly wistful men and women, and drew them to her as if by a spell. But her talk and manner in conversation were so unlike her singing, so little accorded with the look that often came into her eyes while she sang, that she was a perpetual puzzle to such elderly men as Sir Donald Ulford, to such young men as Robin Pierce, and even to some women. They came about her like beggars who have heard a chink of gold, and she showed them a purse that seemed to be empty.

Was it the *milieu* in which she lived, the influence of a vulgar and greedy age, which prevented her from showing her true self except in her art? Or was she that stupefying enigma sometimes met with, an unintelligent genius?

There were some who wondered.

In her singing she seemed to understand, to love, to pity, to enthrone. In her life she often seemed not to understand, not to love, not to pity, not to place high.

She sang of Venice, and those who cannot even think of the city in the sea without a flutter of the heart, a feeling not far from soft pain in its tenderness and gratitude, listened to the magic bells at sunset, and glided in the fairy barques across the liquid plains of gold. She spoke of Venice, and they heard only the famished voice of the mosquito uttering its midnight grace before meat.

Which was the real Venice?

Which was the real woman?

CHAPTER V

ON the following day, which was warm and damp; Lady Holme drove to Bond Street, bought two new hats, had her hand read by a palmist who called himself "Cupido," looked in at a ladies' club and then went to Mrs. Wolfstein, with whom she was engaged to lunch. She did not wish to lunch with her. She disliked Mrs. Wolfstein as she disliked most women, but she had not been able to get out of it. Mrs. Wolfstein had overheard her saying to Lady Cardington that she had nothing particular to do till four that day, and had immediately "pinned her." Besides disliking Mrs. Wolfstein, Lady Holme was a little afraid of her. Like many clever Jewesses, Mrs. Wolfstein was a ruthless conversationalist, and enjoyed showing off at the expense of others, even when they were her guests. She had sometimes made Lady Holme feel stupid, even feel as if a good talker might occasionally gain, and keep, an advantage over a lovely woman who did not talk so well. The sensation passed, but the fact that it had ever been did not draw Lady Holme any closer to the woman with the "pawnbroking expression" in her eyes.

Mrs. Wolfstein was not in the most exclusive set in London, but she was in the smart set, which is no longer exclusive although it sometimes hopes it is. She knew the racing people, nearly all the most fashionable Jews, and those very numerous English patricians who like to go where money is. She also knew the whole of Upper Bohemia, and was a *persona gratissima* in that happy land of talent and jealousy. She entertained a great deal, generally at modish restaurants. Many French and Germans were to be met with at her parties; and it was impossible to be with either them or her for many minutes without hearing the most hearty and whole-souled abuse of English aspirations, art, letters and cooking. The respectability, the pictures, the books and the boiled cabbage of Britain all came impartially under the lash.

Mrs. Wolfstein's origin was obscure. That she was a Jewess was known to everybody, but few could say with certainty whether she was a German, a Spanish, a Polish or an Eastern Jewess. She had much of the covert coarseness and open impudence of a Levantine, and occasionally said things which made people wonder whether, before she became Amalia

Wolfstein, she had not perhaps been—well really—something very strange somewhere a long way off.

Her husband was shocking to look at: small, mean, bald, Semitic and nervous, with large ears which curved outwards from his head like leaves, and cheeks blue from much shaving. He was said to hide behind his anxious manner an acuteness that was diabolic, and to have earned his ill-health by sly dissipations for which he had paid enormous sums. There were two Wolfstein children, a boy and a girl of eleven and twelve; small, swarthy, frog-like, self-possessed. They already spoke three languages, and their protruding eyes looked almost diseased with intelligence.

The Wolfstein house, which was in Curzon Street, was not pretty, Apparently neither Mrs. Wolfstein nor her husband, who was a financier and company promoter on a very large scale, had good taste in furniture and decoration. The mansion was spacious but dingy. There was a great deal of chocolate and fiery yellow paint. There were many stuffy brown carpets, and tables which were unnecessarily solid. In the hall were pillars which looked as if they were made of brawn, and arches with lozenges of azure paint in which golden stars appeared rather meretriciously. A plaster statue of Hebe, with crinkly hair and staring eyeballs, stood in a corner without improving matters. That part of the staircase which was not concealed by the brown carpet was dirty white. An immense oil painting of a heap of dead pheasants, rabbits and wild duck, lying beside a gun and a pair of leather gaiters, immediately faced the hall door, which was opened by two enormous men with yellow complexions and dissipated eyes. Mrs. Wolfstein was at home, and one of the enormous men lethargically showed Lady Holme upstairs into a drawing-room which suggested a Gordon Hotel. She waited for about five minutes on a brown and yellow sofa near a table on which lay some books and several paper-knives, and then Mrs. Wolfstein appeared. She was dressed very smartly in blue and red, and looked either Oriental or Portuguese, as she came in. Lady Holme was not quite certain which.

"Dear person!" she said, taking Lady Holme's hands in hers, which were covered with unusually large rings. "Now, I've got a confession to make. What a delicious hat!"

Lady Holme felt certain the confession was of something unpleasant, but she only said, in the rather languid manner she generally affected towards women:

"Well? My ear is at the grating."

"My lunch is at the Carlton."

Lady Holme was pleased. At the Carlton one can always look about.

"And—it's a woman's lunch."

Lady Holme's countenance fell quite frankly.

"I knew you'd be horrified. You think us such bores, and so we are. But I couldn't resist being malicious to win such a triumph. You at a hen lunch! It'll be the talk of London. Can you forgive me?"

"Of course."

"And can you stand it?"

Lady Holme looked definitely dubious.

"I'll tell you who'll be there—Lady Cardington, Lady Manby, Mrs. Trent—do you know her? Spanish looking, and's divorced two husbands, and's called the scarlet woman because she always dresses in red—Sally Perceval, Miss Burns and Pimpernel Schley."

"Pimpernel Schley! Who is she?"

"The American actress who plays all the improper modern parts. Directly a piece is produced in Paris that we run over to see—you know the sort! the Grand Duke and foreign Royalty species—she has it adapted for her. Of course it's Bowdlerised as to words, but she manages to get back all that's been taken out in her acting. Young America's crazy about her. She's going to play over here."

"Oh!"

Lady Holme's voice was not encouraging, but Mrs. Wolfstein was not sensitive. She chattered gaily all the way to the Haymarket. When they came into the Palm Court they found Lady Cardington already there, seated tragically in an armchair, and looking like a weary empress. The band was playing on the balcony just outside the glass wall which divides the great dining-room from the court, and several people were dotted about waiting for friends, or simply killing time by indulging curiosity. Among them was a large, broad-shouldered young man, with a round face, contemptuous blue eyes and a mouth with chubby, pouting lips. He was well dressed, but there was a touch of horseyness in the cut of his trousers, the arrangement of his tie. He sat close to the band, tipping his green chair backwards and smoking a cigarette.

As Mrs. Wolfstein and Lady Holme went up to greet Lady Cardington, Sally Perceval and Mrs. Trent came in together, followed almost immediately by Lady Manby.

Sally Perceval was a very pretty young married woman, who spent most of her time racing, gambling and going to house parties. She looked excessively fragile and consumptive, but had lived hard and never had a day's illness in her life. She was accomplished, not at all intellectual, clever at games, a fine horsewoman and an excellent swimmer. She had been all over the world with her husband, who was very handsome and almost idiotic, and who could not have told you what the Taj was, whether Thebes was in Egypt or India, or what was the difference, if any, between the Golden Gate and the Golden Horn. Mrs. Trent was large, sultry, well-informed and supercilious; had the lustrous eyes of a Spaniard, and spoke in a warm contralto voice. Her figure was magnificent, and she prided herself on having a masculine intellect. Her enemies said that she had a more than masculine temper.

Lady Manby had been presented by Providence with a face like a teapot, her nose being the spout and her cheeks the bulging sides. She saw everything in caricature. If war were spoken of, her imagination immediately conjured up visions of unwashed majors conspicuously absurd in toeless boots, of fat colonels forced to make merry on dead rats, of field-marshals surprised by the enemy in their nightshirts, and of common soldiers driven to repair their own clothes and preposterously at work on women's tasks. She adored the clergy for their pious humours, the bench for its delicious attempts at dignity, the bar for its grotesque travesties of passionate conviction—lies with their wigs on—the world political for its intrigues dressed up in patriotism. A Lord Chancellor in full state seemed to her the most delightfully ridiculous phenomenon in a delightfully ridiculous universe. And she had once been obliged to make a convulsive exit from an English cathedral, in which one hundred colonial bishops were singing a solemn hymn, entirely devastated by the laughter waked in her by this most sacred spectacle.

Miss Burns, who hurried in breathlessly ten minutes late, was very thin, badly dressed and insignificant-looking, wore her hair short, and could not see you if you were more than four feet away from her. She had been on various lonely and distant travelling excursions, about which she had written books, had consorted merrily with naked savages, sat in the oily huts of Esquimaux, and penetrated into the interior of China dressed as a man. Her lack of affectation hit you in the face on a first meeting, and her sincerity was perpetually embroiling her with the persistent liars who, massed together, formed what is called decent society.

"I know I'm late," she said, pushing her round black hat askew on her shaggy little head. "I know I've kept you all waiting. Pardon!"

"Indeed you haven't," replied Mrs. Wolfstein. "Pimpernel Schley isn't here yet. She lives in the hotel, so of course she'll turn up last."

Mrs. Trent put one hand on her hip and stared insolently at the various groups of people in the court, Lady Cardington sighed, and Lady Holme assumed a vacant look, which suited her mental attitude at the moment. She generally began to feel rather vacant if she were long alone with women.

Another ten minutes passed.

"I'm famishing," said Sally Perceval. "I've been at the Bath Club diving, and I do so want my grub. Let's skip in."

"It really is too bad—oh, here she comes!" said Mrs. Wolfstein.

Many heads in the Palm Court were turned towards the stairs, down which a demure figure was walking with extreme slowness. The big young man with the round face got up from his chair and looked greedy, and the waiters standing by the desk just inside the door glanced round, whispered, and smiled quickly before gliding off to their different little tables.

Pimpernel Schley was alone, but she moved as if she were leading a quiet procession of vestal virgins. She was dressed in white, with a black velvet band round her tiny waist and a large black hat. Her shining, straw-coloured hair was fluffed out with a sort of ostentatious innocence on either side of a broad parting, and she kept her round chin tucked well in as she made what was certainly an effective entrance. Her arms hung down at her sides, and in one hand she carried a black fan. She wore no gloves, and many diamond rings glittered on her small fingers, the rosy nails of which were trimmed into points. As she drew near to Mrs. Wolfstein's party she walked slower and slower, as if she felt that she was arriving at a destination much too soon.

Lady Holme watched her as she approached, examined her with that piercing scrutiny in which the soul of one woman is thrust out, like a spear, towards the soul of another. She noticed at once that Miss Schley resembled her, had something of her charm of fairness. It was a fainter, more virginal charm than hers. The colouring of hair and eyes was lighter. The complexion was a more dead, less warm, white. But there was certainly a resemblance. Miss Schley was almost exactly her height, too, and—

Lady Holme glanced swiftly round the Palm Court. Of all the women gathered there Pimpernel Schley and herself were nearest akin in appearance.

As she recognised this fact Lady Holme felt hostile to Miss Schley.

Not until the latter was almost touching her hostess did she lift her eyes from the ground. Then she stood still, looked up calmly, and said, in a drawling and infantine voice:

"I had to see my trunks unpacked, but I was bound to be on time. I wouldn't have come down to-day for any soul in the world but you. I would not."

It was a pretty speaking voice, clear and youthful, with a choir-boyish sound in it, and remarkably free from nasal twang, but it was not a lady's voice. It sounded like the frontispiece of a summer number become articulate.

Mrs. Wolfstein began to introduce Miss Schley to her guests, none of whom, it seemed, knew her. She bowed to each of them, still with the vestal virgin air, and said, "Glad to know you!" to each in turn without looking at anyone. Then Mrs. Wolfstein led the way into the restaurant.

Everyone looked at the party of women as they came in and ranged themselves round a table in the middle of the big room. Lady Cardington sat on one side of Mrs. Wolfstein and Lady Holme on the other, between her and Mrs. Trent. Miss Schley was exactly opposite. She kept her eyes eternally cast down like a nun at Benediction. All the quite young men who could see her were looking at her with keen interest, and two or three of them—probably up from Sandhurst—had already assumed expressions calculated to alarm modesty. Others looked mournfully fatuous, as if suddenly a prey to lasting and romantic grief. The older men were more impartial in their observation of Mrs. Wolfstein's guests. And all the women, without exception, fixed their eyes upon Lady Holme's hat.

Lady Cardington, who seemed oppressed by grief, said to Mrs. Wolfstein:

"Did you see that article in the *Daily Mail* this morning?"

"Which one?"

"On the suggestion to found a school in which the only thing to be taught would be happiness."

"Who's going to be the teacher?"

"Some man. I forget the name."

"A man!" said Mrs. Trent, in a slow, veiled contralto voice. "Why, men are always furious if they think we have any pleasure which they can't deprive us of at a minute's notice. A man is the last two-legged thing to be a happiness teacher."

"Whom would you have then?" said Lady Cardington.

"Nobody, or a child."

"Of which sex?" said Mrs. Wolfstein.

"The sex of a child," replied Mrs. Trent.

Mrs. Wolfstein laughed rather loudly.

"I think children are the most greedy, unsatisfied individuals in—" she began.

"I was not alluding to Curzon Street children," observed Mrs. Trent, interrupting. "When I speak in general terms of anything I always except London."

"Why?" said Sally Perceval.

"Because it's no more natural, no more central, no more in line with the truth of things than you are, Sally."

"But, my dear, you surely aren't a belated follower of Tolstoi!" cried Mrs. Wolfstein. "You don't want us all to live like day labourers."

"I don't want anybody to do anything, but if happiness is to be taught it must not be by a man or by a Londoner."

"I had no idea you had been caught by the cult of simplicity," said Mrs. Wolfstein. "But you are so clever. You reveal your dislikes but conceal your preferences. Most women think that if they only conceal their dislikes they are quite perfectly subtle."

"Subtle people are delicious," said Lady Manby, putting her mouth on one side. "They remind me of a kleptomaniac I once knew who had a little pocket closed by a flap let into the front of her gown. When she dined out she filled it with scraps. Once she dined with us and I saw her, when she thought no one was watching, peppering her pocket with cayenne, and looking so delightfully sly and thieving. Subtle people are always peppering their little pockets and thinking nobody sees them."

"And lots of people don't," said Mrs. Wolfstein.

"The vices are divinely comic," continued Lady Manby, looking every moment more like a teapot. "I think it's such a mercy. Fancy what a lot of fun we should lose if there were no drunkards, for instance!"

Lady Cardington looked shocked.

"The virtues are often more comic than the vices," said Mrs. Trent, with calm authority. "Dramatists know that. Think of the dozens of good farces whose foundation is supreme respectability in contact with the wicked world."

"I didn't know anyone called respectability a virtue," cried Sally Perceval.

"Oh, all the English do in their hearts," said Mrs. Wolfstein. "Pimpernel, are you Yankees as bad?"

Miss Schley was eating *sole a la Colbert* with her eyes on her plate. She ate very slowly and took tiny morsels. Now she looked up.

"We're pretty respectable over in America, I suppose," she drawled. "Why not? What harm does it do anyway?"

"Well, it limits the inventive faculties for one thing. If one is strictly respectable life is plain sailing."

"Oh, life is never that," said Mrs. Trent, "for women."

Lady Cardington seemed touched by this remark.

"Never, never," she said in her curious voice—a voice in which tears seemed for ever to be lingering. "We women are always near the rocks."

"Or on them," said Mrs. Trent, thinking doubtless of the two husbands she had divorced.

"I like a good shipwreck," exclaimed Miss Burns in a loud tenor voice. "I was in two before I was thirty, one off Hayti and one off Java, and I enjoyed them both thoroughly. They wake folks up and make them show their mettle."

"It's always dangerous to speak figuratively if she's anywhere about," murmured Mrs. Wolfstein to Lady Holme. "She'll talk about lowering boats and life-preservers now till the end of lunch."

Lady Holme started. She had not been listening to the conversation but had been looking at Miss Schley. She had noticed instantly the effect created in the room by the actress's presence in it. The magic of a name flits, like a migratory bird, across the Atlantic. Numbers of the youthful loungers of London had been waiting impatiently during the last weeks for the arrival of this pale and demure star. Now that she had come their interest in her was keen. Her peculiar reputation for ingeniously tricking Mrs. Bowdler, secretary to Mrs. Grundy, rendered her very piquant, and this piquancy was increased by her ostentatiously vestal appearance.

Lady Holme was sometimes clairvoyante. At this moment every nerve in her body seemed telling her that the silent girl, who sat there nibbling her lunch composedly, was going to be the rage in London. It did not matter at all whether she had talent or not. Lady Holme saw that directly, as she glanced from one little table to another at the observant, whispering men.

She felt angry with Miss Schley for resembling her in colouring, for resembling her in another respect—capacity for remaining calmly silent in the midst of fashionable chatterboxes.

"Will she?" she said to Mrs. Wolfstein.

"Yes. If she'd never been shipwrecked she'd have been almost entertaining, but—there's Sir Donald Ulford trying to attract your attention."

"Where?"

She looked and saw Sir Donald sitting opposite to the large young man with the contemptuous blue eyes and the chubby mouth. They both seemed very bored. Sir Donald bowed.

"Who is that with him?" asked Lady Holme.

"I don't know," said Mrs. Wolfstein. "He looks like a Cupid who's been through Sandow's school. He oughtn't to wear anything but wings."

"It's Sir Donald's son, Leo," said Lady Cardington.

Pimpernel Schley lifted her eyes for an instant from her plate, glanced at Leo Ulford, and cast them down again.

"Leo Ulford's a blackguard," observed Mrs. Trent. "And when a fair man's a blackguard he's much more dangerous than a dark man."

All the women stared at Leo Ulford with a certain eagerness.

"He's good-looking," said Sally Perceval. "But I always distrust cherubic people. They're bound to do you if they get the chance. Isn't he married?"

"Yes," said Mrs. Trent. "He married a deaf heiress."

"Intelligent of him!" remarked Mrs. Wolfstein. "I always wish I'd married a blind millionaire instead of Henry. Being a Jew, Henry sees not only all there is to see, but all there isn't. Sir Donald and his Cupid son don't seem to have much to say to one another."

"Oh, don't you know that family affection's the dumbest thing on earth?" said Mrs. Trent.

"Too deep for speech," said Lady Manby. "I love to see fathers and sons together, the fathers trying to look younger than they are and the sons older. It's the most comic relationship, and breeds shyness as the West African climate breeds fever."

"I know the whole of the West African coast by heart," declared Miss Burns, wagging her head, and moving her brown hands nervously among her knives and forks. "And I never caught anything there."

"Not even a husband," murmured Mrs. Wolfstein to Lady Manby.

"In fact, I never felt better in my life than I did at Old Calabar," continued Miss Burns. "But there my mind was occupied. I was studying the habits of alligators."

"They're very bad, aren't they?" asked Lady Manby, in a tone of earnest inquiry.

"I prefer to study the habits of men," said Sally Perceval, who was always surrounded by a troup of young racing men and athletes, who admired her swimming feats.

"Men are very disappointing, I think," observed Mrs. Trent. "They are like a lot of beads all threaded on one string."

"And what's the string?" asked Sally Perceval.

"Vanity. Men are far vainer than we are. Their indifference to the little arts we practise shows it. A woman whose head is bald covers it with a wig. Without a wig she would feel that she was an outcast totally powerless to attract. But a bald-headed man has no idea of diffidence. He does not bother about a wig because he expects to be adored without one."

"And the worst of it is that he is adored," said Mrs. Wolfstein. "Look at my passion for Henry."

They began to talk about their husbands. Lady Holme did not join in. She and Pimpernel Schley were very silent members of the party. Even Miss Burns, who was—so she said—a spinster by conviction not by necessity, plunged into the husband question, and gave some very daring illustrations of the marriage customs of certain heathen tribes.

Pimpernel Schley hardly spoke at all. When someone, turning to her, asked her what she thought about the subject under discussion, she lifted her pale eyes and said, with the choir-boy drawl:

"I've got no husband and never had one, so I guess I'm no kind of a judge."

"I guess she's a judge of other women's husbands, though," said Mrs. Wolfstein to Lady Cardington. "That child is going to devastate London."

Now and then Lady Holme glanced towards Sir Donald and his son. They seemed as untalkative as she was. Sir Donald kept on looking towards Mrs. Wolfstein's table. So did Leo. But whereas Leo Ulford's eyes were fixed on Pimpernel Schley, Sir Donald's met the eyes of Lady Holme. She felt annoyed; not because Sir Donald was looking at her, but because his son was not.

How these women talked about their husbands! Lady Cardington, who was a widow, spoke of husbands as if they were a race which was gradually dying out. She thought the modern woman was beginning to get a little tired of the institution of matrimony, and to care much less for men than was formerly the case. Being contradicted by Mrs. Trent, she gave her reasons for this belief. One was that whereas American matinee girls used to go mad over the "leading men" of the stage they now went mad over the leading women. She also instanced the many beautiful London women, universally admired, who were over thirty and still remained spinsters. Mrs. Trent declared that they were abnormal, and that, till the end of time, women would always wish to be wives. Mrs. Wolfstein agreed with her on various grounds. One was that it was the instinct of woman to buy and to rule, and that if she were rich she could now acquire a husband as, in former days, people acquired slaves—by purchase. This remark led to the old question of American heiresses and the English nobility, and to a prolonged discussion as to whether or not most women ruled their husbands.

Women nearly always argue from personal experience, and consequently Lady Cardington—whose husband had treated her badly—differed on this point from Mrs. Wolfstein, who always did precisely what she pleased, regardless of Mr. Wolfstein's wishes. Mrs. Trent affirmed that for her part she thought women should treat their husbands as they treated their servants, and dismiss them if they didn't behave themselves, without giving them a character. She had done so twice, and would do it a third time if the occasion arose. Sally Perceval attacked her for this, pleading slangily that men would be men, and that their failings ought to be winked at; and Miss Burns, as usual, brought the marital proceedings of African savages upon the carpet. Lady Manby turned the whole thing into a joke by a farcical description of the Private Enquiry proceedings of a jealous woman of her acquaintance, who had donned a canary-coloured wig as a disguise, and dogged her husband's footsteps in the streets of London, only to find that he went out at odd times to visit a grandmother from whom he had expectations, and who happened to live in St. John's Wood.

The foreign waiters, who moved round the table handing the dishes, occasionally exchanged furtive glances which seemed indicative of suppressed amusement, and the men who were lunching near, many of whom were now smoking cigarettes, became more and more intent upon Mrs. Wolfstein and her guests. As they were getting up to go into the Palm Court for coffee and liqueurs, Lady Cardington again referred to the article on the proposed school for happiness, which had apparently made a deep impression upon her.

"I wonder if happiness can be taught," she said. "If it can—"

"It can't," said Mrs. Trent, with more than her usual sledge-hammer bluntness. "We aren't meant to be happy here."

"Who doesn't mean us to be happy?" asked poor Lady Cardington in a deplorable voice.

"First—our husbands."

"It's cowardly not to be happy," cried Miss Burns, pushing her hat over her left eye as a tribute to the close of lunch. "In a savage state you'll always find—"

The remainder of her remark was lost in the *frou-frou* of skirts as the eight women began slowly to thread their way between the tables to the door.

Lady Holme found herself immediately behind Miss Schley, who moved with impressive deliberation and the extreme composure of a well-brought-up child thoroughly accustomed to being shown off to visitors. Her straw-coloured hair was done low in the nape of her snowy neck, and, as she took her little steps, her white skirt trailed over the carpet behind her with a sort of virginal slyness. As she passed Leo Ulford it brushed gently against him, and he drummed the large fingers of his left hand with sudden violence on the tablecloth, at the same time pursing his chubby lips and then opening his mouth as if he were going to say something.

Sir Donald rose and bowed. Mrs. Wolfstein murmured a word to him in passing, and they had not been sipping their coffee for more than two or three minutes before he joined them with his son.

Sir Donald came up at once to Lady Holme.

"May I present my son to you, Lady Holme?" he said.

"Certainly."

"Leo, I wish to introduce you to Lady Holme."

Leo Ulford bowed rather ungracefully. Standing up he looked more than ever like a huge boy, and he had much of the expression that is often characteristic of huge boys—an expression in which impudence seems to float forward from a background of surliness.

Lady Holme said nothing. Leo Ulford sat down beside her in an armchair.

"Better weather," he remarked.

Then he called a waiter, and said to him, in a hectoring voice:

"Bring me a Kummel and make haste about it."

He lit a cigarette that was almost as big as a cigar, and turned again to Lady Holme.

"I've been in the Sahara gazelle shooting," he continued.

He spoke in a rather thick, lumbering voice and very loud, probably because he was married to a deaf woman.

"Just come back," he added.

"Oh!" said Lady Holme.

She was sitting perfectly upright on her chair, and noticed that her companion's eyes travelled calmly and critically over her figure with an unveiled deliberation that was exceptionally brazen even in a modern London man. Lady Holme did not mind it. Indeed, she rather liked it. She knew at once, by that look, the type of man with whom she had to deal. In Leo Ulford there was something of Lord Holme, as in Pimpernel Schley there was perhaps a touch of herself. Having finished his stare, Leo Ulford continued:

"Jolly out there. No rot. Do as you like and no one to bother you. Gazelle are awfully shy beasts though."

"They must have suited you," said Lady Holme, very gravely.

"Why?" he asked, taking the glass of Kummel which the waiter had brought and setting it down on a table by him.

"Aren't you a shy—er—beast?"

He stared at her calmly for a moment, and then said:

"I say, you're too sharp, Lady Holme."

He turned his head towards Pimpernel Schley, who was sitting a little way off with her soft, white chin tucked well in, looking steadily down into a cup half full of Turkish coffee and speaking to nobody.

"Who's that girl?" he asked.

"That's Miss Pimpernel Schley. A pretty name, isn't it?"

"Is it? An American of course."

"Of course."

"What cheek they have? What's she do?"

"I believe she acts in—well, a certain sort of plays."

A slow smile overspread Leo Ulford's face and made him look more like a huge boy than ever.

"What certain sort?" he asked. "The sort I'd like?"

"Very probably. But I know nothing of your tastes."

She did—everything almost. There are a good many Leo Ulfords lounging about London.

"I like anything that's a bit lively, with no puritanic humbug about it."

"Well, you surely can't suppose that there can be any puritanic humbug about Miss Schley or anything she has to do with!"

He glanced again at Pimpernel Schley and then at Lady Holme. The smile on his face became a grin. Then his huge shoulders began to shake gently.

"I do love talking to women," he said, on the tide of a prolonged chuckle. "When they aren't deaf."

Lady Holme still remained perfectly grave.

"Do you? Why?" she inquired.

"Can't you guess why?"

"Our charity to our sister women?"

She was smiling now.

"You teach me such a lot," he said.

He drank his Kummel.

"I always learn something when I talk to a woman. I've learnt something from you."

Lady Holme did not ask him what it was. She saw that he was now more intent on her than he had been on Miss Schley, and she got up to go, feeling more cheerful than she had since she left the *atelier* of "Cupido."

"Don't go."

"I must."

"Already! May I come and call?"

"Your father knows my address."

"Oh, I say—but—"

"You're not going already!" cried Mrs. Wolfstein, who was having a second glass of Benedictine and beginning to talk rather outrageously and with a more than usually pronounced foreign accent.

"I must, really."

"I'm afraid my son has bored you," murmured Sir Donald, in his worn-out voice.

"No, I like him," she replied, loud enough for Leo to hear.

Sir Donald did not look particularly gratified at this praise of his achievement. Lady Holme took an airy leave of everybody. When she came to Pimpernel Schley she said:

"I wish you a great success, Miss Schley."

"Many thanks," drawled the vestal virgin, who was still looking into her coffee cup.

"I must come to your first night. Have you ever acted in London?"

"Never."

"You won't be nervous?"

"Nervous! Don't know the word."

She bent to sip her coffee.

When Lady Holme reached the door of the Carlton, and was just entering one of the revolving cells to gain the pavement, she heard Lady Cardington's low voice behind her.

"Let me drive you home, dear."

At the moment she felt inclined to be alone. She had even just refused Sir Donald's earnest request to accompany her to her carriage. Had any other woman made her this offer she would certainly have refused it. But few people refused any request of Lady Cardington's. Lady Holme, like the rest of the world, felt the powerful influence that lay in her gentleness as a nerve lies in a body. And then had she not wept when Lady Holme sang a tender song to her? In a moment they were driving up the Haymarket together in Lady Cardington's barouche.

The weather had grown brighter. Wavering gleams of light broke through the clouds and lay across the city, giving a peculiarly unctuous look to the slimy streets, in which there were a good many pedestrians more or less splashed with mud. There was a certain hopefulness in the atmosphere, and yet a pathos such as there always is in Spring, when it walks through London ways, bearing itself half nervously, like a country cousin.

"I don't like this time of year," said Lady Cardington.

She was leaning back and glancing anxiously about her.

"But why not?" asked Lady Holme. "What's the matter with it?"

"Youth."

"But surely—"

"The year's too young. And at my age one feels very often as if the advantage of youth were an unfair advantage."

"Dare I ask—?"

She checked herself, looking at her companion's snow-white hair, which was arranged in such a way that it looked immensely thick under the big black hat she wore—a hat half grandmotherly and half coquettish, that certainly suited her to perfection.

"Spring—" she was beginning rather quickly; but Lady Cardington interrupted her.

"Fifty-eight," she said.

She laughed anxiously and looked at Lady Holme.

"Didn't you think I was older?"

"I don't know that I ever thought about it," replied Lady Holme, with the rather careless frankness she often used towards women.

"Of course not. Why should you, or anyone? When a woman's once over fifty it really doesn't matter much whether she's fifty-one or seventy-one. Does it?"

Lady Holme thought for a moment. Then she said:

"I really don't know. You see, I'm not a man."

Lady Cardington's forehead puckered and her mouth drooped piteously.

"A woman's real life is very short," she said. "But her desire for real life can last very long—her silly, useless desire."

"But if her looks remain?"

"They don't."

"You think it is a question of looks?"

"Do you think it is?" asked Lady Cardington. "But how can you know anything about it, at your age, and with your appearance?"

"I suppose we all have our different opinions as to what men are and what men want," Lady Holme said, more thoughtfully than usual.

"Men! Men!" Lady Cardington exclaimed, with a touch of irritation unusual in her. "Why should we women do, and be, everything for men?"

"I don't know, but we do and we are. There are some men, though, who think it isn't a question of looks, or think they think so."

"Who?" said Lady Cardington, quickly.

"Oh, there are some," answered Lady Holme, evasively, "who believe in mental charm more than in physical charm, or say they do. And mental charm doesn't age so obviously as physical—as the body does, I suppose. Perhaps we ought to pin our faith to it. What do you think of Miss Schley?"

Lady Cardington glanced at her with a kind of depressed curiosity.

"She pins her faith to the other thing," she said.

"Yes."

"She's pretty. Do you know she reminds me faintly of you."

Lady Holme felt acute irritation at this remark, but she only said:

"Does she?"

"Something in her colouring. I'm sure she's a man's woman, but I can't say I found her interesting."

"Men's women seldom are interesting to us. They don't care to be," said Lady Holme.

Suddenly she thought that possibly between Pimpernel Schley and herself there were resemblances unconnected with colouring.

"I suppose not. But still—ah, here's Cadogan Square!"

She kissed Lady Holme lightly on the cheek.

"Fifty-eight!" Lady Holme said to herself as she went into the house. "Just think of being fifty-eight if one has been a man's woman! Perhaps it's better after all to be an everybody's woman. Well, but how's it done?"

She looked quite puzzled as she came into the drawing-room, where Robin Pierce had been waiting impatiently for twenty minutes.

"Robin," she said seriously, "I'm very unhappy."

"Not so unhappy as I have been for the last half hour," he said, taking her hand and holding it. "What is it?"

"I'm dreadfully afraid I'm a man's woman. Do you think I am?"

He could not help smiling as he looked into her solemn eyes.

"I do indeed. Why should you be upset about it?"

"I don't know. Lady Cardington's been saying things—and I met a rather abominable little person at lunch, a little person like a baby that's been about a great deal in a former state, and altogether—Let's have tea."

"By all means."

"And now soothe me, Robin. I'm dreadfully strung up. Soothe me. Tell me, I'm an everybody's woman and that I shall never be *de trop* in the world—not even when I'm fifty-eight."

CHAPTER VI

THE success of Pimpernel Schley in London was great and immediate, and preceded her appearance upon the stage. To some people, who thought they knew their London, it was inexplicable. Miss Schley was pretty and knew how to dress. These facts, though of course denied by some, as all facts in London are, were undeniable. But Miss Schley had nothing to say. She was not a brilliant talker, as so many of her countrywomen are. She was not vivacious in manner, except on rare occasions. She was not interested in all the questions of the day. She was not—a great many things. But she was one thing.

She was exquisitely sly.

Her slyness was definite and pervasive. In her it took the place of wit. It took the place of culture. It even took the place of vivacity. It was a sort of maid-of-all-work in her personality and never seemed to tire. The odd thing was that it did not seem to tire others. They found it permanently piquant. Men said of Miss Schley, "She's a devilish clever little thing. She don't say much, but she's up to every move on the board." Women were impressed by her. There was something in her supreme and snowy composure that suggested inflexible will. Nothing ever put her out or made her look as if she were in a false position.

London was captivated by the abnormal combination of snow and slyness which she presented to it, and began at once to make much of her.

At one time the English were supposed to be cold; and rather gloried in the supposition. But recently a change has taken place in the national character—at any rate as exhibited in London. Rigidity has gone out of fashion. It is condemned as insular, and unless you are cosmopolitan nowadays you are nothing, or worse than nothing. The smart Englishwoman is beginning to be almost as restless as a Neapolitan. She is in a continual flutter of movement, as if her body were threaded with trembling wires. She uses a great deal of gesture. She is noisy about nothing. She is vivacious at all costs, and would rather suggest hysteria than British phlegm.

Miss Schley's calm was therefore in no danger of being drowned in any pervasive calm about her. On the contrary, it stood out. It became very individual. Her composed speechlessness in the midst of uneasy chatter—the Englishwoman is seldom really self-possessed—carried with it a certain dignity which took the place of breeding. She was always at her ease, and to be always at your ease makes a deep impression upon London, which is full of self-consciousness.

She began to be the fashion at once. A great lady, who had a passion for supplying smart men with what they wanted, saw that they were going to want Miss Schley and promptly took her up. Other women followed suit. Miss Schley had a double triumph. She was run after by women as well as by men. She got her little foot in everywhere, and in no time. Her personal character was not notoriously bad. The slyness had taken care of that. But even if it had been, if only the papers had not been too busy in the matter, she might have had success. Some people do whose names have figured upon the evening bills exposed at the street corners. Hers had not and was not likely to. It was her art to look deliberately pure and good, and to suggest, in a way almost indefinable and very perpetual, that she could be anything and everything, and perhaps had been, under the perfumed shadow of the rose. The fact that the suggestion seemed to be conveyed with intention was the thing that took corrupt old London's fancy and made Miss Schley a pet.

Her name of Pimpernel was not against her.

Men liked it for its innocence, and laughed as they mentioned it in the clubs, as who should say:

"We know the sort of Pimpernel we mean."

Miss Schley's social success brought her into Lady Holme's set, and people noticed, what Lady Holme had been the first to notice, the faint likeness between them. Lady Holme was not exquisitely sly. Her voice was not like a choir-boy's; her manner was not like the manner of an image; her eyes were not for ever cast down. Even her characteristic silence was far less perpetual than the equally characteristic silence of Miss Schley. But men said they were the same colour. What men said women began to think, and it was not an assertion wholly without foundation. At a little distance there was an odd resemblance in the one white face and fair hair to the other. Miss Schley's way of moving, too, had a sort of reference to Lady Holme's individual walk. There were several things characteristic of Lady Holme which Miss Schley seemed to reproduce, as it were, with a sly exaggeration. Her hair was similar, but paler, her whiteness more dead, her silence more perpetual, her composure more enigmatically serene, her gait slower, with diminished steps.

It was all a little like an imitation, with just a touch of caricature added.

One or two friends remarked upon it to Lady Holme, who heard them very airily.

"Are we alike?" she said. "I daresay, but you mustn't expect me to see it. One never knows the sort of impression one produces on the world. I think Miss Schley a very attractive little creature, and as to her social gifts, I bow to them."

"But she has none," cried Mrs. Wolfstein, who was one of those who had drawn Lady Holme's attention to the likeness.

"How can you say so? Everyone is at her feet."

"Her feet, perhaps. They are lovely. But she has no gifts. That's why she gets on. Gifted people are a drug in the market. London's sick of them. They worry. Pimpernel's found that out and gone in for the savage state. I mean mentally of course."

"Her mind dwells in a wigwam," said Lady Manby. "And wears glass beads and little bits of coloured cloth."

"But her acting?" asked Lady Holme, with careless indifference.

"Oh, that's improper but not brilliant," said Mrs. Wolfstein. "The American critics says it's beneath contempt."

"But not beneath popularity, I suppose?" said Lady Holme.

"No, she's enormously popular. Newspaper notices don't matter to Pimpernel. Are you going to ask her to your house? You might. She's longing to come. Everybody else has, and she knew you first."

Lady Holme began to realise why she could never like Mrs. Wolfstein. The latter would try to manage other people's affairs.

"I had no idea she would care about it," she answered, rather coldly.

"My dear—an American! And your house! You're absurdly modest. She's simply pining to come. May I tell her to?"

"I should prefer to invite her myself," said Lady Holme, with a distinct touch of hauteur which made Mrs. Wolfstein smile maliciously.

When Lady Holme was alone she realised that she had, half unconsciously, meant that Miss Schley should find that there was at any rate one house in London whose door did not at once fly open to welcome her demure presence. But now? She certainly did not intend to be a marked exception to a rule that was apparently very general. If people were going to talk about her exclusion of Miss Schley, she would certainly not exclude her. She asked herself why she wished to, and said to herself that Miss Schley's slyness bored her. But she knew that the real reason of the secret hostility she felt towards the American was the fact of their resemblance to each other. Until Miss Schley appeared in London she—Viola Holme—had been original both in her beauty and in her manner of presenting it to the world. Miss Schley was turning her into a type.

It was too bad. Any woman would have disliked it.

She wondered whether Miss Schley recognised the likeness. But of course people had spoken to her about it. Mrs. Wolfstein was her bosom friend. The Jewess had met her first at Carlsbad and, with that terrible social flair which often dwells in Israel, had at once realised her fitness for a London success and resolved to "get her over." Women of the Wolfstein species are seldom jealously timorous of the triumphs of other women. A certain coarse cleverness, a certain ingrained assurance and unconquerable self-confidence keeps them hardy. And they generally have a noble reliance on the power of the tongue. Being incapable of any fear of Miss Schley, Mrs. Wolfstein, ever on the look-out for means of improving her already satisfactory position in the London world, saw one in the vestal virgin and resolved to launch her in England. She was delighted with the result. Miss Schley had already added several very desirable people to the Wolfstein visiting-list. In return "Henry" had "put her on to" one or two very good things in the City. Everything would be most satisfactory if only Lady Holme were not tiresome about the Cadogan Square door.

"She hates you, Pimpernel," said Mrs. Wolfstein to her friend.

"Why?" drawled Miss Schley.

"You know why perfectly well. You reproduce her looks. I'm perfectly certain she's dreading your first night. She's afraid people will begin to think that extraordinary colourless charm she and you possess stagey. Besides, you have certain mannerisms—you don't imitate her, Pimpernel?"

The pawnbroking expression was remarkably apparent for a moment in Mrs. Wolfstein's eyes.

"I haven't started to yet."

"Yet?"

"Well, if she don't ask me to number thirty-eight—'tis thirty-eight?"

"Forty-two."

"Forty-two Cadogan Square, I might be tempted. I came out as a mimic, you know, at Corsher and Byall's in Philadelphia."

Miss Schley gazed reflectively upon the brown carpet of Mrs. Wolfstein's boudoir.

"Folks said I wasn't bad," she added meditatively.

"I think I ought to warn Viola," said Mrs. Wolfstein.

She was peculiarly intimate with people of distinction when they weren't there. Miss Schley looked as if she had not heard. She often did when anything of importance to her was said. It was important to her to be admitted to Lady Holme's house. Everybody went there. It was one of the very smartest houses in London, and since everybody knew that she had been introduced to Lady Holme, since half the world was comparing their faces and would soon begin to compare their mannerisms—well, it would be better that she should not be forced into any revival of her Philadelphia talents.

Mrs. Wolfstein did not warn Lady Holme. She was far too fond of being amused to do anything so short-sighted. Indeed, from that moment she was inclined to conspire to keep the Cadogan Square door shut against her friend. She did not go so far as that; for she had a firm faith in Pimpernel's cuteness and was aware that she would be found out. But she remained passive and kept her eyes wide open.

Miss Schley was only going to act for a month in London. Her managers had taken a theatre for her from the first of June till the first of July. As she was to appear in a play she had already acted in all over the States, and as her American company was coming over to support her, she had nothing to do in the way of preparation. Having arrived early in the year, she had nearly three months of idleness to enjoy. Her conversation with Mrs. Wolfstein took place in the latter days of March. And it was just at this period that Lady Holme began seriously to debate whether she should, or should not, open her door to the American. She knew Miss Schley was determined to come to her house. She knew her house was one of those to which any woman setting out on the conquest of London would wish to come. She did not want Miss Schley there, but she resolved to invite her if peopled talked too much about her not being invited. And she wished to be informed if they did. One day she spoke to Robin Pierce about it. Lord Holme's treatment of Carey had not yet been applied to him. They met at a private view in Bond Street, given by a painter who was adored by the smart world, and, as yet, totally unknown in every other circle. The exhibition was of portraits of beautiful women, and all the beautiful women and their admirers crowded the rooms. Both Lady Holme and Miss Schley had been included among the sitters of the painter, and—was it by chance or design?—their portraits hung side by side upon the brown-paper-covered walls. Lady Holme was not aware of this when she caught Robin's eye through a crevice in the picture hats and called him to her with a little nod.

"Is there tea?"

"Yes. In the last room."

"Take me there. Oh, there's Ashley Greaves. Avoid him, like a dear, till I've looked at something."

Ashley Greaves was the painter. There was nothing of the Bohemian about him. He looked like a heavy cavalry officer as he stood in the centre of the room talking to a small, sharp-featured old lady in a poke bonnet.

"He's safe. Lady Blower's got hold of him."

"Poor wretch! She ought to have a keeper. Strong tea, Robin."

They found a settee in a corner walled in by the backs of tea-drinking beauties.

"I want to ask you something," said Lady Holme, confidentially. "You go about and hear what they're saying."

"And greater nonsense it seems each new season."

"Nonsense keeps us alive."

"Is it the oxygen self-administered by an almost moribund society?"

"It's the perfume that prevents us from noticing the stuffiness of the room. But, Robin, tell me—what is the nonsense of now?"

"Religious, political, theatrical, divorce court or what, Lady Holme?"

He looked at her with a touch of mischief in his dark face, which told her, and was meant to tell her, that he was on the alert, and had divined that she had a purpose in thus pleasantly taking possession of him.

"Oh, the people—nonsense. You know perfectly what I mean."

"Whom are they chattering about most at the moment? You'll be contemptuous if I tell you."

"It's a woman, then?"

"When isn't it?"

"Do I know her?"

"Slightly."

"Well?"

"Miss Schley."

"Really?"

Lady Holme's voice sounded perfectly indifferent and just faintly surprised. There was no hint of irritation in it.

"And what are they saying about Miss Schley?" she added, sipping her tea and glancing about the crowded room.

"Oh, many things, and among the many one that's more untrue than all the rest put together."

"What's that?"

"It's too absurd. I don't think I'll tell you."

"But why not? If it's too absurd it's sure to be amusing."

"I don't think so."

His voice sounded almost angry.

"Tell me, Robin."

He looked at her quickly with a warm light in his dark eyes.

"If you only knew how I—"

"Hush! Go on about Miss Schley."

"They're saying that she's wonderfully like you, and that—have some more tea?"

"That—?"

"That you hate it."

Lady Holme smiled, as if she were very much entertained.

"But why should I hate it?"

"I don't know. But women invent reasons for everything."

"What have they invented for this?"

"Oh—well—that you like to—I can't tell you it all, really. But in substance it comes to this! They are saying, or implying—"

"Implication is the most subtle of the social arts."

"It's the meanest—implying that all that's natural to you, that sets you apart from others, is an assumption to make you stand out from the rest of the crowd, and that you hate Miss Schley because she happens to have assumed some of the same characteristics, and so makes you seem less unique than you did before."

Lady Holme said nothing for a moment. Then she remarked:

"I'm sure no woman said 'less unique.'"

"Why not?"

"Now did anyone? Confess!"

"What d'you suppose they did say?"

"More commonplace."

He could not help laughing.

"As if you were ever commonplace!" he exclaimed, rather relieved by her manner.

"That's not the question. But then Miss Schley's said to be like me not only in appearance but in other ways? Are we really so Siamese?"

"I can't see the faintest beginning of a resemblance."

"Ah, now you're falling into exaggeration in the other direction."

"Well, not in realities. Perhaps in one or two trifling mannerisms—I believe she imitates you deliberately."

"I think I must ask her to the house."

"Why should you?"

"Well, perhaps you might tell me."

"I don't understand."

"Aren't people saying that the reason I don't ask her is because I am piqued at the supposed resemblance between us?"

"Oh, people will say anything. If we are to model our lives according to their ridiculous ideas—"

"Well, but we do."

"Unless we follow the dictates of our own natures, our own souls."

He lowered his voice almost to a whisper.

"Be yourself, be the woman who sings, and no one—not even a fool—will ever say again that you resemble a nonentity like Miss Schley. You see—you see now that even socially it is a mistake not to be your real self. You can be imitated by a cute little Yankee who has neither imagination nor brains, only the sort of slyness that is born out of the gutter."

"My dear Robin, remember where we are. You—a diplomatist!"

She put her finger to her lips and got up.

"We must look at something or Ashley Greaves will be furious."

They made their way into the galleries, which were almost impassable. In the distance Lady Holme caught sight of Miss Schley with Mrs. Wolfstein. They were surrounded by young men. She looked hard at the American's pale face, saying to herself, "Is that like me? Is that like me?" Her conversation with Robin Pierce had made her feel excited. She had not shown it. She had seemed, indeed, almost oddly indifferent. But something combative was awake within her. She wondered whether the American was consciously imitating her. What an impertinence! But Miss Schley was impertinence personified. Her impertinence was her *raison d'etre*. Without it she would almost cease to be. She would at any rate be as nothing.

Followed by Robin, Lady Holme made her way slowly towards the Jewess and the American.

They were now standing together before the pictures, and had been joined by Ashley Greaves, who was beginning to look very warm and expressive, despite his cavalry moustache. Their backs were towards the room, and Lady Holme and Robin drew near to them without being perceived. Mrs. Wolfstein had a loud voice and did not control it in a crowd. On the contrary, she generally raised it, as if she wished to be heard by those whom she was not addressing.

"Sargent invariably brings out the secret of his sitters," she was saying to Ashley Greaves as Lady Holme and Robin came near and stood for an instant wedged in by people, unable to move forward or backward. "You've brought out the similarities between Pimpernel and Lady Holme. I never saw anything so clever. You show us not only what we all saw but what we all passed over though it was there to see. There is an absurd likeness, and you've blazoned it."

Robin stole a glance at his companion. Ashley Greaves said, in a thin voice that did not accord with his physique:

"My idea was to indicate the strong link there is between the English woman and the American woman. If I may say so, these two portraits, as it were, personify the two countries, and—er—and—er—"

His mind appeared to give way. He strove to continue, to say something memorable, conscious of his conspicuous and central position. But his intellect, possibly over-heated and suffering from lack of air, declined to back him up, and left him murmuring rather hopelessly:

"The one nation—er—and the other—yes—the give and take—the give and take. You see my meaning? Yes, yes."

Miss Schley said nothing. She looked at Lady Holme's portrait and at hers with serenity, and seemed quite unconscious of the many eyes fastened upon her.

"You feel the strong link, I hope, Pimpernel?" said Mrs. Wolfstein, with her most violent foreign accent. "Hands across the Herring Pond!"

"Mr. Greaves has been too cute for words," she replied. "I wish Lady Holme could cast her eye on them."

She looked up at nothing, with a sudden air of seeing something interesting that was happening along way off.

"Philadelphia!" murmured Mrs. Wolfstein, with an undercurrent of laughter.

It was very like Lady Holme's look when she was singing. Robin Pierce saw it and pressed his lips together. At this moment the crowd shifted and left a gap through which Lady Holme immediately glided towards Ashley Greaves. He saw her and came forward to meet her with eagerness, holding out his hand, and smiling mechanically with even more than his usual intention.

"What a success!" she said.

"If it is, your portrait makes it so."

"And where is my portrait?"

Robin Pierce nipped in the bud a rather cynical smile. The painter wiped his forehead with a white silk handkerchief.

"Can't you guess? Look where the crowd is thickest."

The people had again closed densely round the two pictures.

"You are an artist in more ways than one, I'm afraid," said Lady Holme. "Don't turn my head more than the heat has."

The searching expression, that indicated the strong desire to say something memorable, once more contorted the painter's face.

"He who would essay to fix beauty on canvas," he began, in a rather piercing voice, "should combine two gifts."

He paused and lifted his upper lip two or three times, employing his under-jaw as a lever.

"Yes?" said Lady Holme, encouragingly.

"The gift of the brush which perpetuates and the gift of—er—gift of the—"

His intellect once more retreated from him into some distant place and left him murmuring:

"Beauty demands all, beauty demands all. Yes, yes! Sacrifice! Sacrifice! Isn't it so?"

He tugged at his large moustache, with an abrupt assumption of the cavalry officer's manner, which he doubtless deemed to be in accordance with his momentary muddle-headedness.

"And you give it what it wants most—the touch of the ideal. It blesses you. Can we get through?"

She had glanced at Robin while she spoke the first words. Ashley Greaves, with an expression of sudden relief, began very politely to hustle the crowd, which yielded to his persuasive shoulders, and Lady Holme found herself within looking distance of the two portraits, and speaking distance of Mrs. Wolfstein and Miss Schley. She greeted them with a nod that was more gay and friendly than her usual salutations to women, which often lacked *bonhomie*. Mrs. Wolfstein's too expressive face lit up.

"The sensation is complete!" she exclaimed loudly.

"Hope you're well," murmured Miss Schley, letting her pale eyes rest on Lady Holme for about a quarter of a second, and then becoming acutely attentive to vacancy.

Lady Holme was now in front of the pictures. She looked at Miss Schley's portrait with apparent interest, while Mrs. Wolfstein looked at her with an interest that was maliciously real.

"Well?" said Mrs. Wolfstein. "Well?"

"There's an extraordinary resemblance!" said Lady Holme. "It's wonderfully like."

"Even you see it! Ashley, you ought to be triumphant—"

"Wonderfully like—Miss Schley," added Lady Holme, cutting gently through Mrs. Wolfstein's rather noisy outburst.

She turned to the American.

"I have been wondering whether you won't come in one day and see my little home. Everyone wants you, I know, but if you have a minute some Wednesday—"

"I'll be delighted."

"Next Wednesday, then?"

"Thanks. Next Wednesday."

"Cadogan Square—the red book will tell you. But I'll send cards. I must be running away now."

When she had gone, followed by Robin, Mrs. Wolfstein said to Miss Schley:

"She's been conquered by fear of Philadelphia."

"Wait till I give her Noo York," returned the American, placidly.

It seemed that Lady Holme's secret hostility to Miss Schley was returned by the vestal virgin.

CHAPTER VII

LORD HOLME seldom went to parties and never to private views. He thought such things "all damned rot." Few functions connected with the arts appealed to his frankly Philistine spirit, which rejoiced in celebrations linked with the glories of the body; boxing and wrestling matches, acrobatic performances, weight-lifting exhibitions, and so forth. He regretted that bear-baiting and cock-fighting were no longer legal in England, and had, on two occasions, travelled from London to South America solely in order to witness prize fights.

As he so seldom put in an appearance at smart gatherings he had not yet encountered Miss Schley, nor had he heard a whisper of her much-talked-of resemblance to his wife. Her name was known to him as that of a woman whom one or two of his "pals" began to call a "deuced pretty girl" but his interest in her was not greatly awakened. The number of deuced pretty girls that had been in his life, and in the lives of his pals, was legion. They came and went like feathers dancing on the wind. The mere report of them, therefore, casual and drifting, could not excite his permanent attention, or fix their names and the record of their charms in his somewhat treacherous memory. Lady Holme had not once mentioned the American to him. She was a woman who knew how to be silent, and sometimes she was silent by instinct without saying to herself why.

Lord Holme never appeared on her Wednesdays; and, indeed, those days were a rather uncertain factor among the London joys. If Lady Holme was to be found in her house at all, she was usually to be found on a Wednesday afternoon. She herself considered that she was at home on Wednesdays, but this idea of hers was often a mere delusion, especially when the season had fully set in. There were a thousand things to be done. She frequently forgot what the day of the week was. Unluckily she forgot it on the Wednesday succeeding her invitation to Miss Schley. The American duly turned up in Cadogan Square and was informed that Lady Holme was not to be seen. She left her card and drove away in her coupe with a decidedly stony expression upon her white face.

That day it chanced that Lord Holme came in just before his wife and carelessly glanced over the cards which had been left during the afternoon. He was struck by the name of Pimpernel. It tickled his fancy somehow. As he looked at it he grinned. He looked at it again and vaguely recalled some shreds of the club gossip about Miss Schley's attractions. When Lady Holme walked quietly into her drawing-room two or three minutes later he met her with Miss Schley's card in his hand.

"What have you got there, Fritz?" she said.

He gave her the card.

"You never told me you'd run up against her," he remarked.

Lady Holme looked at the card and then, quickly, at her husband.

"Why—do you know Miss Schley?" she asked.

"Not I."

"Well then?"

"Fellows say she's deuced takin'. That's all. And she's got a fetchin' name—eh? Pimpernel."

He repeated it twice and began to grin once more, and to bend and straighten his legs in the way which sometimes irritated his wife. Lady Holme was again looking at the card.

"Surely it isn't Wednesday?" she said.

"Yes, it is. What did you think it was?"

"Tuesday—Monday—I don't know."

"Where'd you meet her?"

"Whom? Miss Schley? At the Carlton. A lunch of Amalia Wolfstein's."

"Is she pretty?"

"Yes."

There was no hesitation before the reply.

"What colour?

"Oh!—not Albino."

Lord Holme stared.

"What d'you mean by that, girlie?"

"That Miss Schley is remarkably fair—fairer than I am."

"Is she as pretty as you?

"You can find out for yourself. I'm going to ask her to something—presently."

In the last word, in the pause that preceded it, there was the creeping sound of the reluctance Lady Holme felt in allowing Miss Schley to draw any closer to her life. Lord Holme did not notice it. He only said:

"Right you are. Pimpernel—I should like to have a squint at her."

"Very well. You shall."

"Pimpernel," repeated Lord Holme, in a loud bass voice, as he lounged out of the room, grinning. The name tickled his fancy immensely. That was evident.

Lady Holme fully intended to ask Miss Schley to the "something" already mentioned immediately. But somehow several days slipped by and it was difficult to find an unoccupied hour. The Holme cards had, of course, duly gone to the Carlton, but there the matter had ended, so far as Lady Holme was concerned. Miss Schley, however, was not so heedless as the woman she resembled. She began to return with some assiduity to the practice of the talent of the old Philadelphia days. In those days she used to do a "turn" in the course of which she imitated some of the popular public favourites of the States, and for each of her imitations she made up to resemble the person mimicked. She now concentrated this talent upon Lady Holme, but naturally the methods she employed in Society were far more subtle than those she had formerly used upon the stage. They were scarcely less effective. She slightly changed her fashion of doing her hair, puffing it out less at the sides, wearing it a little higher at the back. The change accentuated her physical resemblance to Lady Holme. She happened to get the name of the dressmaker who made most of the latter's gowns, and happened to give her an order that was executed with remarkable rapidity. But all this was only the foundation upon which she based, as it were, the structure of her delicate revenge.

That consisted in a really admirable hint—it could not be called more— of Lady Holme's characteristic mannerisms.

Lady Holme was not an affected woman, but, like all women of the world who are greatly admired and much talked about, she had certain little ways of looking, moving, speaking, being quiet, certain little habits of laughter, of gravity, that were her own property. Perhaps originally natural to her, they had become slightly accentuated as time went on, and many tongues and eyes admired them. That which had been unconscious had become conscious. The faraway look came a little more abruptly, went a little more reluctantly; than it had in the young girl's days. The wistful smile lingered more often on the lips of the twenties than on the lips of the teens. Few noticed any change, perhaps, but there had been a slight change, and it made things easier for Miss Schley.

Her eye was observant although it was generally cast down. Society began to smile secretly at her talented exercises. Only a select few, like Mrs. Wolfstein, knew exactly what she was doing and why she was doing it, but the many were entertained, as children are, without analysing the cause of their amusement.

Two people, however, were indignant—Robin Pierce and Rupert Carey.

Robin Pierce, who had an instinct that was almost feminine in its subtlety, raged internally, and Rupert Carey, who, naturally acute, was always specially shrewd when his heart was in the game, openly showed his distaste for Miss Schley, and went about predicting her complete failure to capture the London public as an actress.

"She's done it as a woman," someone replied to him.

"Not the public, only the smart fools," returned Carey.

"The smart fools have more influence on the public every day."

Carey only snorted. He was in one of his evil moods that afternoon. He left the club in which the conversation had taken place, and, casting about for something to do, some momentary solace for his irritation and *ennui,* he bethought him of Sir Donald Ulford's invitation and resolved to make a call at the Albany. Sir Donald would be out, of course, but anyhow he would chance it and shoot a card.

Sir Donald's servant said he was in. Carey was glad. Here was an hour filled up.

With his usual hasty, decisive step he followed the man through a dark and Oriental-looking vestibule into a library, where Sir Donald was sitting at a bureau of teakwood, slowly writing upon a large, oblong sheet of foolscap with a very pointed pen.

He got up, looking rather startled, and held out his hand.

"I am glad to see you. I hoped you would come."

"I'm disturbing a new poem," said Carey.

Sir Donald's faded face acknowledged it.

"Sorry. I'll go."

"No, no. I have infinite leisure, and I write now merely for myself. I shall never publish anything more. The maunderings of the old are really most thoroughly at home in the waste-paper basket. Do sit down."

Carey threw himself into a deep chair and looked round. It was a room of books and Oriental china. The floor was covered with an exquisite Persian carpet, rich and delicate in colour, with one of those vague and elaborate designs that stir the imagination as it is stirred by a strange perfume in a dark bazaar where shrouded merchants sit.

"I light it with wax candles," said Sir Donald, handing Carey a cigar.

"It's a good room to think in, or to be sad in."

He struck a match on his boot.

"You like to shut out London," he continued.

"Yes. Yet I live in it."

"And hate it. So do I. London's like a black-browed brute that gets an unholy influence over you. It would turn Mark Tapley into an Ibsen man. Yet one can't get away from it."

"It holds interesting minds and interesting faces."

"Didn't Persia?"

"Lethargy dwells there and in all Eastern lands."

"You have made up your mind to spend the rest of your days in the fog?"

"No. Indeed, only to-day I acquired a Campo Santo with cypress trees, in which I intend to make a home for any dying romance that still lingers within me."

He spoke with a sort of wistful whimsicality. Carey stared hard at him.

"A Campo Santo's a place for the dead."

"Why not for the dying? Don't they need holy ground as much?"

"And where's this holy ground of yours?"

Sir Donald got up from his chair, went over to the bureau, opened a drawer, and took out of it a large photograph rolled round a piece of wood, which he handed to Carey, who swiftly spread it out on his knees.

"That is it."

"I say, Sir Donald, d'you mind my asking for a whisky-and-soda?"

"I beg your pardon."

He hastily touched a bell and ordered it. Meanwhile Carey examined the photograph.

"What do you think of it?" Sir Donald asked.

"Well—Italy obviously."

"Yes, and a conventional part of Italy."

"Maggiore?"

"No, Como."

"The playground of the honeymoon couple."

"Not where my Campo Santo is. They go to Cadenabbia, Bellagio, Villa D'Este sometimes."

"I see the fascination. But it looks haunted. You've bought it?"

"Yes. The matter was arranged to-day."

The photograph showed a large, long house, or rather two houses divided by a piazza with slender columns. In the foreground was water. Through the arches of the piazza water was also visible, a cascade falling in the black cleft of a mountain gorge dark with the night of cypresses. To the right of the house, rising from the lake, was a tall old wall overgrown with masses of creeping plants and climbing roses. Over it more cypresses looked, and at the base of it, near the house, were a flight of worn steps disappearing into the lake, and an arched doorway with an elaborately-wrought iron grille. Beneath the photograph was written, "*Casa Felice.*"

"Casa Felice, h'm!" said Carey, with his eyes on the photograph.

"You think the name inappropriate?"

"Who knows? One can be wretched among sunbeams. One might be gay among cypresses. And Casa Felice belongs to you?"

"From to-day."

"Old—of course?"

"Yes. There is a romance connected with the house."

"What is it?"

"Long ago two guilty lovers deserted their respective mates and the brilliant world they had figured in, and fled there together."

"And quarrelled and were generally wretched there for how many months?"

"For eight years."

"The devil! Fidelity gone mad!"

"It is said that during those years the mistress never left the garden, except to plunge into the lake on moonlight nights and swim through the silver with her lover."

The Woman with the Fan | 77

Carey was silent. He did not take his eyes from the photograph, which seemed to fascinate him. When the servant came in with the whisky-and-soda he started.

"Not a place to be alone in," he said.

He drank, and stared again at the photograph.

"There's something about the place that holds one even in a photograph," he added.

"One can feel the strange intrigue that made the house a hermitage. It has been a hermitage ever since."

"Ah!"

"An old Italian lady, very rich, owned it, but never lived there. She recently died, and her heir consented to sell it to me."

"Well, I should like to see it in the flesh—or the bricks and mortar. But it's not a place to be alone in," repeated Carey. "It wants a woman if ever a house did."

"What sort of woman?"

Sir Donald had sat down again on the chair opposite, and was looking with his exhausted eyes through the smoke of the cigars at Carey.

"A fair woman, a woman with a white face, a slim woman with eyes that are cords to draw men to her and bind them to her, and a voice that can sing them into the islands of the sirens."

"Are there such women in a world that has forgotten Ulysses?"

"Don't you know it?"

He rolled the photograph round the piece of wood and laid it on a table.

"I can only think of one who at all answers to your description."

"The one of whom I was thinking."

"Lady Holme?"

"Of course."

"Don't you think she would be dreadfully bored in Casa Felice?"

"Horribly, horribly. Unless—"

"Unless?"

"Who knows what? But there's very often an unless hanging about, like a man at a street corner, that—" He broke off, then added abruptly, "Invite me to Casa Felice some day."

"I do."

"When will you be going there?"

"As soon as the London season is over. Some time in August. Will you come then?"

"The house is ready for you?"

"It will be. The necessary repairs will be begun now. I have bought it furnished."

"The lovers' furniture?"

"Yes. I shall add a number of my own things, picked up on my wanderings."

"I'll come in August if you'll have me. But I'll give you the season to think whether you'll have me or whether you won't. I'm a horrible bore in a house—the lazy man who does nothing and knows a lot. Casa Felice—Casa Felice. You won't alter the name?"

"Would you advise me to?"

"I don't know. To keep it is to tempt the wrath of the gods, but I should keep it."

He poured out another whisky-and-soda and suddenly began to curse Miss Schley.

Sir Donald had spoken to her after Mrs. Wolfstein's lunch.

"She's imitating Lady Holme," said Carey.

"I cannot see the likeness," Sir Donald said. "Miss Schley seems to me uninteresting and common."

"She is."

"And Lady Holme's personality is, on the contrary; interesting and uncommon."

"Of course. Pimpernel Schley would be an outrage in that Campo Santo of yours. And yet there is a likeness, and she's accentuating it every day she lives."

"Why?"

"Ask the women why they do the cursed things they do do."

"You are a woman-hater?"

"Not I. Didn't I say just now that Casa Felice wanted a woman? But the devil generally dwells where the angel dwells—cloud and moon together. Now you want to get on with that poem."

Half London was smiling gently at the resemblance between Lady Holme and Miss Schley before the former made up her mind to ask the latter to "something." And when, moved to action by certain evidences of the Philadelphia talent which could not be misunderstood, she did make up her mind, she resolved that the "something" should be very large and by no means very intimate. Safety wanders in crowds.

She sent out cards for a reception, one of those affairs that begin about eleven, are tremendous at half past, look thin at twelve, and have faded away long before the clock strikes one.

Lord Holme hated them. On several occasions he had been known to throw etiquette to the winds and not to turn up when his wife was giving them. He always made what he considered to be a good excuse. Generally he had "gone into the country to look at a horse." As Lady Holme sent out her cards, and saw her secretary writing the words, "Miss Pimpernel Schley," on an envelope which contained one, she asked herself whether her husband would be likely to play her false this time.

"Shall you be here on the twelfth?" she asked him casually.

"Why? What's up on the twelfth?"

"I'm going to have one of those things you hate—before the Arkell House ball. I chose that night so that everyone should run away early! You won't be obliged to look at a horse in the country that particular day?"

She spoke laughingly, as if she wanted him to say no, but would not be very angry if he didn't. Lord Holme tugged his moustache and looked very serious indeed.

"Another!" he ejaculated. "We're always havin' 'em. Any music?"

"No, no, nothing. There are endless dinners that night, and Mrs. Crutchby's concert with Calve, and the ball. People will only run in and say something silly and run out again."

"Who's comin'?"

"Everybody. All the tiresome dears that have had their cards left."

Lord Holme stared at his varnished boots and looked rather like a puzzled boy at a *viva voce* examination.

"The worst of it is, I can't be in the country lookin' at a horse that night," he said with depression.

"Why not?"

She hastily added:

"But why should you? You ought to be here."

"I'd rather be lookin' at a horse. But I'm booked for the dinner to Rowley at the Nation Club that night. I might say the speeches were too long and I couldn't get away. Eh?"

He looked at her for support.

"You really ought to be here, Fritz," she answered.

It ended there. Lady Holme knew her husband pretty well. She fancied that the speeches at the dinner given to Sir Jacob Rowley, ex-Governor of some place she knew nothing about, would turn out to be very lengthy indeed—speeches to keep a man far from his home till after midnight.

On the evening of the twelfth Lord Holme had not arrived when the first of his wife's guests came slowly up the stairs, and Lady Holme began gently to make his excuses to all the tiresome dears who had had their cards left at forty-two Cadogan Square. There were a great many tiresome dears. The stream flowed steadily, and towards half-past eleven resembled a flood-tide.

Lady Cardington, Lady Manby, Mr. Bry, Sally Perceval had one by one appeared, and Robin Pierce's dark head was visible mounting slowly amid a throng of other heads of all shapes, sizes and tints.

Lady Holme was looking particularly well. She was dressed in black. Of course black suits everybody. It suited her even better than most people, and her gown was a triumph. She was going on to the Arkell House ball, and wore the Holme diamonds, which were superb, and which she had recently had reset. She was in perfect health, and felt unusually young and unusually defiant. As she stood at the top of the staircase, smiling, shaking hands with people, and watching Robin Pierce coming slowly nearer, she wondered a little at certain secret uneasinesses—they could scarcely be called tremors—which had recently oppressed her. How absurd of her to have been troubled, even lightly, by the impertinent proceedings of an American actress, a nobody from the States, without position, without distinction, without even a husband. How could it matter to her what such a little person—she always called Pimpernel Schley a little person in her thoughts—did or did not do? As Robin came towards her she almost—but not quite—wished that the speeches at the dinner to Sir Jacob Rowley had not been so long as they evidently had been, and that her husband were standing beside her, looking enormous and enormously bored.

"What a crowd!"

"Yes. We can't talk now. Are you going to Arkell House?"

Robin nodded.

"Take me in to supper there."

"May I? Thank you. I'm going with Rupert Carey."

"Really!"

At this moment Lady Holme's eyes and manner wandered. She had just caught a glimpse of Mrs. Wolfstein, a mass of jewels, and of Pimpernel Schley at the foot of the staircase, had just noticed that the latter happened to be dressed in black.

"Bye-bye!" she added.

Robin Pierce walked on into the drawing-rooms looking rather preoccupied.

Everybody came slowly up the stairs. It was impossible to do anything else. But it seemed to Lady Holme that Miss Schley walked far more slowly than the rest of the tiresome dears, with a deliberation that had a touch of insolence in it. Her straw-coloured hair was done exactly like Lady Holme's, but she wore no diamonds in it. Indeed, she had on no jewels. And this absence of jewels, and her black gown, made her skin look almost startlingly white, if possible whiter than Lady Holme's. She smiled quietly as she mounted the stairs, as if she were wrapt in a pleasant, innocent dream which no one knew anything about.

Amalia Wolfstein was certainly a splendid—a too splendid—foil to her. The Jewess was dressed in the most vivid orange colour, and was very much made up. Her large eyebrows were heavily darkened. Her lips were scarlet. Her eyes, which moved incessantly, had a lustre which suggested oil with a strong light shining on it. "Henry" followed in her wake, looking intensely nervous, and unnaturally alive and observant, as if he were searching in the crowd for a bit of gold that someone had accidentally dropped. When anyone spoke to him he replied with extreme vivacity but in the fewest possible words. He held his spare figure slightly sideways as he walked, and his bald head glistened under the electric lamps. Behind them, in the distance, was visible the yellow and sunken face of Sir Donald Ulford.

When Miss Schley gained the top of the staircase Lady Holme saw that their gowns were almost exactly alike. Hers was sewn with diamonds, but otherwise there was scarcely any difference. And she suddenly felt as if the difference made by the jewels was not altogether in her favour, as if she were one of those women who look their best when they are not wearing any ornaments. Possibly Mrs. Wolfstein made all jewellery seem vulgar for the moment. She looked like an exceedingly smart jeweller's shop rather too

brilliantly illuminated; "as if she were for sale," as an old and valued friend of hers aptly murmured into the ear of someone who had known her ever since she began to give good dinners.

"Here we are! I'm chaperoning Pimpernel. But her mother arrives to-morrow," began Mrs. Wolfstein, with her strongest accent, while Miss Schley put out a limp hand to meet Lady Holme's and very slightly accentuated her smile.

"Your mother? I shall be delighted to meet her. I hope you'll bring her one day," said Lady Holme; thinking more emphatically than ever that for a woman with a complexion as perfect as hers it was a mistake to wear many jewels.

"I'll be most pleased, but mother don't go around much," replied Miss Schley.

"Does she know London?"

"She does not. She spends most of her time sitting around in Susanville, but she's bound to look after me in this great city."

Mrs. Wolfstein was by this time in violent conversation with a pale young man, who always looked as if he were on the point of fainting, but who went literally everywhere. Miss Schley glanced up into Lady Holme's eyes.

"I hoped to make the acquaintance of Lord Holme to-night," she murmured. "Folks tell me he's a most beautiful man. Isn't he anywhere around?"

She looked away into vacancy, ardently. Lady Holme felt a slight tingling sensation in her cool skin. For a moment it seemed to her as if she watched herself in caricature, distorted perhaps by a mirror with a slight flaw in it.

"My husband was obliged to dine out to-night; unfortunately. I hope he'll be here in a moment, but he may be kept, as there are to be some dreadful speeches afterwards. I can't think why elderly men always want to get up and talk nonsense about the Royal family after a heavy dinner. It's so bad for the digestion and the—ah, Sir Donald! Sweet of you to turn up. Your boy's been so unkind. I asked him to call, or he asked to call, and he's never been near me."

Miss Schley drifted away and was swallowed by the crowd. Sir Donald had arrived at the top of the stairs.

"Leo's been away in Scotland ever since he had the pleasure of meeting you. He only came back to-night."

"Then I'm not quite so hurt. He's always running about, I suppose, to kill things, like my husband."

"He does manage a good deal in that way. If you are going to the Arkell House ball you'll meet him there. He and his wife are both—"

"How did do! Oh, Charley, I never expected to see you. I thought it wasn't the thing for the 2nd to turn up at little hay parties like this. Kitty Barringlave is in the far room, dreadfully bored. Go and cheer her up. Tell her what'll win the Cup. She's pale and peaky with ignorance about Ascot this year. Both going to Arkell House, Sir Donald, did you say? Bring your son to me, won't you? But of course you're a wise man trotting off to bed."

"No. The Duke is a very old friend of mine, and so—"

"Perfect. We'll meet then. They say it's really locomotor ataxia, poor fellow I but—ah, there's Fritz!"

Sir Donald looked at her with a sudden inquiring shrewdness, that lit up his faded eyes and made them for a moment almost young. He had caught a sound of vexation in her voice, which reminded him oddly of the sound in her singing voice when Miss Filberte was making a fiasco of the accompaniment. Lord Holme was visible and audible in the hall. His immense form towered above his guests, and his tremendous bass voice dominated the hum of conversation round him. Lady Holme could see from where she stood that he was in a jovial and audacious mood. The dinner to Sir Jacob Rowley had evidently been well cooked and gay. Fritz had the satisfied and rather larky air of a man who has been having one good time and intends to have another. She glanced into the drawing-rooms. They were crammed. She saw in the distance Lady Cardington talking to Sir Donald Ulford. Both of them looked rather pathetic. Mrs. Wolfstein was not far off, standing in the midst of a group and holding forth with almost passionate vivacity and self-possession. Her husband was gliding sideways through the crowd with his peculiarly furtive and watchful air, which always suggested the old nursery game, "Here I am on Tom Tiddler's ground, picking up gold and silver." Lady Manby was laughing in a corner with an archdeacon who looked like a guardsman got up in fancy dress. Mr. Bry, his eyeglass fixed in his left eye, came towards the staircase, moving delicately like Agag, and occasionally dropping a cold or sarcastic word to an acquaintance. He reached Lady Holme when Lord Holme was half-way up the stairs, and at once saw him.

"A giant refreshed with wine," he observed, dropping his eyeglass.

It was such a perfect description of Lord Holme in his present condition that two or three people who were standing with Lady Holme smiled, looking down the staircase. Lady Holme did not smile. She continued chattering, but her face wore a discontented expression. Mr. Bry noticed it. There were very few things he did not notice, although he claimed to be the most short-sighted man in London.

"Why is your husband so dutiful to-night?" he murmured to his hostess. "I thought he always had to go into the country to look at a gee-gee on these occasions."

"He had to be in town for the dinner to Sir Jacob Rowley. I begged him to come back in—How did do! How did do! Yes, very. Mr. Raleigh, do tell the opera people not to put on Romeo too often this season. Of course Melba's splendid in it, and all that, but still—"

Mr. Bry fixed his eyeglass again, and began to smile gently like an evil-minded baby. Lord Holme's brown face was full in view, grinning. His eyes were looking about with unusual vivacity.

"How early you are, Fritz! Good boy. I want you to look after—"

"I say, Vi, why didn't you tell me?"

Mr. Bry, letting his eyeglass fall, looked abstracted and lent an attentive ear. If he were not playing prompter to social comedies he generally stood in the wings, watching and listening to them with a cold amusement that was seldom devoid of a spice of venom.

"Tell you what, Fritz?"

"That Miss Schley was comin' to-night. Everyone's talking about her. I sat next Laycock at dinner and he was ravin'. Told me she was to be here and I didn't know it. Rather ridiculous, you know. Where is she?"

"Somewhere in the rooms."

"What's she like?"

"Oh!—I don't know. She's in black. Go and look for her."

Lord Holme strode on. As he passed Mr. Bry he said:

"I say, Bry, d'you know Miss Pimpernel Schley?"

"Naturally."

"Come with me, there's a good chap, and—what's she like?"

As they went on into the drawing-rooms Mr. Bry dropped out:

"Some people say she's like Lady Holme."

"Like Vi! Is she? Laycock's been simply ravin'—simply ravin'—and Laycock's not a feller to—where is she?

"We shall come to her. So there was no gee-gee to look at in the country to-night?"

Lord Holme burst into a roar of laughter.

"There's the vestal tending her lamp," said Mr. Bry a moment later.

"The what up to what?"

"Miss Pimpernel Schley keeping the fire of adoration carefully alight."

"Where?"

"There."

"Oh, I see! Jove, what a skin, though! Eh! Isn't it? She is deuced like Vi at a distance. Vi looks up just like that when she's singin'. Doesn't she, though? Eh?"

He went on towards her.

Mr. Bry followed him, murmuring.

"The giant refreshed with wine. No gee-gee to-night. No gee-gee."

CHAPTER VIII

"THE brougham is at the door, my lady"

"Tell his lordship."

The butler went out, and Lady Holme's maid put a long black cloak carefully over her mistress's shoulders. While she did this Lady Holme stood quite still gazing into vacancy. They were in the now deserted yellow drawing-room, which was still brilliantly lit, and full of the already weary-looking flowers which had been arranged for the reception. The last guest had gone and the carriage was waiting to take the Holmes to Arkell House.

The maid did something to the diamonds in Lady Holme's hair with deft fingers, and the light touch seemed to wake Lady Holme from a reverie. She went to a mirror and looked into it steadily. The maid stood behind. After a moment Lady Holme lifted her hand suddenly to her head, as if she were going to take off her tiara. The maid could not repress a slight movement of startled astonishment. Lady Holme saw it in the glass, dropped her hand, and said:

"C'est tout, Josephine. Vous pouvez vous en aller."

"Merci, miladi."

She went out quietly.

Two or three minutes passed. Then Lord Holme's deep bass voice was audible, humming vigorously:

> "Ina, Ina, oh, you should have seen her!
> Seen her with her eyes cast down.
> She looked upon the floor,
> And all the Johnnies swore
> That Ina, Ina—oh, you should have seen her!—
> That Ina was the chic-est girl in town."

Lady Holme frowned.

"Fritz!" she called rather sharply.

Lord Holme appeared with a coat thrown over his arm and a hat in his hand. His brown face was beaming with self-satisfaction.

"Well, old girl, ready? What's up now?"

"I wish you wouldn't sing those horrible music-hall songs. You know I hate them."

"Music-hall! I like that. Why, it's the best thing in *The Chick from the Army and Navy* at the Blue Theatre."

"It's disgustingly vulgar."

"What next? Why, I saw the Lord Chan—"

"I daresay you did. Vulgarity will appeal to the Saints of Heaven next season if things go on as they're going now. Come along."

She went out of the room, walking more quickly than she usually walked, and holding herself very upright. Lord Holme followed, forming the words of his favourite song with his lips, and screwing up his eyes as if he were looking at an improper peepshow. When they were in the electric brougham, which spun along with scarcely any noise, he began:

"I say, Vi, how long've you known Miss Schley?"

"I don't know. Some weeks."

"Why didn't you tell me?"

"I did. I said I had met her at Mrs. Wolfstein's lunch."

"No, but why didn't you tell me how like you she was?"

There was complete silence in the brougham for a minute. Then Lady Holme said:

"I had no idea she was like me."

"Then you're blind, old girl. She's like you if you'd been a chorus-girl and known a lot of things you don't know."

"Really. Perhaps she has been a chorus-girl."

"I'll bet she has, whether she says so or not."

He gave a deep chuckle. Lady Holme's gown rustled as she leaned back in her corner.

"And she's goin' to Arkell House. Americans are the very devil for gettin' on. Laycock was tellin' me to-night that—"

"I don't wish to hear Mr. Laycock's stories, Fritz. They don't amuse me."

"Well, p'r'aps they're hardly the thing for you, Vi. But they're deuced amusin' for all that."

He chuckled again. Lady Holme felt an intense desire to commit some act of physical violence. She shut her eyes. In a minute she heard her husband once more beginning to hum the refrain about Ina. How utterly careless he was of her desires and requests. There was something animal in his forgetfulness and indifference. She had loved the animal in him. She did love it. Something deep down in her nature answered eagerly to its call. But at moments she hated it almost with fury. She hated it now and longed to use the whip, as the tamer in a menagerie uses it when one of his beasts shows its teeth, or sulkily refuses to perform one of its tricks.

Lord Holme went on calmly humming till the brougham stopped in the long line of carriages that stretched away into the night from the great portico of Arkell House.

People were already going in to supper when the Holmes arrived. The Duke, upon whom a painful malady was beginning to creep, was bravely welcoming his innumerable guests. He found it already impossible to go unaided up and down stairs, and sat in a large armchair close to the ball-room, with one of his pretty daughters near him, talking brightly, and occasionally stealing wistful glances at the dancers, who were visible through a high archway to his left. He was a thin, middle-aged man, with a curious, transparent look in his face—something crystalline that was nearly beautiful.

The Duchess was swarthy and masterful, very intelligent and *grande dame*. Vivacity was easy to her. People said she had been a good hostess in her cradle, and that she had presided over the ceremony of her own baptism in a most autocratic and successful manner. It was quite likely.

After a word with the Duke, Lady Holme went slowly towards the ballroom with her husband. She did not mean to dance, and began to refuse the requests of would-be partners with charming protestations of fatigue. Lord Holme was scanning the ballroom with his big brown eyes.

"Are you going to dance, Fritz?" asked Lady Holme, nodding to Robin Pierce, whom she had just seen standing at a little distance with Rupert Carey.

The latter had not seen her yet, but as Robin returned her nod he looked hastily round.

"Yes, I promised Miss Schley to struggle through a waltz with her. Wonder if she's dancin'?"

Lady Holme bowed, a little ostentatiously, to Rupert Carey. Her husband saw it and began at once to look pugilistic. He could not say anything, for at this moment two or three men strolled up to speak to Lady Holme. While she was talking to them, Pimpernel Schley came in sight waltzing with Mr. Laycock, one of those abnormally thin, narrow-featured, smart men, with bold, inexpressive ayes, in whom London abounds.

Lord Holme's under-jaw resumed its natural position, and he walked away and was lost in the crowd, following the two dancers.

"Take me in to supper, Robin. I'm tired."

"This way. I thought you were never coming."

"People stayed so late. I can't think why. I'm sure it was dreadfully dull and foolish. How odd Mr. Carey's looking! When I bowed to him just now he didn't return it, but only stared at me as if I were a stranger."

Robin Pierce made no rejoinder. They descended the great staircase and went towards the picture-gallery.

"Find a corner where we can really talk."

"Yes, yes."

He spoke eagerly.

"Here—this is perfect."

They sat down at a table for two that was placed in an angle of the great room. Upon the walls above them looked down a Murillo and a Velasquez. Lady Holme was under the Murillo, which represented three Spanish street boys playing a game in the dust with pieces of money.

"A table for two," said Robin Pierce. "I have always said that the Duchess understands the art of entertaining better than anyone in London, except you—when you choose."

"To-night I really couldn't choose. Later on, I'm going to give two or three concerts. Is anything the matter with Mr. Carey?"

"Do you think so?"

"Well, I hope it isn't true what people are saying."

"What are they saying?"

"That's he's not very judicious in one way."

A footman poured champagne into her glass. Robin Pierce touched the glass.

"That way?"

"Yes. It would be too sad."

"Let us hope it isn't true, then."

"You know him well. Is it true?"

"Would you care if it was?"

He looked at her earnestly.

"Yes. I like Mr. Carey."

There was a rather unusual sound of sincerity in her voice.

"And what is it that you like in him?"

"Oh, I don't know. He talks shocking nonsense, of course, and is down on people and things. And he's absurdly unsophisticated at moments, though he knows the world so well. He's not like you—not a diplomat. But I believe if he had a chance he might do something great."

Robin felt as if the hidden woman had suddenly begun to speak. Why did she speak about Rupert Carey?

"Do you like a man to do something great?" he said.

"Oh, yes. All women do."

"But I perpetually hear you laughing at the big people—the Premiers, the Chancellors, the Archbishops, the Generals of the world."

"Because I've always known them. And really they are so often quite absurd and tiresome."

"And—Rupert Carey?"

"Oh, he's nothing at all, poor fellow! Still there's something in his face that makes me think he could do an extraordinary thing if he had the chance. I saw it there to-night when he didn't bow to me. There's Sir Donald's son. And what a dreadful-looking woman just behind him."

Leo Ulford was coming down the gallery with a gaunt, aristocratic, harsh-featured girl. Behind him walked Mr. Bry, conducting a very young old woman, immensely smart, immensely vivacious, and immensely pink, who moved with an unnecessary alertness that was birdlike, and turned her head about sharply on a long, thin neck decorated with a large diamond dog-collar. Slung at her side there was a tiny jewelled tube.

"That's Mrs. Leo."

"She must be over sixty."

"She is."

The quartet sat down at the next table. Leo Ulford did not see Lady Holme at once. When he caught sight of her, he got up, came to her, stood over her and pressed her hand.

"Been away," he explained. "Only back to-night."

"I've been complaining to your father about you."

A slow smile overspread his chubby face.

"May I see you again after supper?"

"If you can find me."

"I can always manage to find what I want," he returned, still smiling.

When he had gone back to his table Robin Pierce said:

"How insolent Englishmen are allowed to be in Society! It always strikes me after I've been a long time abroad. Doesn't anybody mind it?"

"Do you mean that you consider Mr. Ulford insolent?"

"In manner. Yes, I do."

"Well, I think there's something like Fritz about him."

Robin Pierce could not tell from the way this was said what would be a safe remark to make. He therefore changed the subject.

"Do you know what Sir Donald's been doing?" he said.

"No. What?"

"Buying a Campo Santo."

"A Campo Santo! Is he going to bury himself, then? What do you mean, Robin?"

"He called it a Campo Santo to Carey. It's really a wonderful house in Italy, on Como. Casa Felice is the name of it. I know it well."

"Casa Felice. How delicious! But is it the place for Sir Donald?"

"Why not?"

"For an old, tired man. Casa Felice. Won't the name seem an irony to him when he's there?"

"You think an old man can't be happy anywhere?"

"I can't imagine being happy old."

"Why not?"

"Oh!"—she lowered her voice—"if you want to know, look at Mrs. Ulford."

"Your husk theory again. A question of looks. But you will grow old gracefully—some day in the far future."

"I don't think I shall grow old at all."

"Then—?"

"I think I shall die before that comes—say at forty-five. I couldn't live with wrinkles all over my face. No, Robin, I couldn't. And—look at Mrs. Ulford!—perhaps an ear-trumpet set with opals."

"What do the wrinkles matter? But some day you'll find I'm right. You'll tell me so. You'll acknowledge that your charm comes from within, and has survived the mutilation of the husk."

"Mutilation! What a hideous sound that word has. Why don't all mutilated people commit suicide at once? I should. Is Sir Donald going to live in his happy house?"

"Naturally. He'll be there this August. He's invited Rupert Carey to stay there with him."

"And you?"

"Not yet."

"I suppose he will. Everybody always asks you everywhere. Diplomacy is so universally—"

She broke off. Far away, at the end of the gallery, she had caught sight of Miss Schley coming in with her husband. They sat down at a table near the door. Robin Pierce followed her eyes and understood her silence.

"Are you going on the first?" he asked.

"What to?"

"Miss Schley's first night."

"Is it on the first? I didn't know. We can't. We're dining at Brayley House that evening."

"What a pity!" he said, with a light touch of half playful malice. "You would have seen her as she really is—from all accounts."

"And what is Miss Schley really?"

"The secret enemy of censors."

"Oh!"

"You dislike her. Why?"

"I don't dislike her at all."

"Do you like her?"

"No. I like very few women. I don't understand them."

"At any rate you understand—say Miss Schley—better than a man would."

"Oh—a man!"

"I believe all women think all men fools."

Lady Holme laughed, not very gaily.

"Don't they?" he insisted.

"In certain ways, in certain relations of life, I suppose most men are—rather short-sighted."

"Like Mr. Bry."

"Mr. Bry is the least short-sighted man I know. That's why he always wears an eyeglass."

"To create an illusion?"

"Who knows?"

She looked down the long room. Between the heads of innumerable men and women she could see Miss Schley. Her husband was hidden. She would have preferred to see him. Miss Schley's head was by no means expressive of the naked truth. It merely looked cool, self-possessed, and—so Lady Holme said to herself—extremely American. What she meant by that she could, perhaps, hardly have explained.

"Do you admire Miss Schley's appearance?"

Robin Pierce spoke again with a touch of humorous malice. He knew Lady Holme so well that he had no objection to seem wanting in tact to her when he had a secret end to gain. She looked at him sharply; leaning forward over the table and opening her eyes very wide.

"Why are you forgetting your manners to-night and bombarding me with questions?"

"The usual reason—devouring curiosity."

She hesitated, looking at him. Then suddenly her face changed. Something, some imp of adorable frankness, peeped out of it at him, and her whole body seemed confiding.

"Miss Schley is going about London imitating me. Now, isn't that true? Isn't she?"

"I believe she is. Damned impertinence!"

He muttered the last words under his breath.

"How can I admire her?"

There was something in the way she said that which touched him. He leaned forward to her.

"Why not punish her for it?"

"How?"

"Reveal what she can't imitate."

"What's that?"

"All you hide and I divine."

"Go on."

"She mimics the husk. She couldn't mimic the kernel."

"Ice, my lady?"

Lady Holme started. Till the footman spoke she had not quite realised how deeply interested she was in the conversation. She helped herself to some ice.

"You can go on, Mr. Pierce," she said when the man had gone.

"But you understand."

She shook her head, smiling. Her body still looked soft and attractive, and deliciously feminine.

"Miss Schley happens to have some vague resemblance to you in height and colouring. She is a clever mimic. She used to be a professional mimic."

"Really!"

"That was how she first became known."

"In America?"

"Yes."

"Why should she imitate me?"

"Have you been nice to her?"

"I don't know. Yes. Nice enough."

Robin shook his head.

"You think she dislikes me then?"

"Do women want definite reasons for half the things they do? Miss Schley may not say to herself that she dislikes you, any more than you say to yourself that you dislike her. Nevertheless—"

"We should never get on. No."

"Consider yourselves enemies—for no reasons, or secret woman's reasons. It's safer."

Lady Holme looked down the gallery again. Miss Schley's fair head was bending forward to some invisible person.

"And the mimicry?" she asked, turning again to Robin.

"Can only be applied to mannerisms, to the ninety-ninth part, the inconsiderable fraction of your charm. Miss Schley could never imitate the hidden woman, the woman who sings, the woman who laughs at, denies herself when she is not singing."

"But no one cares for her—if she exists."

There was a hint of secret bitterness in her voice when she said that.

"Give her a chance—and find out. But you know already that numbers do."

He tried to look into her eyes, but she avoided his gaze and got up.

"Take me back to the ballroom."

"You are going to dance?"

"I want to see who's here."

As they passed the next table Lady Holme nodded to Leo Ulford. He bowed in return and indicated that he was following almost immediately. Mrs. Ulford put down her ear-trumpet, turned her head sharply, and looked at Lady Holme sideways, fluttering her pink eyelids.

"How exactly like a bird she is," murmured Lady Holme.

"Exactly—moulting."

Lady Holme meant as she walked down the gallery; to stop and speak a few gay words to Miss Schley and her husband, but when she drew near to their table Lord Holme was holding forth with such unusual volubility, and Miss Schley was listening with such profound attention, that it did not seem worth while, and she went quietly on, thinking they did not see her. Lord Holme did not. But the American smiled faintly as Lady Holme and Robin disappeared into the hall. Then she said, in reply to her animated companion:

"I'm sure if I am like Lady Holme I ought to say *Te Deum* and think myself a lucky girl. I ought, indeed."

Lady Holme had not been in the ballroom five minutes before Leo Ulford came up smiling.

"Here I am," he remarked, as if the statement were certain to give universal satisfaction.

Robin looked black and moved a step closer to Lady Holme.

"Thank you, Mr. Pierce," she said.

She took Leo Ulford's arm, nodded to Robin, and walked away.

Robin stood looking after her. He started when he heard Carey's voice saying:

"Why d'you let her dance with that blackguard?"

"Hulloa, Carey?"

"Come to the supper-room. I want to have a yarn with you. And all this"—he made a wavering, yet violent, gesture towards the dancers—"might be a Holbein."

"A dance of death? What nonsense you talk!"

"Come to the supper-room."

Robin looked at his friend narrowly.

"You're bored. Let's go and take a stroll down Park Lane."

"No. Well, then, if you won't—"

"I'll come."

He put his arm through Carey's, and they went out together.

Lady Holme was generally agreeable to men. She was particularly charming to Leo Ulford that night. He was not an interesting man, but he seemed to interest her very much. They sat out together for a long time in the corner of a small drawing-room, far away from the music. She had said to Robin Pierce that she thought there was something about Leo Ulford that was like her husband, and when she talked to him she found the resemblance even greater than she had supposed.

Lord Holme and Leo Ulford were of a similar type. Both were strong, healthy, sensual, slangy, audacious in a dull kind of fashion—Lady Holme did not call it dull—serenely and perpetually intent upon having everything their own way in life. Both lived for the body and ignored the soul, as they would have ignored a man with a fine brain, a passionate heart, a narrow chest and undeveloped muscles. Such a man they would have summed up as "a rotter." If they ever thought of the soul at all, it was probably under some such comprehensive name. Both had the same simple and blatant aim in life, an aim which governed all their actions and was the generator of most of their thoughts. This aim, expressed in their own terse language, was "to do themselves jolly well." Both had, so far, succeeded in their ambition. Both were, consequently, profoundly convinced of their own cleverness. Intellectual conceit—the conceit of the brain—is as nothing to physical conceit—the conceit of the body. Acute intelligence is always capable of uneasiness, can always make room for a doubt. But the self-satisfaction of the little-brained and big-muscled man who has never had a rebuff or a day's illness is cased in triple brass. Lady Holme knew this self-satisfaction well. She had seen it staring out of her husband's big brown eyes. She saw it now in the boyish eyes of Leo Ulford. She was at home with it and rather liked it. In truth, it had at least one merit—from the woman's point of view—it was decisively masculine.

Whether Leo Ulford was, or was not, a blackguard; as Mrs. Trent had declared, did not matter to her. Three-quarters of the men she knew were blackguards according to the pinched ideas of Little Peddlington; and Mrs. Trent might originally have issued from there.

She got on easily with Leo Ulford because she was experienced in the treatment of his type. She knew exactly what to do with it; how to lead it on, how to fend it off, how to throw cold water on its enterprise without dashing it too greatly, how to banish any little, sulky cloud that might appear on the brassy horizon without seeming to be solicitous.

The type is amazingly familiar to the woman of the London world. She can recognize it at a glance, and can send it in its armchair canter round the circus with scarce a crack of the ring-mistress's whip.

To-night Lady Holme enjoyed governing it more than usual, and for a subtle reason.

In testing her power upon Leo Ulford she was secretly practising her siren's art, with a view that would have surprised and disgusted him, still more amazed him, had he known it. She was firing at the dummy in order that later she might make sure of hitting the living man. Leo Ulford was the dummy. The living man would be Fritz.

Both dummy and living man were profoundly ignorant of her moving principle. The one was radiant with self-satisfaction under her fusillade. The other, ignorant of it so far, would have been furious in the knowledge of it.

She knew—and laughed at the men.

Presently she turned the conversation, which was getting a little too personal—on Leo Ulford's side—to a subject very present in her mind that night.

"Did you have a talk with Miss Schley the other day after I left?" she asked. "I ran away on purpose to give you a chance. Wasn't it good-natured of me, when I was really longing to stay?"

Leo Ulford stretched out his long legs slowly, his type's way of purring.

"I'd rather have gone on yarning with you."

"Then you did have a talk! She was at my house to-night, looking quite delicious. You know she's conquered London?"

"That sort's up to every move on the board."

"What do you mean? What board?"

She looked at him with innocent inquiry.

"I wish men didn't know so much," she added; with a sort of soft vexation. "You have so many opportunities of acquiring knowledge and we so few—if we respect the *convenances*."

"Miss Schley wouldn't respect 'em."

He chuckled, and again drew up and then stretched out his legs, slowly and luxuriously.

"How can you know?"

"She's not the sort that does. She's the sort that's always kicking over the traces and keeping it dark. I know 'em."

"I think you're rather unkind. Miss Schley's mother arrives to-morrow."

Leo Ulford put up his hands to his baby moustache and shook with laughter.

"That's the only thing she wanted to set her up in business," he ejaculated. "A marmar. I do love those Americans!"

"But you speak as if Mrs. Schley were a stage property!"

"I'll bet she is. Wait till you see her. Why, it's a regular profession in the States, being a marmar. I tell you what—"

He leaned forward and fixed his blue eyes on Lady Holme, with an air of profound acuteness.

"Are you going to see her?"

"Mrs. Schley? I daresay."

"Well, you remember what I tell you. She'll be as dry as a dog-biscuit, wear a cap and spectacles with gold rims, and say nothing but 'Oh, my, yes indeed!' to everything that's said to her. Does she come from Susanville?"

"How extraordinary! I believe she does."

Leo Ulford's laugh was triumphant and prolonged.

"That's where they breed marmars!" he exclaimed, when he was able to speak. "Women are stunning."

"I'm afraid I don't quite understand," said Lady Holme, preserving a quiet air of pupilage. "But perhaps it's better I shouldn't. Anyhow, I am quite sure Miss Schley's mother will be worthy of her daughter."

"You may bet your bottom dollar on that. She'll be what they call 'a sootable marmar.' I must get my wife to shoot a card on her."

"I hope you'll introduce me to Mrs. Ulford. I should like to know her."

"Yours isn't the voice to talk down a trumpet," said Leo Ulford, with a sudden air of surliness.

"I should like to know her now I know you and your father."

At the mention of his father Leo Ulford's discontented expression increased.

"My father's a rotter," he said. "Never cared for anything. No shot to speak of. He can sit on a horse all right. Had to, in South America and Morocco and all those places. But he never really cared about it, I don't believe. Why, he'd rather look at a picture than a thoroughbred any day!"

At this moment Sir Donald wandered into the room, with his hands behind his thin back, and his eyes searching the walls. The Duke possessed a splendid collection of pictures.

"There he is!" said Leo, gruffly.

"He doesn't see us. Go and tell him I'm here."

"Why? he might go out again if we keep mum."

"But I want to speak to him. Sir Donald! Sir Donald!"

Sir Donald turned round at the second summons and came towards them, looking rather embarrassed.

"Hulloa, pater!" said Leo.

Sir Donald nodded to his son with a conscientious effort to seem familiar and genial.

"Hulloa!" he rejoined in a hollow voice.

"Your boy has been instructing me in American mysteries," said Lady Holme. "Do take me to the ballroom, Sir Donald."

Leo Ulford's good humour returned as abruptly as it had departed. Her glance at him, as she spoke, had seemed to hint at a secret understanding between them in which no one—certainly not his father—was included.

"Pater can tell you all about the pictures," he said, with a comfortable assurance, which he did not strive to disguise, that she would be supremely bored.

He stared at her hard, gave a short laugh, and lounged away.

When he had gone, Sir Donald still seemed embarrassed. He looked at Lady Holme apologetically, and in his faded eyes she saw an expression that reminded her of Lady Cardington. It was surely old age asking forgiveness for its existence.

She did not feel much pity for it, but with the woman of the world's natural instinct to smooth rough places—especially for a man—she began to devote herself to cheering Sir Donald up, as they slowly made their way through room after room towards the distant sound of the music.

"I hear you've been plunging!" she began gaily.

Sir Donald looked vague.

"I'm afraid I scarcely—"

"Forgive me. I catch slang from my husband. He's ruining my English. I mean that I hear you've been investing—shall I say your romance?—in a wonderful place abroad, with a fascinating name. I hope you'll get enormous interest."

A faint colour, it was like the ghost of a blush, rose in Sir Donald's withered cheeks.

"Ah, Mr. Carey—"

He checked himself abruptly, remembering whet he had heard from Robin Pierce.

"No, Mr. Pierce was my informant. He knows your place and says it's too wonderful. I adore the name."

"Casa Felice. You would not advise me to change it, then?"

"Change it! Why?"

"Well, I—one should not, perhaps, insist beforehand that one is going to have happiness, which must always lie on the knees of the gods."

"Oh, I believe in defiance."

There was an audacious sound in her voice. Her long talk with Leo Ulford had given her back her belief in herself, her confidence in her beauty, her reliance on her youth.

"You have a right to believe in it. But Casa Felice is mine."

"Even to buy it was a defiance—in a way."

"Perhaps so. But then—"

"But then you have set out and you must not turn back, Sir Donald. Baptise your wonderful house yourself by filling it with happiness. Another gave it its name. Give it yourself the reason for the name."

Happiness seemed to shine suddenly in the sound of her speaking voice, as it shone in her singing voice when the theme of her song was joy. Sir Donald's manner lost its self-consciousness, its furtive diffidence.

"You—you come and give my house its real baptism," he said, with a flash of ardour that, issuing from him, was like fire bursting out of a dreary marsh land. "Will you? This August?"

"But," she hesitated. "Isn't Mr. Carey coming?"

At this moment they came into a big drawing-room that immediately preceded the ballroom, with which it communicated by an immense doorway hung with curtains of white velvet. They could see in the distance the dancers moving rather indifferently in a lancers. Lord Holme and Miss Schley were dancing in the set nearest to the doorway, and on the side that faced the drawing-room. Directly Lady Holme saw the ballroom she saw them. A sudden sense of revolt, the defiance of joy carried on into the defiance of anger, rose up in her.

"If Mr. Carey is coming I'll come too, and baptise your house," she said.

Sir Donald looked surprised, but he answered, with a swiftness that did not seem to belong to old age:

"That is a bargain, Lady Holme. I regard that as a bargain."

"I'll not go back on it."

There was a hard sound in her voice.

They entered the ballroom just as the band played the closing bars of the lancers, and the many sets began to break up and melt into a formless crowd which dispersed in various directions. The largest number of people moved towards the archway near which the Duke was still sitting, bravely exerting himself to be cheerful. Lady Holme and Sir Donald became involved in this section of the crowd, and naturally followed its direction. Lord Holme and Miss Schley were at a short distance behind them, and

Lady Holme was aware of this. The double defiance was still alive in her, and was strengthened by a clear sound which reached her ears for a moment, then was swallowed up by the hum of conversation from many intervening voices—the sound of the American's drawling tones raised to say something she could not catch. As she came out into the hall, close to the Duke's chair, she saw Rupert Carey trying to make his way into the ballroom against the stream of dancers. His face was flushed. There were drops of perspiration on his forehead, and the violent expression that was perpetually visible in his red-brown eyes, lighting them up as with a flame, seemed partially obscured as if by a haze. The violence of them was no longer vivid but glassy.

Lady Holme did not notice all this. The crowd was round her, and she was secretly preoccupied. She merely saw that Rupert Carey was close to her, and she knew who was following behind her. A strong impulse came upon her and she yielded to it without hesitation. As she reached Rupert Carey she stopped and held out her hand.

"Mr. Carey," she said, "I've been wanting to speak to you all the evening. Why didn't you ask me to dance?"

She spoke very distinctly. Carey stood still and stared at her, and now she noticed the flush on his face and the unnatural expression in his eyes. She understood at once what was the matter and repented of her action. But it was too late to draw back. Carey stared dully for an instant, as if he scarcely knew who she was. Then, with a lurch, he came closer to her, and, with a wavering movement, tried to find her hand, which she had withdrawn.

"Where is it?" he muttered in a thick voice. "Where is it?"

He groped frantically.

"Sir Donald!" Lady Holme whispered sharply, while the people nearest to them began to exchange glances of surprise or of amusement.

She pressed his arm and he tried to draw her on. But Carey was exactly in front of her. It was impossible for her to escape. He found her hand at last, took it limply in his, bent down and began to kiss it, mumbling some loud but incoherent words.

The Duke, who from his chair, was a witness of the scene, tried to raise himself up, and a vivid spot of scarlet burned in his almost transparent cheeks. His daughter hastened forward to stop his effort. Lady Holme dragged her hand away violently, and Carey suddenly burst into tears. Sir Donald hurried Lady Holme on, and Carey tried to follow, but was forcibly prevented by two men.

When at length Lady Holme found herself at the other end of the great hall, she turned and saw her husband coming towards her with a look of fury on his face.

"I wish to go home," she said to him in a low voice.

She withdrew her hand from Sir Donald's arm and quietly bade him good-bye. Lord Holme did not say a word.

"Where is the Duchess?" Lady Holme added. "Ah, there she is!"

She saw the Duchess hurriedly going towards the place where the Duke was sitting, intercepted her swiftly, and bade her good-night.

"Now, Fritz!" she said.

She was conscious that a number of people were watching her, and her voice and manner were absolutely unembarrassed. A footman took the number of her cloak from Lord Holme and fetched the cloak. A voice cried in the distance, "Lord Holme's carriage!" Another, and nearer voice, echoed the call. She passed slowly between two lines of men over a broad strip of carpet to the portico, and stepped into the brougham.

As it glided away into the night she heard her husband's loud breathing.

He did not speak for two or three minutes, but breathed like a man who had been running, and moved violently in the carriage as if to keep still were intolerable to him. The window next to him was up. He let it down. Then he turned right round to his wife, who was leaning back in her corner wrapped up in her black cloak.

"With the Duke sittin' there!" he said in a loud voice. "With the Duke sittin' there!"

There was a sound of outrage in the voice.

"Didn't I kick that sweep out of the house?" he added. "Didn't I?"

"I believe you asked Mr. Carey not to call anymore."

Lady Holme's voice had no excitement in it.

"Asked him! I—"

"Don't make such a noise, Fritz. The men will hear you."

"I told him if he ever came again I'd have him put out."

"Well, he never has come again."

"What d'you mean by speakin' to him? What d'you mean by it?"

Lady Holme knew that her husband was a thoroughly conventional man, and, like all conventional men, had a horror of a public scene in which any woman belonging to him was mixed up. Such a scene alone was quite enough to rouse his wrath. But there was in his present anger something deeper, more brutal, than any rage caused by a breach of the conventions. His jealousy was stirred.

"He didn't speak to you. You spoke to him."

Lady Holme did not deny it.

"I heard every word you said," continued Lord Holme, beginning to breathe hard again. "I—I—"

Lady Holme felt that he was longing to strike her, that if he had been the same man, but a collier or a labourer, born in another class of life, he would not have hesitated to beat her. The tradition in which he had been brought up controlled him. But she knew that if he could have beaten her he would have hated her less, that his sense of bitter wrong would have at once diminished. In self-control it grew. The spark rose to a flame.

"You're a damned shameful woman!" he said.

The brougham drew up softly before their house. Lord Holme, who was seated on the side next the house, got out first. He did not wait on the pavement to assist his wife, but walked up the steps, opened the door, and went into the hall. Lady Holme followed. She saw her husband, with the light behind him, standing with his hand on the handle of the hall door. For an instant she thought that he was going to shut her out. He actually pushed the door till the light was almost hidden. Then he flung it open with a bang, threw down his hat and strode upstairs.

If he had shut her out! She found herself wondering what would have become of her, where she would have gone. She would have had to go to the Coburg, or to Claridge's, without a maid, without luggage. As she slowly came upstairs she heard her husband go into the drawing-room. Was he waiting for her there? or did he wish to avoid her? When she reached the broad landing she hesitated. She was half inclined to go in audaciously, to laugh in his face; turn his fury into ridicule, tell him she was the sort of woman who is born to do as she likes, to live as she chooses, to think of nothing but her own will, consult nothing but her whims of the moment. But she went on and into her bedroom.

Josephine was there and began to take the diamonds out of her hair. Lady Holme did not say a word. She was listening intently for the sound of any movement below. She heard nothing. When she was undressed, and there was nothing more for the maid to do, she began to feel uneasy, as if she would rather not dismiss the girl. But it was very late. Josephine strangled her yawns with difficulty. There was no excuse for keeping her up any longer.

"You can go."

The maid went out, leaving Lady Holme standing in the middle of the big bedroom. Next to it on one side was Lord Holme's dressing-room. On the other side there was a door leading into Lady Holme's boudoir. Almost directly after Josephine had gone Lady Holme heard the outer door of this room opened, and the heavy step of her husband. It moved about the room, stopped, moved about again. What could he be doing? She stood where she was, listening. Suddenly the door between the rooms was thrown open and Lord Holme appeared.

"Where's the red book?" he said.

"The red book!"

"Where is it? D'you hear?"

"What do you want it for?"

"That sweep's address."

"What are you going to do? Write to him?"

"Write to him!" said Lord Holme, with bitter contempt. "I'm goin' to thrash him. Where is it?"

"You are going now?"

"I've not come up to answer questions. I've come for the red book. Where is it?"

"The little drawer at the top on the right hand of the writing-table."

Lord Holme turned back into the boudoir, went to the writing-table, found the book, opened it, found the address and wrote it down on a bit of paper. He folded the paper up anyhow and thrust it into his waistcoat pocket. Then, without saying another word to his wife, or looking at her, he went out and down the staircase.

She followed him on to the landing, and stood there till she heard the hall door shut with a bang.

A clock below struck four. She went back into the bedroom and sank into an armchair.

A slight sense of confusion floated over her mind for a moment, like a cloud. She was not accustomed to scenes. There had been one certainly when Rupert Carey was forbidden to come to the house any more, but it had been brief, and she had not been present at it. She had only heard of it afterwards. Lord Holme had been angry then, and she had rather liked his anger. She took it as, in some degree, a measure of his attachment to her. And then she had had no feeling of being in the wrong or of humiliation. She had been charming to Carey, as she was charming to all men. He had lost his head. He had mistaken the relations existing between her and her husband, and imagined that such a woman as she was must be unhappily mated with such a man as Lord Holme. The passionate desire to console a perfectly-contented woman had caused him to go too far, and bring down upon himself a fiat of exile, which he could not defy since Lady Holme permitted it to go forth, and evidently was not rendered miserable by it. So the acquaintance with Rupert Carey had ceased, and life had slipped along once more on wheels covered with india-rubber tyres.

And now she had renewed the acquaintance publicly and with disastrous results.

As she sat there she began to wonder at herself, at the strength of her temper, the secret violence of her nature. She had yielded like a child to a sudden impulse. She had not thought of consequences. She had ignored her worldly knowledge. She had considered nothing, but had acted abruptly, as any ignorant, uneducated woman might have acted. She had been the slave of a mood. Or had she been the slave of another woman—of a woman whom she despised?

Miss Schley had certainly been the cause of the whole affair. Lady Holme had spoken to Rupert Carey merely because she knew that her husband was immediately behind her with the American. There had been within her at that moment something of a broad, comprehensive feeling, mingled with the more limited personal feeling of anger against another woman's successful impertinence, a sentiment of revolt in which womanhood seemed to rise up against the selfish tyrannies of men. As she had walked in the crowd, and heard for an instant Miss Schley's drawling voice speaking to her husband, she had felt as if the forbidding of the acquaintance between herself and Rupert Carey had been an act of tyranny, as if the acquaintance between Miss Schley and her husband were a worse act of tyranny. The feeling was wholly unreasonable, of course. How could Lord Holme know that she wished to impose a veto, even as he had? And what reason was there for such a veto? That lay deep down within her as woman's instinct. No man could have understood it.

And now Lord Holme had gone out in the dead of the night to thrash Carey.

She began to think about Carey.

How disgusting he had been. A drunken man must be one of two things—either terrible or absurd. Carey had been absurd—disgusting and absurd. It had been better for him if he had been terrible. But mumblings and tears! She remembered what she had said of Carey to Robin Pierce— that something in his eyes, one of those expressions which are the children of the eyes, or of the lines about the eyes, told her that he was capable of doing something great. What an irony that her remark to Robin had been succeeded by such a scene! And she heard again the ugly sound of Carey's incoherent exclamations, and felt again the limp clasp of his hot, weak hand, and saw again the tears running over his flushed, damp face. It was all very nauseous. And yet—had she been wrong in what she had said of him? Did she even think that she had been wrong now, after what had passed?

What kind of great action had she thought he would be capable of if a chance to do something great were thrown in his way? She said to herself that she had spoken at random, as one perpetually speaks in Society. And then she remembered Carey's eyes. They were ugly eyes. She had always thought them ugly. Yet, now and then, there was something in them, something to hold a woman—no, perhaps not that—but something to startle a woman, to make her think, wonder, even to make her trust. And the scene which had just occurred, with all its weakness, its fatuity, its maundering display of degradation and the inability of any self-government, had not somehow destroyed the impression made upon Lady Holme by that something in Carey's eyes. What she had said to Robin Pierce she might not choose ever to say again. She would not choose ever to say it again—of that she was certain—but she had not ceased to think it.

A conviction based upon no evidence that could be brought forward to convince anyone is the last thing that can be destroyed in a woman's heart.

It was nearly six o'clock when Lady Holme heard a step coming up the stairs. She was still sitting in the deep chair, and had scarcely moved. The step startled her. She put her hands on the arms of the chair and leaned forward. The step passed her bedroom. She heard the door of the dressing-room opened and then someone moving about.

"Fritz!" she called. "Fritz!"

There was no answer. She got up and went quickly to the dressing-room. Her husband was there in his shirt sleeves. His evening coat and waistcoat were lying half on a chair, half on the floor, and he was in the act of unfastening his collar. She looked into his face, trying to read it.

"Well?" she said. "Well?"

"Go to bed!" he said brutally.

"What have you done?"

"That's my business. Go to bed. D'you hear?"

She hesitated. Then she said:

"How dare you speak to me like that? Have you seen Mr. Carey?"

Lord Holme suddenly took his wife by the shoulders; pushed her out of the room, shut the door, and locked it.

They always slept in the same bedroom. Was he not going to bed at all? What had happened? Lady Holme could not tell from his face or manner anything of what had occurred. She looked at her clock and saw her husband had been out of the house for two hours. Indignation and curiosity fought within her; and she became conscious of an excitement such as she had never felt before. Sleep was impossible, but she got into bed and lay there listening to the noises made by her husband in his dressing-room. She could just hear them faintly through the door. Presently they ceased. A profound silence reigned. There was a sofa in the dressing-room. Could he be trying to sleep on it? Such a thing seemed incredible to her. For Lord Holme, although he could rough it when he was shooting or hunting, at home or abroad, and cared little for inconvenience when there was anything to kill, was devoted to comfort in ordinary life, and extremely exigent in his own houses. For nothing, for nobody, had Lady Holme ever known him to allow himself to be put out.

She strained her ears as she lay in bed. For a long time the silence lasted. She began to think her husband must have left the dressing-room, when she heard a noise as if something—some piece of furniture—had been kicked, and then a stentorian "Damn!"

Suddenly she burst out laughing. She shook against the pillows. She laughed and laughed weakly; helplessly, till the tears ran down her cheeks. And with those tears ran away her anger, the hot, strained sensation that had been within her even since the scene at Arkell House. If she had womanly pride it melted ignominiously. If she had feminine dignity—that pure and sacred panoply which man ignores at his own proper peril—it disappeared. The "poor old Fritz" feeling, which was the most human, simple, happy thing in her heart, started into vivacity as she realised the long legs flowing into air over the edge of the short sofa, the pent-up fury—fury of the too large body on the too small resting-place—which found a partial vent in the hallowed objurgation of the British Philistine.

With every moment that she lay in the big bed she was punishing Fritz. She nestled down among the pillows. She stretched out her limbs luxuriously. How easy it was to punish a man! Lying there she recalled her husband's words, each detail of his treatment of her since she had spoken to Carey. He had called her "a damned shameful woman." That was of all the worst offence. She told herself that she ought to, that she must, for that expression alone, hate Fritz for ever. And then, immediately, she knew that she had forgiven it already, without effort, without thought.

She understood the type with which she had to deal, the absurd boyishness that was linked with the brutality of it, the lack of mind to give words their true, their inmost meaning. Words are instruments of torture, or the pattering confetti of a carnival, not by themselves but by the mind that sends them forth. Fritz's exclamation might have roused eternal enmity in her if it had been uttered by another man. Coming from Fritz it won its pardon easily by having a brother, "Damn."

She wondered how long her husband would be ruled by his sense of outrage.

Towards seven she heard another movement; another indignant exclamation, then the creak of furniture, a step, a rattling at the door. She turned on her side towards the wall, shut her eyes and breathed lightly and regularly. The key revolved, the door opened and closed, and she heard feet shuffling cautiously over the carpet. A moment and Fritz was in bed. Another moment, a long sigh, and he was asleep.

Lady Holme still lay awake. Now that her attention was no longer fixed upon her husband's immediate proceedings she began to wonder again what had happened between him and Rupert Carey. She would find out in the morning.

And presently she too slept.

CHAPTER IX

IN the morning Lord Holme woke very late and in a different humour. Lady Holme was already up, sitting by a little table and pouring out tea, when he stretched himself, yawned, turned over, uttered two or three booming, incoherent exclamations, and finally raised himself on one arm, exhibiting a touzled head and a pair of blinking eyes, stared solemnly at his wife's white figure and at the tea-table, and ejaculated:

"Eh?"

"Tea?" she returned, lifting up the silver teapot and holding it towards him with an encouraging, half-playful gesture.

Lord Holme yawned again, put up his hands to his hair, and then looked steadily at the teapot, which his wife was moving about in the sunbeams that were shining in at the window. The morning was fine.

"Tea, Fritz?"

He smiled and began to roll out of bed. But the action woke up his memory, and when he was on his feet he looked at his wife again more doubtfully. She saw that he was beginning, sleepily but definitely, to consider whether he should go on being absolutely furious about the events of the preceding night, and acted with promptitude.

"Don't be frightened," she said quickly. "I've made up my mind to forgive you. You're only a great schoolboy after all. Come along."

She began to pour out the tea. It made a pleasant little noise falling into the cup. The sun was wonderfully bright in the pretty room, almost Italian in its golden warmth. Lady Holme's black Pomeranian, Pixie, stood on its hind legs to greet him. He came up to the sofa, still looking undecided, but with a wavering light of dawning satisfaction in his eyes.

"You behaved damned badly last night," he growled.

He sat down beside his wife with a bump. She put up her hand to his rough, brown cheek.

"We both behaved atrociously," she answered. "There's your tea."

She poured in the cream and buttered a thin piece of toast. Lord Holme sipped. As he put the cup down she held the piece of toast up to his mouth. He took a bite.

"And we both do the Christian act and forgive each other," she added.

He leaned back. Sleep was flowing away from him, full consciousness of life and events returning to him.

"What made you speak to that feller?" he said.

"Drink your tea. I don't know. He looked miserable at being avoided, and—"

"Miserable! He was drunk. He's done for himself in London, and pretty near done for you too."

As he thought about it all a cloud began to settle over his face. Lady Holme saw it and said:

"That depends on you, Fritz."

She nestled against him, put her hand over his, and kept on lifting his hand softly and then letting it fall on his knee, as she went on:

"That all depends on you."

"How?"

He began to look at her hand and his, following their movements almost like a child.

"If we are all right together, obviously all right, very, very par-ti-cu-lar-ly all right—voyez vous, mon petit chou?—they will think nothing of it. 'Poor Mr. Carey! What a pity the Duke's champagne is so good!' That's what they'll say. But if we—you and I—are not on perfect terms, if you behave like a bear that's been sitting on a wasps' nest—why then they'll say—they'll say—"

"What'll they say?"

"They'll say, 'That was really a most painful scene at the Duke's. She's evidently been behaving quite abominably. Those yellow women always bring about all the tragedies—'"

"Yellow women!" Lord Holme ejaculated.

He looked hard at his wife. It was evident that his mind was tacking.

"Miss Schley heard what you said to the feller," he added.

"People who never speak hear everything—naturally."

"How d'you mean—never speak? Why, she's full of talk."

"How well she listened to him!" was Lady Holme's mental comment.

"If half the world heard it doesn't matter if you and I choose it shouldn't. Unless—"

"Unless what?"

"Unless you did anything last night—afterwards—that will make a scandal?"

"Ah!"

"Did you?"

"That's all right."

He applied himself with energy to the toast. Lady Holme recognised, with a chagrin which she concealed, that Lord Holme was not going to allow himself to be "managed" into any revelation. She recognised it so thoroughly that she left the subject at once.

"We'd better forgive and forget," she said. "After all, we are married and I suppose we must stick together."

There was a clever note of regret in her voice.

"Are you sorry?" Lord Holme said, with a manner that suggested a readiness to be surly.

"For what?"

"That we're married?"

She sat calmly considering.

"Am I? Well, I must think. It's so difficult to be sure. I must compare you with other men—"

"If it comes to that, I might do a bit of comparin' too."

"I should be the last to prevent you, old boy. But I'm sure you've often done it already and always made up your mind afterwards that she wasn't quite up to the marrying mark."

"Who wasn't?"

"The other—horrid creature."

He could not repress a chuckle.

"You're deuced conceited," he said.

"You've made me so."

"I—how?"

"By marrying me first and adoring me afterwards."

They had finished tea and were no longer preoccupied with cups and saucers. It was very bright in the room, very silent. Lord Holme looked at his wife and remembered how much she was admired by other men, how many men would give—whatever men are ready to give—to see her as she was just then. It occurred to him that he would have been rather a fool if he had yielded to his violent impulse and shut her out of the house the previous night.

"You're never to speak to that cad again," he said. "D'you hear?"

"Whisper it close in my ear and I'll try to hear. Your voice is so—what's your expression—so infernally soft."

He put his great arm round her.

"D'you hear?"

"I'm trying."

"I'll make you."

Whether Lord Holme succeeded or not, Lady Holme had no opportunity—even if she desired it—of speaking to Rupert Carey for some time. He left London and went up to the North to stay with his mother. The only person he saw before he went was Robin Pierce. He came round to Half Moon Street early on the afternoon of the day after the Arkell House Ball. Robin was at home and Carey walked in with his usual decision. He was very pale, and his face looked very hard. Robin received him coldly and did not ask him to sit down. That was not necessary, of course. But Robin was standing by the door and did not move back into the room.

"I'm going North to-night," said Carey.

"Are you?"

"Yes. If you don't mind I'll sit down."

Robin said nothing. Carey threw himself into an armchair.

"Going to see the mater. A funny thing—but she's always glad to see me."

"Why not?"

"Mothers have a knack that way. Lucky for sons like me."

There was intense bitterness in his voice, but there was a sound of tenderness too. Robin shut the door but did not sit down.

"Are you going to be in the country long?"

"Don't know. What time did you leave Arkell House last night?"

"Not till after Lady Holme left."

"Oh!"

He was silent for a moment, biting his red moustache.

"Were you in the hall after the last lancers?"

"No."

"You weren't?"

He spoke quickly, with a sort of relief, hesitated then added sardonically:

"But of course you know—and much worse than the worst. The art of conversation isn't dead yet, whatever the—perhaps you saw me being got out?"

"No, I didn't."

"But you do know?"

"Naturally."

"I say, I wish you'd let me have—"

He checked himself abruptly, and muttered:

"Good God! What a brute I am."

He sprang up and walked about the room. Presently he stopped in front of the statuette of the "*Danseuse de Tunisie.*"

"Is it the woman that does it all, or the fan?" he said. "I don't know. Sometimes I think it's one, and sometimes the other. Without the fan there's purity, what's meant from the beginning—"

"By whom?" said Robin. "I thought you were an atheist?"

"Oh, God! I don't know what I am."

He turned away from the statuette.

"With the fan there's so much more than purity, than what was meant to complete us—as devils—men. But—mothers don't carry the fan. And I'm going North to-night."

"Do you mean to say that Lady Holme—?"

Robin's voice was stern.

"Why did she say that to me?"

"What did she say?"

"That she wished to speak to me, to dance with me."

"She said that? How can you know?"

"Oh, I wasn't so drunk that I couldn't hear the voice from Eden. Pierce, you know her. She likes you. Tell her to forgive as much as she can. Will you? And tell her not to carry the fan again when fools like me are about."

And then, without more words, he went out of the room and left Robin standing alone.

Robin looked at the statuette, and remembered what Sir Donald Ulford had said directly he saw it—"Forgive me, that fan makes that statuette wicked."

"Poor old Carey!" he murmured.

His indignation at Carey's conduct, which had been hot, had nearly died away.

"If I had told him what she said about him at supper!" he thought.

And then he began to wonder whether Lady Holme had changed her mind on that subject. Surely she must have changed it. But one never knew—with women. He took up his hat and gloves and went out. If Lady Holme was in he meant to give her Carey's message. It was impossible to be jealous of Carey now.

Lady Holme was not in.

As Robin walked away from Cadogan Square he was not sure whether he was glad or sorry that he had not been able to see her.

After his cup of early morning tea Lord Holme had seemed to be "dear old Fritz" again, and Lady Holme felt satisfied with herself despite the wagging tongues of London. She knew she had done an incautious thing. She knew, too, that Carey had failed her. Her impulse had been to use him as a weapon. He had proved a broken reed. And this failure on his part was likely to correct for ever her incautious tendencies. That was what she told herself, with some contempt for men. She did not tell herself that the use to which she had intended to put Carey was an unworthy one. Women as beautiful, and as successful in their beauty, as she was seldom tell themselves these medicinal truths.

She went about as usual, and on several occasions took Lord Holme with her. And though she saw a light of curiosity in many eyes, and saw lips almost forced open by the silent questions lurking within many minds, it was as she had said it would be. The immediate future had been in Fritz's hands, and he had made it safe enough.

He had made it safe. Even the Duchess of Arkell was quite charming, and laid the whole burden of blame—where it always ought to be laid, of course—upon the man's shoulders. Rupert Carey was quite done for socially. Everyone said so. Even Upper Bohemia thought blatant intemperance—in a Duke's house—an unnecessary defiance flung at the Blue Ribbon Army. Only Amalia Wolfstein, who had never succeeded in getting an invitation to Arkell House, remarked that "It was probably the champagne's fault. She had always noticed that where the host and hostess were dry the champagne was apt to be sweet."

Yes, Fritz had made it safe, but:

Circumstances presently woke in Lady Holme's mind a rather disagreeable suspicion that though Fritz had "come round" with such an admirable promptitude he had reserved to himself a right to retaliate, that he perhaps presumed to fancy that her defiant action, and its very public and unpleasant result, gave to him a greater license than he had possessed before.

Some days after the early morning tea Lord Holme said to his wife:

"I say, Vi, we've got nothing on the first, have we?"

There was a perceptible pause before she replied.

"Yes, we have. We've accepted a dinner at Brayley House."

Lord Holme looked exceedingly put out.

"Brayley House. What rot!" he exclaimed. "I hate those hind-leg affairs. Why on earth did you accept it?"

"Dear boy, you told me to. But why?"

"Why what?"

"Why are you so anxious to be free for the first?"

"Well, it's Miss Schley's *debut* at the British. Everyone's goin' and Laycock says—"

"I'm not very interested in Mr. Laycock's aphorisms, Fritz. I prefer yours, I truly do."

"Oh, well, I'm as good as Laycock, I know. Still—"

"You're a thousand times better. And so everybody's going, on Miss Schley's first night? I only wish we could, but we can't. Let's put up with number two. We're free on the second."

Lord Holme did not look at all appeased.

"That's not the same thing," he said.

"What's the difference? She doesn't change the play, I suppose?"

"No. But naturally on the first night she wants all her friends to come up to the scratch, muster round—don't you know?—and give her a hand."

"And she thinks your hand, being enormous, would be valuable? But we can't throw over Brayley House."

Lord Holme's square jaw began to work, a sure sign of acute irritation.

"If there's a dull, dreary house in London, it's Brayley House," he grumbled. "The cookin's awful—poison—and the wine's worse. Why, last time Laycock was there they actually gave him—"

"Poor dear Mr. Laycock! Did they really? But what can we do? I'm sure I don't want to be poisoned either. I love life."

She was looking brilliant. Lord Holme began to straddle his legs.

"And there's the box!" he said. "A box next the stage that holds six in a row can't stand empty on a first night, eh? It'd throw a damper on the whole house."

"I'm afraid I don't quite understand. What box?"

"Hang it all!—ours."

"I didn't know we had a box for this important social function."

Lady Holme really made a great effort to keep the ice out of her voice, but one or two fragments floated in nevertheless.

"Well, I tell you I've taken a box and asked Laycock—"

The reiterated mention of this hallowed name was a little too much for Lady Holme's equanimity.

"If Mr. Laycock's going the box won't be empty. So that's all right," she rejoined. "Mr. Laycock will make enough noise to give the critics a lead. And I suppose that's all Miss Schley wants."

"But it isn't!" said Lord Holme, violently letting himself down at the knees and shooting himself up again.

"What does she want?"

"She wants you to be there."

"Me! Why?"

"Because she's taken a deuce of a fancy to you."

"Really!"

An iceberg had entered the voice now.

"Yes, thinks you the smartest woman in London, and all that. So you are."

"I'm very sorry, but even the smartest woman in London can't throw over the Brayley's. Take another box for the second."

Lord Holme looked fearfully sulky and lounged out of the room.

On the following morning he strode into Lady Holme's boudoir about twelve with a radiant face.

"It's all right!" he exclaimed. "Talk of diplomatists! I ought to be an ambassador."

He flung himself into a chair, grinning with satisfaction like a schoolboy.

"What is it?" asked Lady Holme, looking up from her writing-table.

"I've been to Lady Brayley, explained the whole thing, and got us both off. After all, she was a friend of my mother's, and knew me in kilts and all that, so she ought to be ready to do me a favour. She looked a bit grim, but she's done it. You've—only got to tip her a note of thanks."

"You're mad then, Fritz!"

Lady Holme stood up suddenly.

"Never saner."

He put one hand into the breast pocket of his coat and pulled out an envelope.

"Here's what she says to you."

Lady Holme tore the note open.

> "BRAYLEY HOUSE, W.
>
> "DEAR VIOLA, —Holme tells me you made a mistake when you accepted my invitation for the first, and that you have long been pledged to be present on that date at some theatrical performance or other.
>
> I am sorry I did not know sooner, but of course I release you with pleasure from your engagement with me, and I have already filled up your places. —Believe me, yours always sincerely,
>
> "MARTHA BRAYLEY."

Lady Holme read this note carefully, folded it up, laid it quietly on the writing-table and repeated:

"You're mad, Fritz."

"What d'you mean—mad?"

"You've made Martha Brayley my enemy for life."

"Rubbish!"

"I beg your pardon. And for—for—"

She stopped. It was wiser not to go on. Perhaps her face spoke for her, even to so dull an observer as Lord Holme, for he suddenly said, with a complete change of tone:

"I forgave you about Carey."

"Oh, I see! You want a *quid pro quo*. Thank you, Fritz."

"Don't forget to tip Lady Brayley a note of thanks," he said rather loudly, getting up from his chair.

"Oh, thanks! You certainly ought to be an ambassador—at the court of some savage monarch."

He said nothing, but walked out of the room whistling the refrain about Ina.

When he had gone Lady Holme sat down and wrote two notes. One was to Lady Brayley and was charmingly apologetic, saying that the confusion was entirely owing to Fritz's muddle-headedness, and that she was in despair at her misfortune—which was almost literally true. The other was to Sir Donald Ulford, begging him to join them in their box on the first, and asking whether it was possible to persuade Mr. and Mrs. Leo Ulford to come with him. If he thought so she would go at once and leave cards on Mrs. Ulford, whom she was longing to know.

Both notes went off by hand before lunch.

CHAPTER X

THE Ulfords accepted for the first. Lady Holme left cards on Mrs. Leo and told her husband that the box was filled up. He received the information with indifference. So long as his wife was there to please Miss Schley, and Mr. Laycock to "give her a hand and show 'em all whether she was popular," he was satisfied. Having gained his point, he was once again in excellent humour. Possibly Lady Holme would have appreciated his large gaieties more if she had not divined their cause. But she expressed no dissatisfaction with them, and indeed increased them by her own brilliant serenity during the days that intervened between the Martha Brayley incident and the first night.

Lord Holme had no suspicion that during these days she was inwardly debating whether she would go to the theatre or not.

It would be very easy to be unwell. She was going out incessantly and could be over-fatigued. She could have woman's great stand-by in moments of crisis—a bad attack of neuralgia. It was the simplest matter in the world. The only question was—all things considered, was it worth while? By "all things considered" she meant Leo Ulford. The touch of Fritz in him made him a valuable ally at this moment. Fritz and Miss Schley were not going to have things quite all their own way. And then Mrs. Leo! She would put Fritz next the ear-trumpet. She had enough sense of humour to smile to herself at the thought of him there. On the whole, she fancied the neuralgia would not attack her at the critical instant.

Only when she thought of what her husband had said about the American's desire for her presence did she hesitate again. Her suspicions were aroused. Miss Schley was not anxious that she should be conspicuously in the theatre merely because she was the smartest woman in London. That was certain. Besides, she was not the smartest woman in London. She was far too well-born to be that in these great days of the *demi-mondaine*. She remembered Robin Pierce's warning at the Arkell House ball—"Consider yourselves enemies for no reasons or secret woman's reasons. It's safer."

When do women want the bulky, solid reasons obtusely demanded by men before they can be enemies? Where man insists on an insult, a blow, they will be satisfied with a look—perhaps not even at them but only at the skirt of their gown—with a turn of the head, with nothing at all. For what a man calls nothing can be the world and all that there is in it to a woman. Lady Holme knew that she and the American had been enemies since the moment when the latter had moved with the tiny steps that so oddly caricatured her own individual walk down the stairs at the Carlton. She wanted no tiresome reasons; nor did Miss Schley. Robin was right, of course. He understood women. But then—?

Should she go to the theatre?

The night came and she went. Whether an extraordinary white lace gown, which arrived from Paris in the morning, and fitted too perfectly for words, had anything to do with the eventual decision was not known to anybody but herself.

Boxes are no longer popular in London except at the Opera. The British Theatre was new, and the management, recognising that people prefer stalls, had given up all the available space to them, and only left room for two large boxes, which faced each other on a level with the dress circle and next the stage. Lord Holme had one. Mrs. Wolfstein had taken the other.

Miss Schley's personal success in London brought together a rather special audience. There were some of the usual people who go to first nights—critics, ladies who describe dresses, fashionable lawyers and doctors. But there were also numbers of people who are scarcely ever seen on these occasions, people who may be found in the ground and grand tier boxes at Covent Garden during the summer season. These thronged the stalls, and every one of them was a dear friend of Lady Holme's. Among them were Lady Cardington, Lady Manby, Sally Perceval with her magnificently handsome and semi-idiotic husband, old Lady Blower, in a green cap that suggested the bathing season, Robin Pierce and Mr. Bry. Smart Americans were scattered all over the house. Most of them had already seen the play in New York during the preceding winter, and nearly everyone in the stalls had seen the French original in Paris. The French piece had been quite shocking and quite delicious. Every Royalty *de passage* in Paris had been to see it, and one wandering monarch had gone three nights running, and had laughed until his gentleman-in-waiting thought the heir to his throne was likely to succeed much sooner than was generally expected.

The Holmes came in early. Lady Holme hated arriving anywhere early, but Lord Holme was in such a prodigious fuss about being in plenty of time to give Miss Schley a "rousin' welcome," that she yielded to his bass protestations, and had the satisfaction of entering their box at least seven minutes before the curtain went up. The stalls, of course, were empty, and as they gradually filled she saw the faces of her friends looking up at her with an amazement that under other circumstances might have been amusing, but under these was rather irritating. Mr. Laycock arrived two minutes after they did, and was immediately engaged in a roaring conversation by Fritz. He was a man who talked a great deal without having anything to say, who had always had much success with women, perhaps because he had always treated them very badly, who dressed, danced and shot well, and who had never, even for a moment, really cared for anyone but himself. A common enough type.

Sir Donald appeared next, looking even more ghostly than usual. He sat down by Lady Holme, a little behind her. He seemed depressed, but the expression in his pale blue eyes when they first rested upon her made her thoroughly realise one thing—that it was one of her conquering nights. His eyes travelled quickly from her face to her throat, to her gown. She wore no jewels. Sir Donald had a fastidious taste in beauty—the taste that instinctively rejects excess of any kind. Her appeal to it had never been so great as to-night. She knew it, and felt that she had never found Sir Donald so attractive as to-night.

Mr. and Mrs. Ulford came in just as the curtain was going up, and the introductions had to be gone through with a certain mysterious caution, and the sitting arrangements made with as little noise as possible. Lady Holme managed them deftly. Mr. Laycock sat nearest the stage, then Leo Ulford next to her, on her right. Sir Donald was on her other side, Mrs. Leo sat in the place of honour, with Lord Holme between her and Sir Donald. She was intensely pink. Even her gown was of that colour, and she wore a pink aigrette in her hair, fastened with a diamond ornament. Her thin, betraying throat was clasped by the large dog-collar she had worn at Arkell House. She cast swift, bird-like glances, full of a sort of haggard inquiry, towards Lady Holme as she settled down in her arm-chair in the corner. Lord Holme looked at her and at her ear-trumpet, and Lady Holme was glad she had decided not to have neuralgia. There are little compensations about all women even in the tiresome moments of their lives. Whether this moment was going to be tiresome or not she could not yet decide.

The Wolfstein party had come in at the same time as the Leo Ulfords, and the box opposite presented an interesting study of Jewish types. For Mrs. Wolfstein and "Henry" were accompanied by four immensely rich compatriots, three of whom were members of the syndicate that was "backing" Miss Schley. The fourth was the wife of one of them, and a cousin of Henry's, whom she resembled, but on a greatly enlarged scale. Both she and Amalia blazed with jewels, and both were slightly overdressed and looked too animated. Lady Holme saw Sir Donald glance at them, and then again at her, and began to think more definitely that the evening would not be tiresome.

Leo Ulford seemed at present forced into a certain constraint by the family element in the box. He looked at his father sideways, then at Lady Holme, drummed one hand on his knee, and was evidently uncertain of himself. During the opening scene of the play he found an opportunity to whisper to Lady Holme:

"I never can talk when pater's there!"

She whispered back:

"We mustn't talk now."

Then she looked towards the stage with apparent interest. Mrs. Leo sat sideways with her trumpet lifted up towards her ear, Lord Holme had his eyes fixed on the stage, and held his hands ready for the "rousin' welcome." Mr. Laycock, at the end of the row, was also all attention. Lady Holme glanced from one to the other, and murmured to Sir Donald with a smile:

"I think we shall find to-night that the claque is not abolished in England."

He raised his eyebrows and looked distressed.

"I have very little hope of her acting," he murmured back.

Lady Holme put her fan to her lips.

"'Sh! No sacrilege!" she said in an under voice.

She saw Leo Ulford shoot an angry glance at his father. Mrs. Wolfstein nodded and smiled at her from the opposite box, and it struck Lady Holme that her smile was more definitely malicious than usual, and that her large black eyes were full of a sort of venomous anticipation. Mrs. Wolfstein had at all times an almost frightfully expressive face. To-night it had surely discarded every shred of reticence, and proclaimed an eager expectation of something which Lady Holme could not divine, but which must surely be very disagreeable to her. What could it possibly be? And was it in any way connected with Miss Schley's anxiety that she should be there that night? She began to wish that the American would appear, but Miss Schley had nothing to do in the first act till near the end, and then had only one short scene to bring down the curtain. Lady Holme knew this because she had seen the play in Paris. She thought the American version very dull. The impropriety had been removed and with it all the fun. People began to yawn and to assume the peculiar blank expression—the bankrupt face— that is indicative of thwarted anticipation. Only the Americans who had seen the piece in New York preserved their lively looks and an appearance of being on the *qui vive.*

Lord Holme's blunt brown features gradually drooped, seemed to become definitely elongated. As time went on he really began to look almost lantern-jawed. He bent forward and tried to catch Mr. Laycock's eye and to telegraph an urgent question, but only succeeded in meeting the surly blue eyes of Leo Ulford, whom he met to-night for the first time. In his despair he turned towards Mrs. Leo, and at once encountered the ear-trumpet. He glanced at it with apprehension, and, after a moment of vital hesitation, was about to pour into it the provender, "Have you any notion when she's comin' on?" when there was a sudden rather languid slapping of applause, and he jerked round hastily to find Miss Schley already on the stage and welcomed without any of the assistance which he was specially there to give. He lifted belated hands, but met a glance from his wife which made him drop them silently. There was a satire in her eyes, a sort of humorous, half-urging patronage that pierced the hide of his self-satisfied and lethargic mind. She seemed sitting there ready to beat time to his applause, nod her head to it as to a childish strain of jigging music. And this apparent preparation for a semi-comic, semi-pitiful benediction sent his hands suddenly to his knees.

He stared at the stage. Miss Schley was looking wonderfully like Viola, he thought, on the instant, more like than she did in real life; like Viola gone to the bad, though become a very reticent, yet very definite, *cocotte.* There was not much in the scene, but Miss Schley, without apparent effort and with a profound demureness, turned the dulness of it into something that was—not French, certainly not that—but that was quite as outrageous as the French had been, though in a different way; something without definite nationality, but instinct with the slyness of acute and unscrupulous womankind. The extraordinary thing was the marvellous resemblance this acute and unscrupulous womanhood bore to Lady Holme's, even through all its obvious difference from hers. All her little mannerisms of voice, look, manner and movement, were there but turned towards commonness, even towards a naive but very self-conscious impropriety. Had she been a public performer instead of merely a woman of the world, the whole audience must have at once recognised the imitation. As it was, her many friends in the house noticed it, and during the short progress of the scene various heads were turned in her direction, various faces glanced up at the big box in which she sat, leaning one arm on the ledge, and looking towards Miss Schley with an expression of quiet observation—a little indifferent—on her white face. Even Sir Donald, who was next to her, and who once—in the most definite moment of Miss Schley's ingenious travesty—looked at her for an instant, could not discern that she was aware of what was amusing or enraging all her acquaintances.

Naturally she had grasped the situation at once, had discovered at once why Miss Schley was anxious for her to be there. As she sat in the box looking on at this gross impertinence, she seemed to herself to be watching herself after a long *degringolade*, which had brought her, not to the gutter, but to the smart restaurant, the smart music-hall, the smart night club; the smart everything else that is beyond the borderland of even a lax society. This was Miss Schley's comment upon her. The sting of it lay in this fact, that it followed immediately upon the heels of the unpleasant scene at Arkell House. Otherwise, she thought it would not have troubled her. Now it did trouble her. She felt not only indignant with Miss Schley. She felt also secretly distressed in a more subtle way. Miss Schley's performance was calculated, coming at this moment, to make her world doubtful just when it had been turned from doubt. A good caricature fixes the attention upon the oddities, or the absurdities, latent in the original. But this caricature did more. It suggested hidden possibilities which she, by her own indiscreet action at the ball, had made perhaps to seem probabilities to many people.

Here, before her friends, was set a woman strangely like her, but evidently a bad woman. Lady Holme was certain that the result of Miss Schley's performance would be that were she to do things now which, done before the Arkell House ball and this first night, would not have been noticed, or would have been merely smiled at, they would be commented upon with acrimony, exaggerated, even condemned.

Miss Schley was turning upon her one of those mirrors which distorts by enlarging. Society would be likely to see her permanently distorted, and not only in mannerisms but in character.

It happened that this fact was specially offensive to her on this particular evening, and at this particular moment of her life.

While she sat there and watched the scene run its course, and saw, without seeming to see, the effect it had upon those whom she knew well in the house—saw Mrs. Wolfstein's eager delight in it, Lady Manby's broad amusement, Robin Pierce's carefully-controlled indignation, Mr. Bry's sardonic and always cold gratification, Lady Cardington's surprised, half-tragic wonder—she was oscillating between two courses, one a course of reserve, of stern self-control and abnegation, the other a course of defiance, of reckless indulgence of the strong temper that dwelt within her, and that occasionally showed itself for a moment, as it had on the evening of Miss Filberte's fiasco. That temper was flaming now unseen. Was she going to throw cold water over the flame, or to fan it? She did not know.

When the curtain fell, the critics, who sometimes seem to enjoy personally what they call very sad and disgraceful in print, were smiling at one another. The blank faces of the men about town in the stalls were shining almost unctuously. The smart Americans were busily saying to everyone, "Didn't we say so?" The whole house was awake. Miss Schley might not be much of an actress. Numbers of people were already bustling about to say that she could not act at all. But she had banished dulness. She had shut the yawning lips, and stopped that uneasy cough which is the expression of the relaxed mind rather than of the relaxed throat.

Lady Holme sat back a little in the box.

"What d'you think of her?" she said to Sir Donald. "I think she's rather piquant, not anywhere near Granier, of course, but still—"

"I think her performance entirely odious," he said, with an unusual emphasis that was almost violent. "Entirely odious."

He got up from his seat, striking his thin fingers against the palms of his hands.

"Vulgar and offensive," he said, almost as if to himself, and with a sort of passion. "Vulgar and offensive!"

Suddenly he turned away and went out of the box.

"I say—"

Lady Holme, who had been watching Sir Donald's disordered exit, looked round to Leo.

"I say—" he repeated. "What's up with pater?"

"He doesn't seem to be enjoying the play."

Leo Ulford looked unusually grave, even thoughtful, as if he were pondering over some serious question. He kept his blue eyes fixed upon Lady Holme. At last he said, in a voice much lower than usual:

"Poor chap!"

"Who's a poor chap?"

Leo jerked his head towards the door.

"Your father? Why?"

"Why—at his age!"

The last words were full of boyish contempt.

"I don't understand."

"Yes, you do. To be like that at his age. What's the good? As if—" He smiled slowly at her. "I'm glad I'm young," he said.

"I'm glad you're young too," she answered. "But you're quite wrong about Sir Donald."

She let her eyes rest on his. He shook his head.

"No, I'm not. I guessed it that day at the Carlton. All through lunch he looked at you."

"But what has all this to do with Miss Schley's performance?"

"Because she's something like you, but low down, where you'd never go."

He drew his chair a little closer to hers.

"Would you?" he added, almost in a whisper.

Mr. Laycock, who was in raptures over Miss Schley's performance, had got up to speak to Fritz, but found the latter being steadily hypnotised by Mrs. Leo's trumpet, which went up towards his mouth whenever he opened it. He bellowed distracted nothings but could not make her hear, obtaining no more fortunate result than a persistent flutter of pink eyelids, and a shrill, reiterated "The what? The what?"

A sharp tap came presently on the box door, and Mrs. Wolfstein's painted face appeared. Lord Holme sprang up with undisguised relief.

"What d'you think of Pimpernel? Ah, Mr. Laycock—I heard your faithful hands."

"Stunnin'!" roared Lord Holme, "simply stunnin'!"

"Stunnin'! stunnin'!" exclaimed Mr. Laycock; "Rippin'! There's no other word. Simply rippin'!"

"The what? The what?" cried Mrs. Ulford.

Mrs. Wolfstein bent down, with expansive affection, over Lady Holme's chair, and clasped the left hand which Lady Holme carelessly raised to a level with her shoulder.

"You dear person! Nice of you to come, and in such a gown too! The angels wear white lace thrown together by Victorine—it is Victorine? I was certain!—I'm sure. D'you like Pimpernel?"

Her too lustrous eyes—even Mrs. Wolfstein's eyes looked over-dressed—devoured Lady Holme, and her large, curving features were almost riotously interrogative.

"Yes," Lady Holme said. "Quite."

"She's startled everybody."

"Startled!—why?"

"Oh, well—she has! There's money in it, don't you think?"

"Henry," who had accompanied his wife, and who was standing sideways at the back of the box looking like a thief in the night, came a step forward at the mention of money.

"I'm afraid I'm no judge of that. Your husband would know better."

"Plenty of money," said "Henry," in a low voice that seemed to issue from the bridge of his nose; "it ought to bring a good six thousand into the house for the four weeks. That's—for Miss Schley—for the Syndicate—ten per cent. on the gross, and twenty-five per cent.—"

He found himself in mental arithmetic.

"The—swan with the golden eggs!" said Lady Holme, lightly, turning once more to Leo Ulford. "You mustn't kill Miss Schley."

Mrs. Wolfstein looked at Mr. Laycock and murmured to him:

"Pimpernel does any killing that's going about—for herself. What d'you say, Franky?"

They went out of the box together, followed by "Henry," who was still buzzing calculations, like a Jewish bee.

Lord Holme resolutely tore himself from the ear-trumpet, and was preparing to follow, with the bellowed excuse that he was "sufferin' from toothache" and had been ordered to "do as much smokin' as possible," when the curtain rose on the second act.

Miss Schley was engaged to a supper-party that evening and did not wish to be late. Lord Holme sat down again looking scarcely pleasant.

"Do as much—the what?" cried Mrs. Ulford, holding the trumpet at right angles to her pink face.

Leo Ulford leant backwards and hissed "Hush!" at her. She looked at him and then at Lady Holme, and a sudden expression of old age came into her bird-like face and seemed to overspread her whole body. She dropped the trumpet and touched the diamonds that glittered in the front of her low gown with trembling hands.

Mr. Laycock slipped into the box when the curtain had been up two or three minutes, but Sir Donald did not return.

"I b'lieve he's bolted," Leo whispered to Lady Holme. "Just like him."

"Why?"

"Oh!—I'm here, for one thing."

He looked at her victoriously.

"You'll have a letter from him to-morrow. Poor old chap!"

He spoke contemptuously.

For the first time Lord Holme seemed consciously and unfavourably observant of his wife and Leo. His under-jaw began to move. But Miss Schley came on to the stage again, and he thrust his head eagerly forward.

During the rest of the evening Miss Schley did not relax her ingenious efforts of mimicry, but she took care not to make them too prominent. She had struck her most resonant note in the first act, and during the two remaining acts she merely kept her impersonation to its original lines. Lady Holme watched the whole performance imperturbably, but before the final curtain fell she knew that she was not going to throw cold water on that flame which was burning within her. Fritz's behaviour, perhaps, decided which of the two actions should be carried out—the douching or the fanning. Possibly Leo Ulford had something to say in the matter too. Or did the faces of friends below in the stalls play their part in the silent drama which moved step by step with the spoken drama on the stage? Lady Holme did not ask questions of herself. When Mr. Laycock and Fritz were furiously performing the duties of a claque at the end of the play, she got up smiling, and nodded to Mrs. Wolfstein in token of her pleasure in Miss Schley's success, her opinion that it had been worthily earned. As she nodded she touched one hand with the other, making a silent applause that Mrs. Wolfstein and all her friends might see. Then she let Leo Ulford put on her cloak and called pretty words down Mrs. Leo's trumpet, all the while nearly deafened by Fritz's demonstrations, which even outran Mr. Laycock's.

When at last they died away she said to Leo:

"We are going on to the Elwyns. Shall you be there?"

He stood over her, while Mrs. Ulford watched him, drooping her head sideways.

"Yes."

"We can talk it all over quietly. Fritz!"

"What's that about the Elwyns?" said Lord Holme.

"I was telling Mr. Ulford that we are going on there."

"I'm not. Never heard of it."

Lady Holme was on the point of retorting that it was he who had told her to accept the invitation on the ground that "the Elwyns always do you better than anyone in London, whether they're second-raters or not," but a look in Leo Ulford's eyes checked her.

"Very well," she said. "Go to the club if you like; but I must peep in for five minutes. Mrs. Ulford, didn't you think Miss Schley rather delicious—?"

She went out of the box with one hand on a pink arm, talking gently into the trumpet.

"You goin' to the Elwyns?" said Lord Holme, gruffly, to Leo Ulford as they got their coats and prepared to follow.

"Depends on my wife. If she's done up—"

"Ah!" said Lord Holme, striking a match, and holding out his cigarette case, regardless of regulations.

A momentary desire to look in at the Elwyns' possessed him. Then he thought of a supper-party and forgot it.

CHAPTER XI

MRS. WOLFSTEIN was right. There was money in Miss Schley's performance. Her sly impropriety appealed with extraordinary force to the peculiar respectability characteristic of the British temperament, and her celebrity, hitherto mainly social, was suddenly and enormously increased. Already a popular person, she became a popular actress, and was soon as well-known to the world in the streets and the suburbs as to the world in the drawing-rooms of Mayfair. And this public celebrity greatly increased the value that was put upon her in private—especially the value put upon her by men.

The average man adores being connected openly with the woman who is the rage of the moment. It flatters his vanity and makes him feel good all over. It even frequently turns his head and makes him almost as intoxicated as a young girl with adulation received at her first ball.

The combination of Miss Schley herself and Miss Schley's celebrity—or notoriety—had undoubtedly turned Lord Holme's head. Perhaps he had not the desire to conceal the fact. Certainly he had not the finesse. He presented his turned head to the world with an audacious simplicity that was almost laughable, and that had in it an element of boyishness not wholly unattractive to those who looked on—the casual ones to whom even the tragedies of a highly-civilised society bring but a quiet and cynical amusement.

Lady Holme was not one of these. Her strong temper was token of a vivid temperament. Till now this vivid temperament had been rocked in the cradle of an easy, a contented, a very successful life. Such storms as had come to her had quickly passed away. The sun had never been far off. Her egoism had been constantly flattered. Her will had been perpetually paramount. Even the tyranny of Lord Holme had been but as the tyranny of a selfish, thoughtless, pleasure-seeking boy who, after all, was faithful to her and was fond of her. His temperamental indifference to any feelings but his own had been often concealed and overlaid by his strong physical passion for his wife's beauty, his profound satisfaction in having carried off and in possessing a woman admired and sought by many others.

Suddenly life presented to Lady Holme its seamy side; Fate attacking her in her woman's vanity, her egoism, even in her love. The vision startled.

The blow stung. She was conscious of confusion, of cloud, then of a terrible orderliness, of a clear light. In the confusion she seemed to hear voices never heard before, voices that dared to jeer at her; in the cloud to see phantoms of gigantic size menacing her, impending over her. The orderliness, the clear light were more frightful to her. They left less to her imagination; had, as it were, no ragged edges. In them she faced a definite catastrophe, saw it whole, as one sees a near object in the magical atmosphere of the East, outlined with burning blue, quivering with relentless gold. She saw herself in the dust, pelted, mocked at.

That seemed at first to be incredible. But she saw it so plainly that she could not even pretend to herself that she was deceived by some unusual play of light or combination of shadows. What she saw—was:

Her husband had thrown off his allegiance to her and transferred his admiration, perhaps his affection, to the woman who had most deftly and delicately insulted her in the face of all her world. And he had done this with the most abominable publicity. That was what she saw in a clear light like the light of the East. That was what sent a lash across her temperament, scarring it perhaps, but waking it into all it could ever have of life. In each woman there is hidden a second woman, more fierce and tender, more evil and good, more strong and fervent than the woman who hides her in the ordinary hours of life; a woman who weeps blood where the other woman weeps tears, who strikes with a flaming sword where the other woman strikes with a willow wand.

This woman now rose up in Lady Holme, rose up to do battle.

The laughing, frivolous world was all unconscious of her. Lord Holme was unconscious of her. But she was at last fully conscious of herself.

This woman remembered Robin Pierce's odd belief and the light words with which she had chastised it. He had persistently kept faith in, and sought for, a far-away being. But she was a being of light and glory. His kernel of the husk was still a siren, but a siren with a heart, with an exquisite imagination, with a fragrance of dreams about her, a lilt of eternal music in her voice, the beaming, wonder of things unearthly in her eyes. Poor Robin! Lady Holme found it in her heart to pity him as she realised herself. But then she turned her pity aside and concentrated it elsewhere. The egoism of her was not dead though the hidden woman had sprung up in vivid life. Her intellect was spurred into energy by the suffering of her pride and of her heart. Memory was restless and full of the passion of recall.

She remembered the night when she softly drew up the hood of her dressing-gown above her head and, rocking herself to and fro, murmured the "Allah-Akbar" of a philosophic fatalist—"I will live for the day. I will live for the night." What an absurd patter that was on the lips of a woman. And she remembered the conversation with Fritz that had preceded her monologue. She had asked him then whether he could love her if her beauty were taken from her. It had never occurred to her that while her beauty still remained her spell upon him might be weakened, might be broken. That it was broken now she did not say to herself. All she did say to herself was that she must strike an effective blow against this impertinent woman. She had some pride but not enough to keep her passive. She was not one of those women who would rather lose all they have than struggle to keep it. She meant to struggle, but she had no wish that the world should know what she was doing. Pride rose in her when she thought of cold eyes watching the battle, cold voices commenting on it—Amalia Wolfstein's eyes, Mr. Bry's voice, a hundred other eyes and voices. Her quickened intellect, her woman's heart would teach her to be subtle. The danger lay in her temper. But since the scene at Arkell House she had thoroughly realised its impetuosity and watched it warily as one watches an enemy. She did not intend to be ruined by anything within her. The outside chances of life were many enough and deadly enough to deal with. Strength and daring were needed to ward them off. The chances that had their origin within the soul, the character—not really chances at all—must be controlled, foreseen, forestalled.

And yet she had not douched the flame of defiance which she had felt burning within her on the night of Pimpernel Schley's first appearance on the London stage. She had fanned it. At the Elwyns' ball she had fanned it. Temper had led her that night. Deliberately, and knowing perfectly well who was her guide, she had let it lead her. She had been like a human being who says, "To do this will be a sin. Very well, I choose to sin. But I will sin carefully." At the Elwyns she had discovered why her husband had not come with her. She had stayed late to please Leo Ulford. Mr. Laycock had come in about two in the morning and had described to Leo the festivity devised by Lord Holme in honour of Miss Schley, at which he had just been present. And Leo Ulford had repeated the description to her. She had deceived him into thinking that she had known of the supper-party and approved of it. But, after this deception, she had given a looser rein to her temper. She had let herself go, careless whether she set the poor pink eyelids of Mrs. Leo fluttering or not.

The hint of Fritz which she recognised in Leo Ulford had vaguely attracted her to him from the first. How her world would have laughed at such a domestic sentiment! She found herself wondering whether it were Miss Schley's physical resemblance to her which had first attracted Fritz, the touch of his wife in a woman who was not his wife and who was what men call "a rascal." Perhaps Fritz loved Miss Schley's imitation of her. She thought a great deal about that—turning it over and over in her mind, bringing to bear on it the white light of her knowledge of her husband's character. Did he see in the American his wife transformed, made common, sly, perhaps wicked, set on the outside edge of decent life, or further—over the border? And did he delight in that? If so, ought she not to—? Then her mind was busy. Should she change? If herself changed were his ideal, why not give him what he wanted? Why let another woman give it to him? But at this point she recognised a fact recognised by thousands of women with exasperation, sometimes with despair—that men would often hate in their wives the thing that draws them to women not their wives. The Pimpernel Schleys of the world know this masculine propensity of seeking different things—opposites, even—in the wife and the woman beyond the edge of the hearthstone, a propensity perhaps more tragic to wives than any other that exists in husbands. And having recognised this fact, Lady Holme knew that it would be worse than useless for her to imitate Miss Schley's imitation of her. Then, travelling along the road of thought swiftly as women in such a case always travel, she reached another point. She began to consider the advice of Robin Pierce, given before she had begun to feel with such intensity, to consider it as a soldier might consider a plan of campaign drawn up by another.

Should she, instead of descending, of following the demure steps of the American to the lower places, strive to ascend?

Could she ascend? Was Robin Pierce right? She thought for a long time about his conception of her. The singing woman; would she be the most powerful enemy that could confront Miss Schley? And, if she would be, could the singing woman be made continuous in the speech and the actions of the life without music? She remembered a man she had known who stammered when he spoke, but never stammered when he sang. And she thought she resembled this man. Robin Pierce had always believed that she could speak without the stammer even as she sang without it. She had never cared to. She had trusted absolutely in her beauty. Now her trust was shaken. She thought of the crutch.

Realising herself she had said within herself, "Poor Robin!" seeing perhaps the tigress where he saw the angel. Now she asked herself whether the angel could conquer where the tigress might fail. People had come round her like beggars who have heard the chink of gold and she had showed them an empty purse. Could she show them something else? And if she could, would her husband join the beggars? Would he care to have even one piece of gold?

Whether Lord Holme's obvious infatuation had carried him very far she did not know. She did not stop to ask. A woman capable, as she was, of retrospective jealousy, an egoist accustomed to rule, buffeted in heart and pride, is swift not sluggish. And then how can one know these things? Jealousy rushes because it is ignorant.

Lord Holme and she were apparently on good terms. She was subtle, he was careless. As she did not interfere with him his humour was excellent. She had carried self-control so far as never to allude to the fact that she knew about the supper-party. Yet it had actually got into the papers. Paragraphs had been written about a wonderful ornament of ice, representing the American eagle perched on the wrist of a glittering maiden, which had stood in the middle of the table. Of course she had seen them, and of course Lord Holme thought she had not seen them as she had never spoken of them. He went his way rejoicing, and there seemed to be sunshine in the Cadogan Square house. And meanwhile the world was smiling at the apparent triumph of impertinence, and wondering how long it would last, how far it would go. The few who were angry—Sir Donald was one of them—were in a mean minority.

Robin Pierce was angry too, but not with so much single-heartedness as was Sir Donald. It could not quite displease him if the Holmes drifted apart. Yet he was fond enough of Lady Holme, and he was subtle enough, to be sorry for any sorrow of hers, and to understand it—at any rate, partially—without much explanation. Perhaps he would have been more sorry if Leo Ulford had not come into Lady Holme's life, and if the defiance within her had not driven her into an intimacy that distressed Mrs. Leo and puzzled Sir Donald.

Robin's time in London was very nearly at an end. The season was at its height. Every day was crowded with engagements. It was almost impossible to find a quiet moment even to give to a loved one. But Robin was determined to have at least one hour with Lady Holme before he started for Italy. He told her so, and begged her to arrange it. She put him off again and again, then at last made an engagement, then broke it. In her present condition of mind to break faith with a man was a pleasure with a bitter savour. But Robin was not to be permanently avoided. He had obstinacy. He meant to have his hour, and perhaps Lady Holme always secretly meant that he should have it. At any rate she made another appointment and kept it.

She came one afternoon to his house in Half Moon Street. She had never been there before. She had never meant to go there. To do so was an imprudence. That fact was another of the pleasures with a bitter savour.

Robin met her at the head of the stairs, with an air of still excitement not common in his look and bearing. He followed her into the blue room where Sir Donald had talked with Carey. The *"Danseuse de Tunisie"* still presided over it, holding her little marble fan. The open fireplace was filled with roses. The tea-table was already set by the great square couch. Robin shut the door and took out a matchbox.

"I am going to make tea," he said.

"Bachelor fashion?"

She sat down on the couch and looked round quickly, taking in all the details of the room. He saw her eyes rest on the woman with the fan, but she said nothing about it. He lit a silver spirit lamp and then sat down beside her.

"At last!" he said.

Lady Holme leaned back in her corner. She was dressed in black, with a small, rather impertinent black toque, in which one pale blue wing of a bird stood up. Her face looked gay and soft, and Robin, who had cunning, recognised that quality of his in her.

"I oughtn't to be here."

"Absurd. Why not?"

"Fritz has a jealous temperament."

She spoke with a simple naturalness that moved the diplomat within him to a strong admiration.

"You can act far better than Miss Schley," he said, with intentional bluntness.

"I love her acting."

"I'm going away. I shan't see you for an age. Don't give me a theatrical performance to-day."

"Can a woman do anything else?"

"Yes. She can be a woman."

"That's stupid—or terrible. What a dear little lamp that is! I like your room."

Robin looked at the blue-grey linen on the walls, at the pale blue wing in her hat, then at her white face.

"Viola," he said, leaning forward, "it's bad to waste anything in this life, but the worst thing of all is to waste unhappiness. If I could teach you to be niggardly of your tears!"

"What do you mean?"

She spoke with sudden sharpness.

"I never cry. Nothing's worth a tear," she added.

"Yes, some things are. But not what you are going to weep for."

Her face had changed. The gaiety had gone out of it, and it looked hesitating.

"You think I am going to shed tears?" she said. "Why?"

"I am glad you let me tell you. For the loss of nothing—a coin that never came out of the mint, that won't pass current anywhere."

"I've lost nothing," she exclaimed, "nothing. You're talking nonsense."

He made no reply, but looked at the small, steady flame of the lamp. She followed his eyes, and, when he saw that she was looking at it too, he said:

"Isn't a little, steady flame like that beautiful?"

She laughed.

"When it means tea—yes. Does it mean tea?"

"If you can wait a few minutes."

"I suppose I must. Have you heard anything of Mr. Carey?"

Robin looked at her narrowly.

"What made you think of him just then?"

"I don't know. Being here, I suppose. He often comes here, doesn't he?"

"Then this room holds more of his personality than of mine?"

There was an under sound of vexation in his voice.

"Have you heard anything?"

"No. But no doubt he's still in the North with his mother."

"How domestic. I hope there is a stool of repentance in the family house."

"I wonder if you could ever repent of anything."

"Do you think there is anything I ought to repent of?"

"Oh, yes."

"What?"

"You might have married a man who knew the truth of you, and you married a man incapable of ever knowing it."

138 | The Woman with the Fan

He half expected an outburst of anger to follow his daring speech, but she sat quite still, looking at him steadily. She had taken off her gloves, and her hands lay lightly, one resting on the other.

"You mean, I might have married you."

"I'm not worth much, but at least I could never have betrayed the white angel in you."

She leaned towards him and spoke earnestly, almost like a child to an older person in whom it has faith.

"Do you think such an angel could do anything in—in this sort of world?"

"Modern London?"

She nodded, keeping her eyes still on him. He guessed at once of what she was thinking.

"Do anything—is rather vague," he replied evasively. "What sort of thing?"

Suddenly she threw off all reserve and let her temper go.

"If an angel were striving with a common American, do you mean to tell me you don't know which would go to the wall in our world?" she cried. "Robin, you may be a thousand things, but you aren't a fool. Nor am I—not *au fond*. And yet I have thought—I have wondered—"

She stopped.

"What?" he asked.

"Whether, if there is an angel in me, it mightn't be as well to trot it out."

The self-consciousness of the slang prevented him from hating it.

"Ah!" he said. "When have you wondered?"

"Lately. It's your fault. You have insisted so much upon the existence of the celestial being that at last I've become almost credulous. It's very absurd and I'm still hanging back."

"Call credulity belief and you needn't be ashamed of it."

"And if I believe, what then?"

"Then a thousand things. Belief sheds strength through all the tissues of the mind, the heart, the temperament. Disbelief sheds weakness. The one knits together, the other dissolves."

"There are people who think angels frightfully boring company."

"I know."

"Well then?"

Suddenly Robin got up and spoke almost brutally.

"Do you think I don't see that you are trying to find out from me what I think would be the best means of—"

The look in her face stopped him.

"I think the water is boiling," he said, going over to the lamp.

"It ought to bubble," she answered quietly.

He lifted up the lid of the silver bowl and peeped in.

"It is bubbling."

For a moment he was busy pouring the water into the teapot. While he did this there was a silence between them. Lady Holme got up from the sofa and walked about the room. When she came to the *"Danseuse de Tunisie"* she stopped in front of it.

"How strange that fan is," she said.

Robin shut the lid of the teapot and came over to her.

"Do you like it?"

"The fan?"

"The whole thing?"

"It's lovely, but I fancy it would have been lovelier without the fan."

"Why?"

She considered, holding her head slightly on one side and half closing her eyes.

"The woman's of eternity, but the fan's of a day," she said presently. "It belittles her, I think. It makes her *chic* when she might have been—"

She stopped.

"Throw away your fan!" he said in a low, eager voice.

"I?"

"Yes. Be the woman, the eternal woman. You've never been her yet, but you could be. Now is the moment. You're unhappy."

"No," she said sharply.

"Yes, you are. Viola, don't imagine I can't understand. You care for him and he's hurting you—hurting you by being just himself, all he can ever be. It's the fan he cares for."

"And you tell me to throw it away!"

She spoke with sudden passion. They stood still for a moment in front of the statuette, looking at each other silently. Then Robin said, with a sort of bitter surprise:

"But you can't love him like that!"

"I do."

It gave her an odd, sharp pleasure to speak the truth to him.

"What are you going to do, then?" he asked, after a pause.

He spoke without emotion, accepting the situation.

"To do? What do you mean?"

"Come and sit down. I'll tell you."

He took her hand and led her back to the sofa. When she had sat down, he poured out tea, put in cream and gave it to her.

"Nothing to eat," she said.

He poured out his tea and sat down in a chair opposite to her, and close to her.

"May I dare to speak frankly?" he asked. "I've known you so long, and I've—I've loved you very much, and I still do."

"Go on!" she answered.

"You thought your beauty was everything, that so long as it lasted you were safe from unhappiness. Well, to-day you are beautiful, and yet—"

"But what does he care for?" she said. "What do men care for? You pretend that it's something romantic, something good even. Really, it's impudent—just that—cold and impudent. You're a fool, Robin, you're a fool!"

"Am I? Thank God there are men—and men. You can't be what Carey said."

For once he had spoken incautiously. He had blurted out something he never meant to say.

"Mr. Carey!" she exclaimed quickly, curiously. "What did Mr. Carey say I was?"

"Oh—"

"No, Robin, you are to tell me. No diplomatic lies."

A sudden, almost brutal desire came into him to tell her the truth, to revel in plain speaking for once, and to see how she would bear it.

"He said you were an egoist, that you were fine enough in your brilliant selfishness to stand quite alone—"

A faint smile moved the narrow corners of her lips at the last words. He went on.

"—That your ideal of a real man, the sort of man a woman loses her head for, was—"

He stopped. Carey's description of the Lord Holme and Leo Ulford type had not been very delicate.

"Was—?" she said, with insistence. "Was—?"

Robin thought how she had hurt him, and said:

"Carey said, a huge mass of bones, muscles, thews, sinews, that cares nothing for beauty."

"Beauty! That doesn't care for beauty! But then—?"

"Carey meant—yes, I'm sure Carey meant real beauty."

"What do you mean by 'real beauty'?"

"An inner light that radiates outward, but whose abiding-place is hidden—perhaps. But one can't say. One can only understand and love."

"Oh. And Mr. Carey said that. Was he—was he at all that evening as he was at Arkell House? Was he talking nonsense or was he serious?"

"Difficult to say! But he was not as he was at Arkell House. Which knows you best—Carey or I?"

"Neither of you. I don't know myself."

"What are you going to do?"

"I don't know. The only thing I know is that you can't tell me what to do."

"No, I can't."

"But perhaps I can tell you."

She put down her cup and looked at him with a sort of grave kindness that he had never seen in her face before.

"What to do?"

"Yes."

"Well?"

"Give up loving the white angel. Perhaps it isn't there. Perhaps it doesn't exist. And if it does—perhaps it's a poor, feeble thing that's no good to me, no good to me."

Suddenly she put her arms on the back of the couch, leaned her face on them and began to cry gently.

Robin was terribly startled. He got up, stretched out his hands to her in an impulsive gesture, then drew them back, turned and went to the window.

She was crying for Fritz.

That was absurd and horrible. Yet he knew that those tears came from the heart of the hidden woman he had so long believed in, proved her existence, showed that she could love.

CHAPTER XII

AS Lady Holme had foreseen, the impertinent mimicry of Miss Schley concentrated a great deal of attention upon the woman mimicked. Many people, accepting the American's cleverness as a fashionable fact, also accepted her imitation as the imitation of a fact more surreptitious, and credited Lady Holme with a secret leading towards the improper never before suspected by them. They remembered the break between the Holmes and Carey, the strange scene at the Arkell House ball, and began to whisper many things of Lady Holme, and to turn a tide of pity and of sympathy upon her husband. On this tide Lord Holme and the American might be said to float merrily like corks, unabashed in the eye of the sun. Their intimacy was condoned on all sides as a natural result of Lady Holme's conduct. Most of that which had been accomplished by Lord and Lady Holme together after their reconciliation over the first breakfast was undone. The silent tongue began to wag, and to murmur the usual platitudes about the poor fellow who could not find sympathy at home and so was obliged, against his will, to seek for it outside.

All this Lady Holme had foreseen as she sat in her box at the British Theatre.

The wrong impression of her was enthroned. She had to reckon with it. This fact, fully recognised by her, made her wish to walk warily where otherwise her temper might have led her to walk heedlessly. She wanted to do an unusual thing, to draw her husband's attention to an intimacy which was concealed from the world—the intimacy between herself and Leo Ulford.

After her visit to the house in Half Moon Street she began to see a great deal of Leo Ulford. Carey had been right when he said that they would get on together. She understood him easily and thoroughly, and for that very reason he was attracted by her. Men delight to feel that a woman is understanding them; women that no man can ever understand them. Under the subtle influence of Lady Holme's complete comprehension of him, Leo Ulford's nature expanded, stretched itself as his long legs stretched themselves when his mind was purring. There was not much in him to reveal, but what there was he revealed, and Lady Holme seemed to be profoundly interested in the contents of his soul.

But she was not interested in the contents of his soul in public places on which the world's eye is fixed. She refused to allow Leo to do what he desired, and assumed an air of almost possessive friendship before Society. His natural inclination for the blatant was firmly checked by her. She cared nothing for him really, but her woman's instinct had divined that he was the type of man most likely to rouse the slumbering passion of Fritz, if Fritz were led to suspect that she was attracted to him. Men like Lord Holme are most easily jealous of the men who most closely resemble them. Their conceit leads them to put an exaggerated value upon their own qualities in others, upon the resemblance to their own physique exhibited by others.

Leo Ulford was rather like a younger and coarser Lord Holme. In him Lady Holme recognised an effective weapon for the chastisement, if not for the eventual reclamation, of her husband. It was characteristic of her that this was the weapon she chose, the weapon she still continued to rely on even after her conversation with Robin Pierce. Her faith in white angels was very small. Perpetual contact with the world of to-day, with life as lived by women of her order, had created within her far other faiths, faiths in false gods, a natural inclination to bow the knee in the house of Rimmon rather than before the altars guarded by the Eternities.

And then—she knew Lord Holme; knew what attracted him, what stirred him, what moved him to excitement, what was likely to hold him. She felt sure that he and such men as he yield the homage they would refuse to the angel to the siren. Instead of seeking the angel within herself, therefore, she sought the siren. Instead of striving to develope that part of her which was spiritual, she fixed all her attention upon that part of her which was fleshly, which was physical. She neglected the flame and began to make pretty patterns with the ashes.

Robin came to bid her good-bye before leaving London for Rome. The weeping woman was gone. He looked into the hard, white face of a woman who smiled. They talked rather constrainedly for a few minutes. Then suddenly he said:

"Once it was a painted window, now it's an iron shutter."

He got up from his chair and clasped his hands together behind his back.

"What on earth do you mean?" she asked, still smiling.

"Your face," he answered. "One could see you obscurely before. One can see nothing now."

"You talk great nonsense, Robin. It's a good thing you're going back to Rome."

"At least I shall find the spirit of beauty there," he said, almost with bitterness. "Over here it is treated as if it were Jezebel. It's trodden down. It's thrown to the dogs."

"Poor spirit!"

She laughed lightly.

"Do you understand what they're saying of you?" he went on.

"Where?"

"All over London."

"Perhaps."

"But—do you?"

"Perhaps I don't care to."

"They're saying—'Poor thing! But it's her own fault.'"

There was a silence. In it he looked at her hard, mercilessly. She returned his gaze, still smiling.

"And it is your own fault," he went on after a moment. "If you had been yourself she couldn't have insulted you first and humiliated you afterwards. Oh, how I hate it! And yet—yet there are moments when I am like the others, when I feel—'She has deserved it.'"

"When will you be in Rome?" she said.

"And even now," he continued, ignoring her remark, "even now, what are you doing? Oh, Viola, you're a prey to the modern madness for crawling in the dirt instead of walking upright in the sun. You might be a goddess and you prefer to be an insect. Isn't it mad of you? Isn't it?"

He was really excited, really passionate. His face showed that. There was fire in his eyes. His lips worked convulsively when he was not speaking. And yet there was just a faint ring of the accomplished orator's music in his voice, a music which suggests a listening ear—and that ear the orator's own.

Perhaps she heard it. At any rate his passionate attack did not seem to move her.

"I prefer to be what I am," was all she said.

"What you are! But you don't know what you are."

"And how can you pretend to know?" she asked. "Is a man more subtle about a woman than she is about herself?"

He did not answer for a moment. Then he said bluntly:

"Promise me one thing before I go away."

"I don't know. What is it?"

"Promise me not to—not to—"

He hesitated. The calm of her face seemed almost to confuse him.

"Well?" she said. "Go on."

"Promise me not to justify anything people are saying, not to justify it with—with that fellow Ulford."

"Good-bye," she answered, holding out her hand.

He recognised that the time for his advice had gone by, if it had ever been.

"What a way—what a way for us to—" he almost stammered.

He recovered his self-possession with an effort and took her hand.

"At least," he said in a low, quiet voice, "believe it is less jealousy that speaks within me than love—love for you, for the woman you are trampling in the dust."

He looked into her eyes and went out. She did not see him again before he left England. And she was glad. She did not want to see him. Perhaps it was the first time in her life that the affection of a man whom she really liked was distasteful to her. It made her uneasy, doubtful of herself just then, to be loved as Robin loved her.

Carey had come back to town, but he went nowhere. He was in bad odour. Sir Donald Ulford was almost the only person he saw anything of at this time. It seemed that Sir Donald had taken a fancy to Carey. At any rate, such friendly feeling as he had did not seem lessened after Carey's exhibition at Arkell House. When Carey returned to Stratton Street, Sir Donald paid him a visit and stayed some time. No allusion was made to the painful circumstances under which they had last seen each other until Sir Donald was on the point of going away. Then he said:

"You have not forgotten that I expect you at Casa Felice towards the end of August?"

Carey looked violently astonished.

"Still?" he said.

"Yes."

Suddenly Carey shot out his hand and grasped Sir Donald's.

"You aren't afraid to have a drunken beast like me in Casa Felice! It's a damned dangerous experiment."

"I don't think so."

"It's your own lookout, you know. I absolve you from the invitation."

"I repeat it, then."

"I accept it, then—again."

Sir Donald went away thoughtfully. When he reached the Albany he found Mrs. Leo Ulford waiting for him in tears. They had a long interview.

Many people fancied that Sir Donald looked more ghostly, more faded even than usual as the season wore on. They said he was getting too old to go about so much as he did, and that it was a pity Society "got such a hold" on men who ought to have had enough of it long ago. One night he met Lady Holme at the Opera. She was in her box and he in the stalls. After the second act she called him to her with a gay little nod of invitation. Lady Cardington had been with her during the act, but left the box when the curtain fell to see some friends close by. When Sir Donald tapped at the door Lady Holme was quite alone. He came in quietly—even his walk was rather ghostly—and sat down beside her.

"You don't look well," she said after they had greeted each other.

"I am quite well," he answered, with evident constraint.

"I haven't seen you to speak to since that little note of yours."

A very faint colour rose in his faded cheeks.

"After Miss Schley's first night?" he murmured.

His yellow fingers moved restlessly.

"Do you know that your son told me you would write?" she continued.

She was leaning back in her chair, half hidden by the curtain of the box.

"Leo!"

Sir Donald's voice was almost sharp and startling.

"How should he—you spoke about me then?"

There was a flash of light in his pale, almost colourless eyes.

"I wondered where you had gone, and he said you would write next day."

"That was all?"

"Why, how suspicious you are!"

She spoke banteringly.

"Suspicious! No—but Leo does not understand me very well. I was rather old when he was born, and I have never been able to be much with him. He was educated in England, and my duties of course lay abroad."

He paused, looking at her and moving his thin white moustache. Then, in an uneasy voice, he added:

"You must not take my character altogether from Leo."

"Nor you mine altogether from Miss Schley," said Lady Holme.

She scarcely knew why she said it. She thought herself stupid, ridiculous almost, for saying it. Yet she could not help speaking. Perhaps she relied on Sir Donald's age. Or perhaps—but who knows why a woman is cautious or incautious in moments the least expected? God guides her, perhaps, or the devil—or merely a bottle imp. Men never know, and that is why they find her adorable.

Sir Donald said nothing for a moment, only made the familiar movement with his hands that was a sign in him of concealed excitement or emotion. His eyes were fixed upon the ledge of the box. Lady Holme was puzzled by his silence and, at last, was on the point of making a remark on some other subject—Plancon's singing—when he spoke, like a man who had made up his mind firmly to take an unusual, perhaps a difficult course.

"I wish to take it from you," he said. "Give me the right one, not an imitation of an imitation."

She knew at once what he meant and was surprised. Had Leo Ulford been talking?

"Lady Holme," he went on, "I am taking a liberty. I know that. It's a thing I have never done before, knowingly. Don't think me unconscious of what I am doing. But I am an old man, and old men can sometimes venture—allowance is sometimes made for them. I want to claim that allowance now for what I am going to say."

"Well?" she said, neither hardly nor gently.

In truth she scarcely knew whether she wished him to speak or not.

"My son is—Leo is not a safe friend for you at this moment."

Again the dull, brick-red flush rose in his cheeks. There was an odd, flattened look just above his cheekbones near his eyes, and the eyes themselves had a strange expression as of determination and guilt mingled.

"Your son?" Lady Holme said. "But—"

"I do not wish to assume anything, but I—well, my daughter-in-law sometimes comes to me."

"Sometimes!" said Lady Holme.

"Leo is not a good husband," Sir Donald said. "But that is not the point. He is also a bad—friend."

"Why don't you say lover?" she almost whispered.

He grasped his knee with one hand and moved the hand rapidly to and fro.

"I must say of him to you that where his pleasure or his vanity is concerned he is unscrupulous."

"Why say all this to a woman?"

"You mean that you know as much as I?"

"Don't you think it likely?"

"Henrietta—"

"Who is that?"

"My daughter-in-law has done everything for Leo—too much. She gets nothing—not even gratitude. I am sorry to say he has no sense of chivalry towards women. You know him, I daresay. But do you know him thwarted?"

"Ah, you don't think so badly of me after all?" she said quickly.

"I—I think of you that—that—"

He stopped.

"I think that I could not bear to see the whiteness of your wings smirched by a child of mine." he added.

"You too!" she said.

Suddenly tears started into her eyes.

"Another believer in the angel!" she thought.

"May I come in?"

It was Mr. Bry's cold voice. His discontented, sleek face was peeping round the door.

Sir Donald got up to go.

As Lady Holme drove away from Covent Garden that night she was haunted by a feverish, embittering thought:

"Will everyone notice it but Fritz?"

Lord Holme indeed seemed scarcely the same man who had forbidden Carey to come any more to his house, who had been jealous of Robin Pierce, who had even once said that he almost wished his wife were an ugly woman. The Grand Turk nature within him, if not actually dead, was certainly in abeyance. He was so intent on his own affairs that he paid no heed at all to his wife's, even when they might be said to be also his. Leo Ulford was becoming difficult to manage, and Lord Holme still gaily went his way. As Lady Holme thought over Sir Donald's words she felt a crushing weight of depression sink down upon her. The brougham rolled smoothly on through the lighted streets. She did not glance out of the windows, or notice the passing crowds. In the silence and darkness of her own soul she was trying not to feel, trying to think.

A longing to be incautious, to do something startling, desperate, came to her.

It was evident that Mrs. Ulford had been complaining to Sir Donald about his son's conduct. With whom? Lady Holme could not doubt that it was with herself. She had read, with one glance at the fluttering pink eyelids, the story of the Leo Ulford's *menage*. Now, she was not preoccupied with any regret for her own cruelty or for another woman's misery. The egoism spoken of by Carey was not dead in her yet, but very much alive. As she sat in the corner of the brougham, pressing herself against the padded wall, she was angry for herself, pitiful for herself. And she was jealous— horribly jealous. That woke up her imagination, all the intensity of her. Where was Fritz to-night? She did not know. Suddenly the dense ignorance in which every human being lives, and must live to the end of time, towered above her like a figure in a nightmare. What do we know, what can we ever know of each other? In each human being dwells the most terrible, the most ruthless power that exists—the power of silence.

Fritz had that power; stupid, blundering, self-contented Fritz.

She pulled the check-string and gave the order, "Home!"

In her present condition she felt unable to go into Society.

When she got to Cadogan Square she said to the footman who opened the door:

"His lordship isn't in yet?"

"No, my lady."

"Did he say what time he would be in to-night?"

"No, my lady."

The man paused, then added:

"His lordship told Mr. Lucas not to wait up."

"Mr. Lucas" was Lord Holme's valet.

It seemed to Lady Holme as if there were a significant, even a slightly mocking, sound in the footman's voice. She stared at him. He was a thin, swarthy young man, with lantern jaws and a very long, pale chin. When she looked at him he dropped his eyes.

"Bring me some lemonade to the drawing-room in ten minutes," she said.

"Yes, my lady."

"In ten minutes, not before. Turn on all the lights in the drawing-room."

"Yes, my lady."

The man went before her up the staircase, turned on the lights, stood aside to let her pass and then went softly down. Lady Holme rang for Josephine.

"Take my cloak and then go to bed," she said.

Josephine took the cloak and went out, shutting the door.

"Ten minutes!" Lady Holme said to herself.

She sat down on the sofa on which she had sat for a moment alone after her song at the dinner-party, the song murdered by Miss Filberte. The empty, brilliantly-lit rooms seemed unusually large. She glanced round them with inward-looking eyes. Here she was at midnight sitting quite alone in her own house. And she wished to do something decisive, startling as the cannon shot sometimes fired from a ship to disperse a fog wreath. That was the reason why she had told the footman to come in ten minutes. She thought that in ten minutes she might make up her mind. If she decided upon doing something that required an emissary the man would be there.

She looked at the little silver box she had taken up that night when she was angry, then at the grand piano in the further room. The two things suggested to her two women—the woman of hot temper and the woman of sweetness and romance. What was she to-night, and what was she going to do? Nothing, probably. What could she do? Again she glanced round the rooms. It seemed to her that she was like an actress in an intense, passionate *role*, who is paralysed by what is called in the theatre "a stage wait." She ought to play a tremendous scene, now, at once, but the person with whom she was to play it did not come on to the stage. She had worked herself up for the scene. The emotion, the passion, the force, the fury were alive, were red hot within her, and she could not set them free. She remained alone upon the stage in a sort of horror of dumbness, a horror of inaction.

The footman came in quietly with the lemonade on a tray. He put it down on a table by Lady Holme.

"Is there anything else, my lady?"

She supposed that the question was meant as a very discreet hint to her that the man would be glad to go to bed. For a moment she did not reply, but kept him waiting. She was thinking rapidly, considering whether she would do the desperate thing or not, whether she would summon one of the actors for the violent scene her nature demanded persistently that night.

After the opera she had been due at a ball to which Leo Ulford was going. She had promised to go in to supper with him and to arrive by a certain hour. He was wondering, waiting, now, at this moment. She knew that. The house was in Eaton Square, not far off. Should she send the footman with a note to Leo, saying that she was too tired to come to the ball but that she was sitting up at home? That was what she was rapidly considering while the footman stood waiting. Leo would come, and then—presently—Lord Holme would come. And then? Then doubtless would happen the scene she longed for, longed for with a sort of almost crazy desire such as she had never felt before.

She glanced up and saw an astonished expression upon the footman's pale face. How long had she kept him there waiting? She had no idea.

"There is nothing else," she said slowly.

She paused, then added, reluctantly:

"You can go to bed."

The man went softly out of the room. As he shut the door she breathed a deep sigh, that was almost a sob. So difficult had she found it to govern herself, not to do the crazy thing.

She poured out the lemonade and put ice into it.

As she did so she made grimaces, absurd grimaces of pain and misery, like those on the faces of the two women in Mantegna's picture of Christ and the Marys in the Brera at Milan. They are grotesque, yet wonderfully moving in their pitiless realism. But tears fall from the eyes of Mantegna's women and no tears fell from Lady Holme's eyes. Still making grimaces, she sipped the lemonade. Then she put down the glass, leaned back on the sofa and shut her eyes. Her face ceased to move, and became beautiful again in its stillness. She remained motionless for a long time, trying to obtain the mastery over herself. In act she had obtained it already, but not in emotion.

Indeed, the relinquishing of violence, the sending of the footman to bed, seemed to have increased the passion within her. And now she felt it rising till she was afraid of being herself, afraid of being this solitary woman, feeling intensely and able to do nothing. It seemed to her as if such a passion of jealousy, and desire for immediate expression of it in action, as flamed within her, must wreak disaster upon her like some fell disease, as if she were in immediate danger, even in immediate physical danger. She lay still like one determined to meet it bravely, without flinching, without a sign of cowardice.

But suddenly she felt that she had made a mistake in dismissing the footman, that the pain of inaction was too great for her to bear. She could not just—do nothing. She could not, and she got up swiftly and rang the bell. The man did not return. She pressed the bell again. After three or four minutes he came in, looking rather flushed and put out.

"I want you to take a note to Eaton Square," she said. "It will be ready in five minutes."

"Yes, my lady."

She went to her writing table and wrote this note to Leo Ulford:

> "DEAR MR. ULFORD,—I am grieved to play you false, but I am too tired to-night to come on. Probably you are amusing yourself. I am sitting here alone over such a dull book. One can't go to bed at twelve, somehow, even if one is tired. The habit of the season's against early hours and one couldn't sleep. Be nice and come in for five minutes on your way home, and tell me all about it. I know you pass the end of the square, so it won't be out of your way.—Yours very sincerely, V. H."

After writing this note Lady Holme hesitated for a moment, then she went to a writing table, opened a drawer and took out a tiny, flat key. She enclosed it in two sheets of thick note paper, folded the note also round it, and put it into an envelope which she carefully closed. After writing Leo Ulford's name on the envelope she rang again for the footman.

"Take this to Eaton Square," she said, naming the number of the house. "And give it to Mr. Ulford yourself. Go in a hansom. When you have given Mr. Ulford the note come straight back in the hansom and let me know. After that you can go to bed. Do you understand?"

"Yes, my lady."

The man went out.

Lady Holme stood up to give him the note. She remained standing after he had gone. An extraordinary sensation of relief had come to her. Action had lessened her pain, had removed much of the pressure of emotion upon her heart. For a moment she felt almost happy.

She sat down again and took up a book. It was a book of poems written by a very young girl whom she knew. There was a great deal about sorrow in the poems, and sorrow was always alluded to as a person; now flitting through a forest in the autumn among the dying leaves, now bending over a bed, now walking by the sea at sunset watching departing ships, now standing near the altar at a wedding. The poems were not good. On the other hand, they were not very bad.

They had some grace, some delicacy here and there, now and then a touch of real, if by no means exquisite, sentiment. At this moment Lady Holme found them soothing. There was a certain music in them and very little reality. They seemed to represent life as a pensive phantasmagoria of bird songs, fading flowers, dying lights, soft winds and rains and sighing echoes.

She read on and on. Sometimes a hard thought intruded itself upon her mind—the thought of Leo Ulford with the latch-key of her husband's house in his hand. That thought made the poems seem to her remarkably unlike life.

She looked at the clock. The footman had been away long enough to do his errand. Just as she was thinking this he came into the room.

"Well?" she said.

"I gave Mr. Ulford the note, my lady."

"Then you can go to bed. Good-night. I'll put out the lights here."

"Thank you, my lady."

As he went away she turned again to the poems; but now she could not read them. Her eyes rested upon them, but her mind took in nothing of their meaning. Presently—very soon—she laid the book down and sat listening. The footman had shut the drawing-room door. She got up and opened it. She wanted to hear the sound of the latch-key being put into the front door by Leo Ulford. It seemed to her as if that sound would be like the *leit motif* of her determination to govern, to take her own way, to strike a blow against the selfish egoism of men. After opening the door she sat down close to it and waited, listening.

Some minutes passed. Then she heard—not the key put into the hall door; it had not occurred to her that she was much too far away to hear that—but the bang of the door being shut.

Quickly she closed the drawing-room door, went back to the distant sofa, sat down upon it and began to turn over the poems once more. She even read one quite carefully. As she finished it the door was opened.

She looked up gaily to greet Leo and saw her husband coming into the room.

She was greatly startled. It had never occurred to her that Fritz was quite as likely to arrive before Leo Ulford as Leo Ulford to arrive before Fritz. Why had she never thought of so obvious a possibility? She could not imagine. The difference between the actuality and her intense and angry conception of what it would be, benumbed her mind for an instant. She was completely confused. She sat still with the book of poems on her lap, and gazed at Lord Holme as he came towards her, taking long steps and straddling his legs as if he imagined he had a horse under him. The gay expression had abruptly died away from her face and she looked almost stupid.

"Hulloa!" said Lord Holme, as he saw her.

She said nothing.

"Thought you were goin' to the Blaxtons to-night," he added.

She made a strong effort and smiled.

"I meant to, but I felt tired after the opera."

"Why don't you toddle off to bed then?"

"I feel tired, I don't feel sleepy."

Lord Holme stared at her, put his hand into his trousers pocket and pulled out his cigarette-case. Lady Holme knew that he had been in a good humour when he came home, and that the sight of her sitting up in the drawing-room had displeased him. She had seen a change come into his face. He had been looking gay. He began to look glum and turned his eyes away from her.

"What have you been up to?" she asked, with a sudden light gaiety and air of comradeship.

"Club—playin' bridge," he answered, lighting a cigarette.

He shot a glance at her sideways as he spoke, a glance that was meant to be crafty. If she had not been excited and horribly jealous, such a glance would probably have amused her, even made her laugh. Fritz's craft was very transparent. But she could not laugh now. She knew he was telling her the first lie that had occurred to him.

"Lucky?" she asked, still preserving her light and casual manner.

"Middlin'," he jerked out.

He sat down in an armchair and slowly stretched his legs, staring up at the ceiling. Lady Holme began to think rapidly, feverishly.

Had he locked the front door when he came in? Very much depended upon whether he had or had not. The servants had all gone to bed. Not one of them would see that the house was closed for the night. Fritz was a very casual person. He often forgot to do things he had promised to do, things that ought to be done. On the other hand, there were moments when his memory was excellent. If she only knew which mood had been his to-night she thought she would feel calmer. The uncertainty in which she was made mind and body tingle. If Fritz had remembered to lock the door, Leo Ulford would try to get in, fail, and go away. But if he had not remembered, at any moment Leo Ulford might walk into the room triumphantly with the latch-key in his hand. And it was nearly half-past twelve.

She wished intensely that she knew what Fritz had done.

"What's up?" he said abruptly.

"Up?" she said with an uncontrollable start.

"Yes, with you?"

"Nothing. What d'you mean?"

"Why, you looked as if—don't you b'lieve I've been playin' bridge?"

"Of course I do. Really, Fritz, how absurd you are!"

It was evident that he, too, was not quite easy to-night. If he had a conscience, surely it was pricking him. Fierce anger flamed up again suddenly in Lady Holme, and the longing to lash her husband. Yet even this anger did not take away the anxiety that beset her, the wish that she had not done the crazy thing. The fact of her husband's return before Leo's arrival seemed to have altered her action, made it far more damning. To have been found with Leo would have been compromising, would have roused Fritz's anger. She wanted to rouse his anger. She had meant to rouse it. But when she looked at Fritz she did not like the thought of Leo walking in at this hour holding the latch-key in his hand. What had Fritz done that night to Rupert Carey? What would he do to-night if—?

"What the deuce is up with you?"

Lord Holme drew in his legs, sat up and stared with a sort of uneasy inquiry which he tried to make hard. She laughed quickly, nervously.

"I'm tired, I tell you. It was awfully hot at the opera."

She put some more ice into the lemonade, and added:

"By the way, Fritz, I suppose you locked up all right?"

"Locked up what?"

"The front door. All the servants have gone to bed, you know."

No sooner had she spoken the last words than she regretted them. If Leo did get in they took away all excuse. She might have pretended he had been let in. He would have had to back her up. It would have been mean of her, of course. Still, seeing her husband there, Leo would have understood, would have forgiven her. Women are always forgiven such subterfuges in unfortunate moments. What a fool she was to-night!

"That don't matter," said her husband, shortly.

"But—but it does. You know how many burglaries there are. Why, only the other night Mrs. Arthur came home from a ball and met two men on the stairs."

"I pity any men I found on my stairs," he returned composedly, touching the muscle of his left arm with his right hand.

He chuckled.

"They'd be sorry for themselves, I'll bet," he added.

He put down his cigarette and took out another slowly, leisurely. Lady Holme longed to strike him. His conceited composure added fuel to the flame of her anxiety.

"Well, anyhow, I don't care to run these risks in a place like London, Fritz," she said almost angrily. "Have you locked up or not?"

"Damned if I remember," he drawled.

She did not know whether he was deliberately trying to irritate her or whether he really had forgotten, but she felt it impossible to remain any longer in uncertainty.

"Very well, then, I shall go down and see," she said.

And she laid the book of poems on a table and prepared to get up from the sofa.

"Rot!" said Lord Holme; "if you're nervous, I'll go."

She leaned back.

"Very well."

"In a minute."

He struck a match and let it out.

"Do go now, there's a good dog," she said coaxingly.

He struck another match and held it head downwards.

"You needn't hurry a feller."

He tapped his cigarette gently on his knee, and applied the flame to it.

"That's better."

Lady Holme moved violently on the sofa. She had a pricking sensation all over her body, and her face felt suddenly very hot, as if she had fever. A ridiculous, but painful idea started up suddenly in her mind. Could Fritz suspect anything? Was he playing with her? She dismissed it at once as the distorted child of a guilty conscience. Fritz was not that sort of man. He might be a brute sometimes, but he was never a subtle brute. He blew two thin lines of smoke out through his nostrils, now with a sort of sensuous, almost languid, deliberation, and watched them fade away in the brilliantly-lit room. Lady Holme resolved to adopt another manner, more in accord with her condition of tense nervousness.

"When I ask you to do a thing, Fritz, you might have the decency to do it," she said sharply. "You're forgetting what's due to me—to any woman."

"Don't fuss at this time of night."

"I want to go to bed, but I'm not going till I know the house is properly shut up. Please go at once and see."

"I never knew you were such a coward," he rejoined without stirring. "Who was at the opera?"

"I won't talk to you till you do what I ask."

"That's a staggerin' blow."

She sprang up with an exclamation of anger. Her nerves were on edge and she felt inclined to scream out.

"I never thought you could be so—such a cad to a woman, Fritz," she said.

She moved towards the door. As she did so she heard a cab in the square outside, a rattle of wheels, then silence. It had stopped. Her heart seemed to stand still too. She knew now that she was a coward, though not in the way Fritz meant. She was a coward with regard to him. Her jealousy had prompted her to do a mad thing. In doing it she had actually meant to produce a violent scene. It had seemed to her that such a scene would relieve the tension of her nerves, of her heart, would clear the air. But now that the scene seemed imminent—if Fritz had forgotten, and she was certain he had forgotten, to lock the door—she felt heart and nerves were failing her. She felt that she had risked too much, far too much. With almost incredible swiftness she remembered her imprudence in speaking to Carey at Arkell House and how it had only served to put a weapon into her husband's hand, a weapon he had not scrupled to use in his selfish way to further his own pleasure and her distress. That stupid failure had not sufficiently warned her, and now she was on the edge of some greater disaster. She was positive that Leo Ulford was in the cab which had just stopped, and it was too late now to prevent him from entering the house. Lord Holme had got up from his chair and stood facing her. He looked quite pleasant. She thought of the change that would come into his face in a moment and turned cold.

"Don't cut up so deuced rough," he said; "I'll go and lock up."

So he had forgotten. He took a step towards the drawing-room door. But now she felt that at all costs she must prevent him from going downstairs, must gain a moment somehow. Suddenly she swayed slightly.

"I feel—awfully faint," she said.

She went feebly, but quickly, to the window which looked on to the Square, drew away the curtain, opened the window and leaned out. The cab had stopped before their door, and she saw Leo Ulford standing on the pavement with his back to the house. He was feeling in his pocket, evidently for some money to give to the cabman. If she could only attract his attention somehow and send him away! She glanced back. Fritz was coming towards her with a look of surprise on his face.

"Leave me alone," she said unevenly. "I only want some air."

"But—"

"Leave me—oh, do leave me alone!"

He stopped, but stood staring at her in blank amazement. She dared not do anything. Leo Ulford stretched out his arm towards the cabman, who bent down from his perch. He took the money, looked at it, then bent down again, showing it to Leo and muttering something. Doubtless he was saying that it was not enough. She turned round again sharply to Fritz.

"Fritz," she said, "be a good dog. Go upstairs to my room and fetch me some eau de Cologne, will you?"

"But—"

"It's on my dressing-table—the gold bottle on the right. You know. I feel so bad. I'll stay here. The air will bring me round perhaps."

She caught hold of the curtain, like a person on the point of swooning.

"All right," he said, and he went out of the room.

She watched till he was gone, then darted to the window and leaned out.

She was too late. The cab was driving off and Leo was gone. He must have entered the house.

CHAPTER XIII

BEFORE she had time to leave the window she heard a step in the room. She turned and saw Leo Ulford, smiling broadly—like a great boy—and holding up the latch-key she had sent him. At the sight of her face his smile died away.

"Go—go!" she whispered, putting out her hand. "Go at once!"

"Go! But you told me—"

"Go! My husband's come back. He's in the house. Go quickly. Don't make a sound. I'll explain to-morrow."

She made a rapid, repeated gesture of her hands towards the door, frowning. Leo Ulford stood for an instant looking heavy and sulky, then, pushing out his rosy lips in a sort of indignant pout, he swung round on his heels. As he did so, Lord Holme came into the room holding the bottle of eau de Cologne. When he saw Leo he stopped. Leo stopped too, and they stood for a moment staring at each other. Lady Holme, who was still by the open window, did not move. There was complete silence in the room. Then Leo dropped the latch-key. It fell on the thick carpet without a noise. He made a hasty, lumbering movement to pick it up, but Lord Holme was too quick for him. When Lady Holme saw the key in her husband's hand she moved at last and came forward into the middle of the room.

"Mr. Ulford's come to tell me about the Blaxtons' dance," she said.

She spoke in her usual light voice, without tremor or uncertainty. Her face was perfectly calm and smiling. Leo Ulford cleared his throat.

"Yes," he said loudly, "about the Blaxtons' dance."

Lord Holme stood looking at the latch-key. Suddenly his face swelled up and became bloated, and large veins stood out in his brown forehead.

"What's this key?" he said.

He held it out towards his wife. Neither she nor Leo Ulford replied to his question.

"What's this key?" he repeated.

"The key of Mr. Ulford's house, I suppose," said Lady Holme. "How should I know?"

"I'm not askin' you," said her husband.

He came a step nearer to Leo.

"Why the devil don't you answer?" he said to him.

"It's my latch-key," said Leo, with an attempt at a laugh.

Lord Holme flung it in his face.

"You damned liar!" he said. "It's mine."

And he struck him full in the face where the key had just struck him.

Leo returned the blow. When she saw that, Lady Holme passed the two men and went quickly out of the room, shutting the door behind her. Holding her hands over her ears, she hurried upstairs to her bedroom. It was in darkness. She felt about on the wall for the button that turned on the electric light, but could not find it. Her hands, usually deft and certain in their movements, seemed to have lost the sense of touch. It was as if they had abruptly been deprived of their minds. She felt and felt. She knew the button was there. Suddenly the room was full of light. Without being aware of it she had found the button and turned it. In the light she looked down at her hands and saw that they were trembling violently. She went to the door and shut it. Then she sat down on the sofa at the foot of the bed. She clasped her hands together in her lap, but they went on trembling. Pulses were beating in her eyelids. She felt utterly degraded, like a scrupulously clean person who has been rolled in the dirt. And she fancied she heard a faint and mysterious sound, pathetic and terrible, but very far away—the white angel in her weeping.

And the believers in the angel—were they weeping too?

She found herself wondering as a sleeper wonders in a dream.

Presently she got up. She could not sit there and see her hands trembling. She did not walk about the room, but went over to the dressing-table and stood by it, resting her hands upon it and leaning forward. The attitude seemed to relieve her. She remained there for a long time, scarcely thinking at all, only feeling degraded, unclean. The sight of physical violence in her own drawing-room, caused by her, had worked havoc in her. She had always thought she understood the brute in man. She had often consciously administered to it. She had coaxed it, flattered it, played upon it even—

surely—loved it. Now she had suddenly seen it rush out into the full light, and it had turned her sick.

The gold things on the dressing-table—bottles, brushes, boxes, trays—looked offensive. They were like lies against life, frauds. Everything in the pretty room was like a lie and a fraud. There ought to be dirt, ugliness about her. She ought to stand with her feet in mud and look on blackness. The angel in her shuddered at the siren in her now, as at a witch with power to evoke Satanic things, and she forgot the trembling of her hands in the sensation of the trembling of her soul. The blow of Fritz, the blow of Leo Ulford, had both struck her. She felt a beaten creature.

The door opened. She did not turn round, but she saw in the glass her husband come in. His coat was torn. His waistcoat and shirt were almost in rags. There was blood on his face and on his right hand. In his eyes there was an extraordinary light, utterly unlike the light of intelligence, but brilliant, startling; flame from the fire by which the animal in human nature warms itself. In the glass she saw him look at her. The light seemed to stream over her, to scorch her. He went into his dressing-room without a word, and she heard the noise of water being poured out and used for washing. He must be bathing his wounds, getting rid of the red stains.

She sat down on the sofa at the foot of the bed and listened to the noise of the water. At last it stopped and she heard drawers being violently opened and shut, then a tearing sound. After a silence her husband came into the room again with his forehead bound up in a silk handkerchief, which was awkwardly knotted behind his head. Part of another silk handkerchief was loosely tied round his right hand. He came forward, stood in front of her and looked at her, and she saw now that there was an expression almost of exultation on his face. She felt something fall into her lap. It was the latch-key she had sent to Leo Ulford.

"I can tell you he's sorry he ever saw that—damned sorry," said Lord Holme.

And he laughed.

Lady Holme took the key up carefully and put it down on the sofa. She was realising something, realising that her husband was feeling happy. When she had laid down the key she looked up at him and there was an intense scrutiny in her eyes. Suddenly it seemed to her as if she were standing up and looking down on him, as if she were the judge, he the culprit in this matter. The numbness left her mind. She was able to think swiftly again and her hands stopped trembling. That look of exultation in her husband's eyes had changed everything.

"Sit down, I want to speak to you," she said.

She was surprised by the calm sound of her own voice.

Lord Holme looked astonished. He shifted the bandage on his hand and stood where he was.

"Sit down," she repeated.

"Well!" he said.

And he sat down.

"I suppose you came up here to turn me out of the house?" she said.

"You deserve it," he muttered.

But even now he did not look angry. There was a sort of savage glow on his face. It was evident that the violent physical effort he had just made, and the success of it, had irresistibly swept away his fury for the moment. It might return. Probably it would return. But for the moment it was gone. Lady Holme knew Fritz, and she knew that he was feeling good all over. The fact that he could feel thus in such circumstances set the brute in him before her as it had never been set before—in a glare of light.

"And what do you deserve?" she asked.

All her terror had gone utterly. She felt mistress of herself.

"When I went to thrash Carey he was so drunk I couldn't touch him. This feller showed fight but he was a baby in my hands. I could do anything I liked with him," said Lord Holme. "Gad! Talk of boxin'—"

He looked at his bandaged hand and laughed again triumphantly. Then, suddenly, a sense of other things than his physical strength seemed to return upon him. His face changed, grew lowering, and he thrust forward his under jaw, opening his mouth to speak. Lady Holme did not give him time.

"Yes, I sent Leo Ulford the latch-key," she said. "You needn't ask. I sent it, and told him to come to-night. D'you know why?"

Lord Holme's face grew scarlet.

"Because you're a—"

She stopped him before he could say the irrevocable word.

"Because I mean to have the same liberty as the man I've married," she said. "I asked Leo Ulford here, and I intended you should find him here."

"You didn't. You thought I wasn't comin' home."

"Why should I have thought such a thing?" she said, swiftly, sharply.

Her voice had an edge to it.

"You meant not to come home, then?"

She read his stupidity at a glance, the guilty mind that had blundered, thinking its intention known when it was not known. He began to deny it, but she stopped him. At this moment, and exactly when she ought surely to have been crushed by the weight of Fritz's fury, she dominated him. Afterwards she wondered at herself, but not now.

"You meant not to come home?"

For once Lord Holme showed a certain adroitness. Instead of replying to his wife he retorted:

"You meant me to find Ulford here! That's a good 'un! Why, you tried all you knew to keep him out."

"Yes."

"Well, then?"

"I wanted—but you'd never understand."

"He does," said Lord Holme.

He laughed again, got up and walked about the room, fingering his bandages. Then suddenly, he turned on Lady Holme and said savagely:

"And you do."

"I?"

"Yes, you. There's lots of fellers that would—"

"Stop!" said Lady Holme, in a voice of sharp decision.

She got up too. She felt that she could not say what she meant to say sitting down.

"Fritz," she added, "you're a fool. You may be worse. I believe you are. But one thing's certain—you're a fool. Even in wickedness you're a blunderer."

"And what are you?" he said.

"I!" she answered, coming a step nearer. "I'm not wicked."

A sudden, strange desire came to her, a desire—as she had slangily expressed it to Robin Pierce—to "trot out" the white angel whom she had for so long ignored or even brow-beaten. Was the white angel there? Some there were who believed so. Robin Pierce, Sir Donald, perhaps others. And these few believers gave Lady Holme courage. She remembered them, she relied on them at this moment.

"I'm not wicked," she repeated.

She looked into her husband's face.

"Don't you know that?"

He was silent.

"Perhaps you'd rather I was," she continued. "Don't men prefer it?"

He stared first at her, then at the carpet. A puzzled look came into his face.

"But I don't care," she said, gathering resolution, and secretly calling, calling on the hidden woman, yet always with a doubt as to whether she was there in her place of concealment. "I don't care. I can't change my nature because of that. And surely—surely there must be some men who prefer refinement to vulgarity, purity to—"

"Ulford, eh?" he interrupted.

The retort struck like a whip on Lady Holme's temper. She forgot the believers in the angel and the angel too.

"How dare you?" she exclaimed. "As if I—"

He took up the latch-key and thrust it into her face. His sense of physical triumph was obviously dying away, his sense of personal outrage returning.

"Good women don't do things like that," he said. "If it was known in London you'd be done for."

"And you—may you do what you like openly, brazenly?"

"Men's different," he said.

The words and the satisfied way in which they were said made Lady Holme feel suddenly almost mad with rage. The truth of the statement, and the disgrace that it was truth, stirred her to the depths. At that moment she hated her husband, she hated all men. She remembered what Lady Cardington had said in the carriage as they were driving away from the Carlton after Mrs. Wolfstein's lunch, and her sense of impotent fury was made more bitter by the consciousness that women had chosen that men should be "different," or at least—if not that—had smilingly given them a license to be so. She wanted to say, to call out, so much that she said nothing. Lord Holme thought that for once he had been clever, almost intellectual. This was indeed a night of many triumphs for him. An intoxication of power surged up to his brain.

"Men's made different and treated differently," he said. "And they'd never stand anything else."

Lady Holme sat down again on the sofa. She put her right hand on her left hand and held it tightly in her lap.

"You mean," she said, in a hard, quiet voice, "that you may humiliate your wife in the eyes of London and that she must just pretend that she enjoys it and go on being devoted to you? Well, I will not do either the one or the other. I will not endure humiliation quietly, and as to my devotion to you—I daresay it wouldn't take much to kill it. Perhaps it's dead already."

No lie, perhaps, ever sounded more like truth than hers. At that moment she thought that probably it was truth.

"Eh?" said Lord Holme.

He looked suddenly less triumphant. His blunt features seemed altered in shape by the expression of blatant, boyish surprise, even amazement, that overspread them. His wife saw that, despite the incident of Leo Ulford's midnight visit, Fritz had not really suspected her of the uttermost faithlessness, that it had not occurred to him that perhaps her love for him was dead, that love was alive in her for another man. Had his conceit then no limits?

And then suddenly another thought flashed into her mind. Was he, too, a firm, even a fanatical, believer in the angel? She had never numbered Fritz among that little company of believers. Him she had always set among the men who worship the sirens of the world. But now—? Can there be two men in one man as there can be two women in one woman? Suddenly Fritz was new to her, newer to her than on the day when she first met him. And he was complex. Fritz complex! She changed the word conceit. She called it trust. And tears rushed into her eyes. There were tears in her heart too. She looked up at her husband. The silk bandage over his forehead had been white. Now it was faintly red. As she looked she thought that the colour of the red deepened.

"Come here, Fritz," she said softly.

He moved nearer.

"Bend down!"

"Eh?"

"Bend down your head."

He bent down his huge form with a movement that had in it some resemblance to the movement of a child. She put up her hand and touched the bandage where it was red. She took her hand away. It was damp.

A moment later Fritz was sitting in a low chair by the wash-hand stand in an obedient attitude, and a woman—was she siren or angel?—was bathing an ugly wound.

CHAPTER XIV

AFTER that night Lady Holme began to do something she had never done before—to idealise her husband. Hitherto she had loved him without weaving pretty fancies round him, loved him crudely for his strength, his animalism, his powerful egoism and imperturbable self-satisfaction. She had loved him almost as a savage woman might love, though without her sense of slavery. Now a change came over her. She thought of Fritz in a different way, the new Fritz, the Fritz who was a believer in the angel. It seemed to her that he could be kept faithful most easily, most surely, by such an appeal as Robin Pierce would have loved. She had sought to rouse, to play upon the instincts of the primitive man. She had not gone very far, it is true, but her methods had been common, ordinary. She had undervalued Fritz's nature. That was what she felt now. He had behaved badly to her, had wronged her, but he had believed in her very much. She resolved to make his belief more intense. An expression on his face—only that—had wrought a vital change in her feeling towards him, her conception of him. She ranged him henceforth with Sir Donald, with Robin Pierce. He stood among the believers in the angel.

She called upon the angel passionately, feverishly.

There was strength in Lady Holme's character, and not merely strength of temper. When she was roused, confident, she could be resolute, persistent; could shut her eyes to side issues and go onward looking straight before her. Now she went onward and she felt a new force within her, a force that would not condescend to pettiness, to any groping in the mud.

Lord Holme was puzzled. He felt the change in his wife, but did not understand it. Since the fracas with Leo Ulford their relations had slightly altered. Vaguely, confusedly, he was conscious of being pitied, yes, surely pitied by his wife. She shed a faint compassion, like a light cloud, over the glory of his wrongdoing. And the glory was abated. He felt a little doubtful of himself, almost as a son feels sometimes in the presence of his mother. For the first time he began to think of himself, now and then, as the inferior of his wife, began even, now and then, to think of man as the inferior of woman—in certain ways. Such a state of mind was very novel in him. He stared at it as a baby stares at its toes, with round amazement, inwardly saying, "Is this phenomenon part of me?"

There was a new gentleness in Viola, a new tenderness. Both put him—as one lifted and dropped—a step below her. He pulled his bronze moustache over it with vigour.

His wife showed no desire to control his proceedings, to know what he was about. When she spoke of Miss Schley she spoke kindly, sympathetically, but with a dainty, delicate pity, as one who secretly murmurs, "If she had only had a chance!" Lord Holme began to think it a sad thing that she had not had a chance. The mere thought sent the American a step down from her throne. She stood below him now, as he stood below Viola. It seemed to him that there was less resemblance between his wife and Miss Schley than he had fancied. He even said so to Lady Holme. The angel smiled. Somebody else in her smiled too. Once he remarked to the angel, *a propos de bottes*, "We men are awful brutes sometimes." Then he paused. As she said nothing, only looked very kind, he added, "I'll bet you think so, Vi?"

It sounded like a question, but she preferred to give no answer, and he walked away shaking his head over the brutishness of men.

The believers in the angel naturally welcomed the development in Lady Holme and the unbelievers laughed at it, especially those who had been at Arkell House and those who had been influenced by Pimpernel Schley's clever imitation. One night at the opera, when *Tannhauser* was being given, Mr. Bry said of it, "I seem to hear the voice of Venus raised in the prayer of Elizabeth." Mrs. Wolfstein lifted large eyebrows over it, and remarked to Henry, in exceptionally guttural German:

"If this goes on Pimpernel's imitation will soon be completely out of date."

To be out of date—in Mrs. Wolfstein's opinion—was to be irremediably damned. Lady Cardington, Sir Donald Ulford, and one or two others began to feel as if their dream took form and stepped out of the mystic realm towards the light of day. Sir Donald seemed specially moved by the change. It was almost as if something within him blossomed, warmed by the breath of spring.

Lady Holme wondered whether he knew of the fight between her husband and his son. She dared not ask him and he only mentioned Leo once. Then he said that Leo had gone down to his wife's country place in Hertfordshire. Lady Holme could not tell by his intonation whether he had guessed that there was a special reason for this departure. She was glad Leo had gone. The developing angel did not want to meet the man who had suffered from the siren's common conduct. Leo was not worth much. She knew that. But she realised now the meanness of having used him merely as a weapon against Fritz, and not only the meanness, but the vulgarity of the action. There were moments in which she was fully conscious that, despite her rank, she had not endured unsmirched close contact with the rampant commonness of London.

One of the last great events of the season was to be a charity concert, got up by a Royal Princess in connection with a committee of well-known women to start a club for soldiers and sailors. Various amateurs and professionals were asked to take part in it, among them Lady Holme and Miss Schley. The latter had already accepted the invitation when Lady Holme received the Royal request, which was made *viva voce* and was followed by a statement about the composition of the programme, in which "that clever Miss Schley" was named.

Lady Holme hesitated. She had not met the American for some time and did not wish to meet her. Since she had bathed her husband's wound she knew—she could not have told how—that Miss Schley's power over him had lessened. She did not know what had happened between them. She did not know that anything had happened. And, as part of this new effort of hers, she had had the strength to beat down the vehement, the terrible curiosity—cold steel and fire combined—that is a part of jealousy. That curiosity, she told herself, belonged to the siren, not to the angel. But at this Royal request her temper waked, and with it many other children of her temperament. It was as if she had driven them into a dark cave and had rolled a great stone to the cave's mouth. Now the stone was pushed back, and in the darkness she heard them stirring, whispering, preparing to come forth.

The Royal lady looked slightly surprised. She coughed and glanced at a watch she wore at her side.

"I shall be delighted to do anything, ma'am," Lady Holme said quickly.

When she received the programme she found that her two songs came immediately after "Some Imitations" by Miss Pimpernel Schley.

She stood for a moment with the programme in her hand.

"Some Imitations"; there was a certain crudeness about the statement, a crudeness and an indefiniteness combined. Who were to be the victims? At this moment, perhaps, they were being studied. Was she to be pilloried again as she had been pilloried that night at the British Theatre? The calm malice of the American was capable of any impudent act. It seemed to Lady Holme that she had perhaps been very foolish in promising to appear in the same programme with Miss Schley. Was it by accident that their names were put together? Lady Holme did not know who had arranged the order of the performances, but it occurred to her that there was attraction to the public in the contiguity, and that probably it was a matter of design. No other two women had been discussed and compared, smiled over and whispered about that season by Society as she and Miss Schley had been.

For a moment, while she looked at the programme, she thought of the strange complications of feeling that are surely the fruit of an extreme civilisation. She saw herself caught in a spider's web of apparently frail, yet really powerful, threads spun by an invisible spider. Her world was full of gossamer playing the part of iron, of gossamer that was compelling, that made and kept prisoners. What freedom was there for her and women like her, what reality of freedom? Even beauty, birth, money were gossamer to hold the fly. For they concentrated the gaze of those terrible watchful eyes which govern lives, dominating actions, even dominating thoughts.

She moved, had always moved, in a maze of complications. She saw them tiny yet intense, like ants in their hill. They stirred minds, hearts, as the ants stirred twigs, leaves, blossoms, and carried them to the hill for their own purposes. In this maze free will was surely lost. The beautiful woman of the world seems to the world to be a dominant being, to be imposing the yoke of her will on those around her. But is she anything but a slave?

Why were she and Miss Schley enemies? Why had they been enemies from the moment they met? There was perhaps a reason for their hostility now, a reason in Fritz. But at the beginning what reason had there been? Civilisation manufactures reasons as the spider manufactures threads, because it is the deadly enemy of peace—manufactures reasons for all those thoughts and actions which are destructive of inward and exterior peace.

For a moment it seemed to Lady Holme as if she and the American were merely victims of the morbid conditions amid which they lived; conditions which caused the natural vanity of women to become a destroying fever, the natural striving of women to please a venomous battle, the natural desire of women to be loved a fracas, in which clothes were the armour, modes of hair-dressing, manicure, perfumes, dyes, powder-puffs the weapons.

What a tremendous, noisy nothingness it was, this state of being! How could an angel be natural in it,—be an angel at all?

She laid down the programme and sighed. She felt a vague yet violent desire for release, for a fierce change, for something that would brush away the spider's web and set free her wings. Yet where would she fly? She did not know; probably against a window-pane. And the change would never come. She and Fritz—what could they ever be but a successful couple known in a certain world and never moving beyond its orbit?

Perhaps for the first time the longing that she had often expressed in her singing, obedient to poet and composer, invaded her own soul. Without music she was what with music she had often seemed to be—a creature of wayward and romantic desires, a yearning spirit, a soaring flame.

At that moment she could have sung better than she had ever sung.

On the programme the names of her songs did not appear. They were represented by the letters A and B. She had not decided yet what she would sing. But now, moved by feeling to the longing for some action in which she might express it, she resolved to sing something in which she could at least flutter the wings she longed to free, something in which the angel could lift its voice, something that would delight the believers in the angel and be as far removed from Miss Schley's imitations as possible.

After a time she chose two songs. One was English, by a young composer, and was called "Away." It breathed something of the spirit of the East. The man who had written it had travelled much in the East, had drawn into his lungs the air, into his nostrils the perfume, into his soul the meaning of desert places. There was distance in his music. There was mystery. There was the call of the God of Gold who lives in the sun. There was the sound of feet that travel. The second song she chose was French. The poem was derived from a writing of Jalalu'd dinu'r Rumi, and told this story.

One day a man came to knock upon the door of the being he loved. A voice cried from within the house, "*Qui est la?*" "*C'est moi!*" replied the man. There was a pause. Then the voice answered, "This house cannot shelter us both together." Sadly the lover went away, went into the great solitude, fasted and prayed. When a long year had passed he came once more to the house of the one he loved, and struck again upon the door. The voice from within cried, "*Qui est la?*" "*C'est toi!*" whispered the lover. Then the door was opened swiftly and he passed in with outstretched arms.

Having decided that she would sing these two songs, Lady Holme sat down to go through them at the piano. Just as she struck the first chord of the desert song a footman came in to know whether she was at home to Lady Cardington. She answered "Yes." In her present mood she longed to give out her feeling to an audience, and Lady Cardington was very sympathetic.

In a minute she came in, looking as usual blanched and tired, dressed in black with some pale yellow roses in the front of her gown. Seeing Lady Holme at the piano she said, in her low voice with a thrill in it:

"You are singing? Let me listen, let me listen."

She did not come up to shake hands, but at once sat down at a short distance from the piano, leaned back, and gazed at Lady Holme with a strange expression of weary, yet almost passionate, expectation.

Lady Holme looked at her and at the desert song. Suddenly she thought she would not sing it to Lady Cardington. There was too wild a spell in it for this auditor. She played a little prelude and sang an Italian song, full, as a warm flower of sweetness, of the sweetness of love. The refrain was soft as golden honey, soft and languorous, strangely sweet and sad. There was an exquisite music in the words of the refrain, and the music they were set to made their appeal more clinging, like the appeal of white arms, of red, parting lips.

> *"Torna in fior di giovinezza*
> *Isaotta Blanzesmano,*
> *Dice: Tutto al mondo e vano:*
> *Nell'amore ogni dolcezza."*

Tears came into Lady Cardington's eyes as she listened, brimmed over and fell down upon her blanched cheeks. Each time the refrain recurred she moved her lips: "Dice: Tutto al mondo e vano: Nell'amore ogni dolcezza."

Lady Holme's voice was like honey as she sang, and tears were in her eyes too. Each time the refrain fell from her heart she seemed to see another world, empty of gossamer threads, a world of spread wings, a world of— but such poetry and music do not tell you! Nor can you imagine. You can only dream and wonder, as when you look at the horizon line and pray for the things beyond.

> *"Tutto—tutto al mondo a vano:*
> *Nell'amore ogni dolcezza."*

"Why do you sing like that to-day?" said Lady Cardington, wiping her eyes gently.

"I feel like that to-day," Lady Holme said, keeping her hands on the keys in the last chord. There was a vagueness in her eyes, a sort of faint cloud of fear. While she was singing she had thought, "Have I known the love that shows the vanity of the world? Have I known the love in which alone all sweetness lives?" The thought had come in like a firefly through an open window. "Have I? Have I?"

And something within her felt a stab of pain, something within her soul and yet surely a thousand miles away.

"Tutto—tutto al mondo e vano," murmured Lady Cardington. "We feel that and we feel it, and—do you?"

"To-day I seem to," answered Lady Holme.

"When you sing that song you look like the love that gives all sweetness to men. Sing like that, look like that, and you—If Sir Donald had heard you!"

Lady Holme got up from the piano.

"Sir Donald!" she said.

She came to sit down near Lady Cardington.

"Sir Donald! Why do you say that?"

And she searched Lady Cardington's eyes with eyes full of inquiry.

Lady Cardington looked away. The wistful power that generally seemed a part of her personality had surely died out in her. There was something nervous in her expression, deprecating in her attitude.

"Why do you speak about Sir Donald?" Lady Holme said.

"Don't you know?"

Lady Cardington looked up. There was an extraordinary sadness in her eyes, mingled with a faint defiance.

"Know what?"

"That Sir Donald is madly in love with you?"

"Sir Donald! Sir Donald—madly anything!"

She laughed, not as if she were amused, but as if she wished to do something else and chose to laugh instead. Lady Cardington sat straight up.

"You don't understand anything but youth," she said.

There was a sound of keen bitterness in her low voice.

"And yet," she added, after a pause, "you can sing till you break the heart of age—break its heart."

Suddenly she burst into a flood of tears. Lady Holme was so surprised that she did absolutely nothing, did not attempt to console, to inquire. She sat and looked at Lady Cardington's tall figure swayed by grief, listened to the sound of her hoarse, gasping sobs. And then, abruptly, as if someone came into the room and told her, she understood.

"You love Sir Donald," she said.

Lady Cardington looked up. Her tear-stained, distorted face seemed very old.

"We both regret the same thing in the same way," she said. "We were both wretched in—in the time when we ought to have been happy. I thought—I had a ridiculous idea we might console each other. You shattered my hope."

"I'm sorry," Lady Holme said.

And she said it with more tenderness than she had ever before used to a woman.

Lady Cardington pressed a pocket-handkerchief against her eyes.

"Sing me that song again," she whispered. "Don't say anything more. Just sing it again and I'll go."

Lady Holme went to the piano.

"Torna in fior di giovinezza

Isaotta Blanzesmano,

Dice: Tutto al mondo a vano:

Nell'amore ogni dolcezza."

When the last note died away she looked towards the sofa. Lady Cardington was gone. Lady Holme leaned her arm on the piano and put her chin in her hand.

"How awful to be old!" she thought.

Half aloud she repeated the last words of the refrain: "Nell'amore ogni dolcezza." And then she murmured:

"Poor Sir Donald!"

And then she repeated, "Poor—" and stopped. Again the faint cloud of fear was in her eyes.

CHAPTER XV

THE Charity Concert was to be given in Manchester House, one of the private palaces of London, and as Royalty had promised to be present, all the tickets were quickly sold. Among those who bought them were most of the guests who had been present at the Holmes' dinner-party when Lady Holme lost her temper and was consoled by Robin Pierce. Robin of course was in Rome, but Lady Cardington, Lady Manby, Mrs. Wolfstein, Sir Donald, Mr. Bry took seats. Rupert Carey also bought a ticket. He was not invited to great houses any more, but on this public occasion no one with a guinea to spend was unwelcome. To Lady Holme's surprise the day before the concert Fritz informed her that he was going too.

"You, Fritz!" she exclaimed. "But it's in the afternoon."

"What o' that?"

"You'll be bored to death. You'll go to sleep. Probably you'll snore."

"Not I."

He straddled his legs and looked attentively at the toes of his boots. Lady Holme wondered why he was going. Had Miss Schley made a point of it? She longed to know. The cruel curiosity which the angel was ever trying to beat down rose up in her powerfully.

"I say—"

Her husband was speaking with some hesitation.

"Well?"

"Let's have a squint at the programme, will you?"

"Here it is."

She gave it to him and watched him narrowly as he looked quickly over it.

"Hulloa!" he said.

"What's the matter?"

"Some Imitations," he said. "What's that mean?"

"Didn't you know Miss Schley was a mimic?"

"A mimic—not I! She's an actress."

"Yes—now."

"Now? When was she anythin' else?"

"When she began in America. She was a mimic in the music-halls."

"The deuce she was!"

He stood looking very grave and puzzled for a minute, then he stared hard at his wife.

"What did she mimic?"

"I don't know—people."

Again there was a silence. Then he said—

"I say, I don't know that I want you to sing at that affair to-morrow."

"But I must. Why not?"

He hesitated, shifting from one foot to the other almost like a great boy.

"I don't know what she's up to," he answered at last.

"Miss Schley?"

"Ah!"

Lady Holme felt her heart beat faster. Was her husband going to open up a discussion of the thing that had been turning her life to gall during these last weeks—his flirtation, his *liaison*—if it were a *liaison*; she did not know—with the American? The woman who had begun to idealise Fritz and the woman who was desperately jealous of him both seemed to be quivering within her.

"Do you mean—?" she began.

She stopped, then spoke again in a quiet voice.

"Do you mean that you think Miss Schley is going to do something unusual at the concert tomorrow?"

"I dunno. She's the devil."

There was a reluctant admiration in his voice, as there always is in the voice of a man when he describes a woman as gifted with infernal attributes, and this sound stung Lady Holme. It seemed to set that angel upon whom she was calling in the dust, to make of that angel a puppet, an impotent, even a contemptible thing.

"My dear Fritz," she said in a rather loud, clear voice, like the voice of one speaking to a child, "my dear Fritz, you're surely aware that I have been the subject of Miss Schley's talent ever since she arrived in London?"

"You! What d'you mean?"

"You surely can't be so blind as not to have seen what all London has seen?"

"What's all London seen?'

"Why, that Miss Schley's been mimicking me!"

"Mimickin' you!"

The brown of his large cheeks was invaded by red.

"But you have noticed it. I remember your speaking about it."

"Not I!" he exclaimed with energy.

"Yes. You spoke of the likeness between us, in expression, in ways of looking and moving."

"That—I thought it was natural."

"You thought it was natural?"

There was a profound, if very bitter, compassion in her voice.

"Poor old boy!" she added.

Lord Holme looked desperately uncomfortable. His legs were in a most violent, even a most pathetic commotion, and he tugged his moustache with the fingers of both hands.

"Damned cheek!" he muttered. "Damned cheek!"

He turned suddenly as if he were going to stride about the room.

"Don't get angry," said his wife. "I never did."

He swung round and faced her.

"D'you mean you've always known she was mimickin' you?"

"Of course. From the very start."

His face got redder.

"I'll teach her to let my wife alone," he muttered. "To dare—my wife!"

"I'm afraid it's a little late in the day to begin now," Lady Holme said. "Society's been laughing over it, and your apparent appreciation of it, the best part of the season."

"My what?"

"Your apparent enjoyment of the performance."

And then she went quietly out of the room and shut the door gently behind her. But directly the door was shut she became another woman. Her mouth was distorted, her eyes shone, she rushed upstairs to her bedroom, locked herself in, threw herself down on the bed and pressed her face furiously against the coverlet.

The fact that she had spoken at last to her husband of the insult she had been silently enduring, the insult he had made so far more bitter than it need have been by his conduct, had broken down something within her, some wall of pride behind which had long been gathering a flood of feeling. She cried now frantically, with a sort of despairing rage, cried and crushed herself against the bed, beating the pillows with her hands, grinding her teeth.

What was the use of it all? What was the use of being beautiful, of being young, rich? What was the use of having married a man she had loved? What was the use? What was the use?

"What's the use?" she sobbed the words out again and again.

For the man was a fool, Fritz was a fool. She thought of him at that moment as half-witted. For he saw nothing, nothing. He was a blind man led by his animal passions, and when at last he was forced to see, when she came and, as it were, lifted his eyelids with her fingers, and said to him, "Look! Look at what has been done to me!" he could only be angry for himself, because the insult had attained him, because she happened to be his wife. It seemed to her, while she was crying there, that stupidity combined with egoism must have the power to kill even that vital, enduring thing, a woman's love. She had begun to idealise Fritz, but how could she go on idealising him? And she began for the first time really to understand—or to begin to understand—that there actually was something within her which was hungry, unsatisfied, something which was not animal but mental, or was it spiritual?—something not sensual, not cerebral, which cried aloud for sustenance. And this something did not, could never, cry to Fritz. It knew he could not give it what it wanted. Then to whom did it cry? She did not know.

Presently she grew calmer and sat upon the bed, looking straight before her. Her mind returned upon itself. She seemed to go back to that point of time, just before Lady Cardington called, when she had the programme in her hand and thought of the gossamer threads that were as iron in her life, and in such lives as hers; then to move on to that other point of time when she laid down the programme, sighed, and was conscious of a violent desire for release, for something to come and lift a powerful hand and brush away the spider's web.

But now, returning to this further moment in her life, she asked herself what would be left to her if the spider's web were gone? The believers in the angel? Perhaps she no longer included Fritz among them. The impotence of his mind seemed to her an impotence of heart just then. He was to her like a numbed creature, incapable of movement, incapable of thought, incapable of belief. Credulity—yes, but not belief. And so, when she looked at the believers, she saw but a few people: Robin Pierce, Sir Donald—whom else?

And then she heard, as if far off, the song she would sing on the morrow at Manchester House.

> "*Torna in fior di giovinezza*
>
> *Isaotta Blanzesmano,*
>
> *Dice: Tutto al mondo a vano:*
>
> *Nell'amore ogni dolcezza.*"

And then she cried again, but no longer frantically; quietly, with a sort of childish despair and confusion. In her heart there had opened a dark space, a gulf. She peered into it and heard, deep down in it, hollow echoes resounding, and she recoiled from a vision of emptiness.

On the following day Fritz drove her himself to Manchester House in a new motor he had recently bought. All the morning he had stayed at home and fidgeted about the house. It was obvious to his wife that he was in an unusually distracted frame of mind. He wanted to tell her something, yet could not do so. She saw that plainly, and she felt almost certain that since their interview of the previous day he had seen Miss Schley. She fancied that there had been a scene of some kind between them, and she guessed that Fritz had been hopelessly worsted in it and was very sorry for himself. There was a beaten look in his face, a very different look from that which had startled her when he came into her room after thrashing Leo Ulford. This time, however, her curiosity was not awake, and the fact that it was not awake marked a change in her. She felt to-day as if she did not care what Fritz had been doing or was going to do. She had suffered, she had concealed her suffering, she had tried vulgarly to pay Fritz out, she had failed. At the critical moment she had played the woman after he had played the man. He had thrashed the intruder whom she was using as a weapon, and she had bathed his wounds, made much of him, idealised him. She had done what any uneducated street woman would have done for "her man." And now she had suddenly come to feel as if there had always been an emptiness in her life, as if Fritz never had, never could fill it. The abruptness of the onset of this new feeling confused her. She did not know that a woman could be subject to a change of this kind. She did not understand it, realise what it portended, what would result from it. But she felt that, for the moment, at any rate, she could not get up any excitement about Fritz, his feelings, his doings. Whenever she thought of him she thought of his blundering stupidity, his blindness, sensuality and egoism. No doubt she loved him. Only, to-day, she did not feel as if she loved him or anyone. Yet she did not feel dull. On the contrary, she was highly strung, unusually sensitive. What she was most acutely conscious of was a sensation of lonely excitement, of solitary expectation. Fritz fidgeted about the house, and the fact that he did so gave her no more concern than if a little dog had been running to and fro. She did not want him to tell her what was the matter. On the other hand, she did want him not to tell her. Simply she did not care.

He said nothing. Perhaps something in her look, her manner, kept him dumb.

When they were in the motor on the way to Manchester House, he said:

"I bet you'll cut out everybody."

"Oh, there are all sorts of stars."

"Well, mind you put 'em all out."

It was evident to her that for some reason or other he was particularly anxious she should shine that afternoon. She meant to. She knew she was going to. But she had no desire to shine in order to gratify Fritz's egoism. Probably he had just had a quarrel with Miss Schley and wanted to punish her through his wife. The idea was not a pretty one. Unfortunately that circumstance did not ensure its not being a true one.

"Mind you do, eh?" reiterated her husband, giving the steering wheel a twist and turning the car up Hamilton Place.

"I shall try to sing well, naturally," she replied coldly. "I always do."

"Of course—I know."

There was something almost servile in his manner, an anxiety which was quite foreign to it as a rule.

"That's a stunnin' dress," he added. "Keep your cloak well over it."

She said nothing.

"What's the row?" he asked. "Anythin' up?"

"I'm thinking over my songs."

"Oh, I see."

She had silenced him for the moment.

Very soon they were in a long line of carriages and motors moving slowly towards Manchester House.

"Goin' to be a deuce of a crowd," said Fritz.

The Woman with the Fan | 183

"Naturally."

"Wonder who'll be there?"

"Everybody who's still in town."

She bowed to a man in a hansom.

"Who's that?"

"Plancon. He's singing."

"How long'll it be before you come on?"

"Quite an hour, I think."

"Better than bein' first, isn't it?"

"Of course."

"What are you goin' to sing?"

"Oh—"

She was about to say something impatient about his not knowing one tune from another, but she checked herself, and answered quietly:

"An Italian song and a French song."

"What about?"

"Take care of that carriage in front—love."

He looked at her sideways.

"You're the one to sing about that," he said.

She felt that he was admiring her beauty as if it were new to him. She did not care.

At last they reached Manchester House. Fritz's place was taken by his chauffeur, and they got out. The crowd was enormous. Many people recognised Lady Holme and greeted her. Others, who did not know her personally, looked at her with open curiosity. A powdered footman came to show her to the improvised artists' room. Fritz prepared to follow.

"Aren't you going into the concert-room?" she said.

"Presently."

"But—"

"I'll take you up first."

"Very well," she said. "But it isn't the least necessary."

He only stuck out his under jaw. She realised that Miss Schley would be in the artists' room and said nothing more. They made their way very slowly to the great landing on the first floor of the house, from which a maze of reception rooms opened. Mr. and Mrs. Ongrin, the immensely rich Australians who were the owners of the house, were standing there ready to receive the two Royal Princesses who were expected, and Mr. Ongrin took from a basket on a table beside him a great bouquet of honey-coloured roses, and offered it to Lady Holme with a hearty word of thanks to her for singing.

She took the roses with a look of pleasure.

"How sweet of you! They suit my song," she said.

She was thinking of the Italian song.

Mr. Ongrin, who was a large, loose-limbed man, with straw-coloured hair turning grey, and a broken nose, looked genial and confused, and she went on, still closely followed by Fritz.

"This is the room for the performers, my lady," said the footman, showing them into a large, green drawing-room, with folding doors at one end shut off by an immense screen.

"Is the platform behind the screen?" Lady Holme asked.

"Yes, my lady. The ladies' cloak-room is on the left—that door, my lady."

There were already several people in the room, standing about and looking tentative. Lady Holme knew most of them. One was a French actor who was going to give a monologue; very short, very stout, very intelligent-looking, with a face that seemed almost too flexible to be human. Two or three were singers from the Opera House. Another was an aristocratic amateur, an intimate friend of Lady Holme's, who had a beautiful contralto voice. Several of the committee were there too, making themselves agreeable to the artists. Lady Holme began to speak to the French actor. Fritz stood by. He scarcely understood a word of French, and always looked rather contemptuous when it was talked in his presence. The French actor appealed to him on some point in the conversation. He straddled his legs, uttered a loud, "Oh, wee! Oh, wee! wee!" and laughed.

"Lord Holme est tout a fait de mon avis!" cried the comedian.

"Evidemment," she answered, wishing Fritz would go. Miss Schley had not come yet. She was certain to be effectively late, as she had been at Mrs. Wolfstein's lunch-party. Lady Holme did not feel as if she cared whether she came early or late, whether she were there or not. She was still companioned by her curious sensation of the morning, a sensation of odd loneliness and detachment, combined with excitement—but an excitement which had nothing to do with the present. It seemed to her as if she were a person leaning out of a window and looking eagerly along a road. People were in the room behind her, voices were speaking, things were happening there, but they had nothing to do with her. That which had to do with her was coming down the road. She could not see yet what it was, but she could hear the faint sound of its approach.

The comedian spoke to someone else. She went into the cloak-room and took off her motor cloak. As she glanced into a mirror to see if all the details of her gown were perfect, she was struck by the expression on her face, as if she had seen it on the face of a stranger. For a moment she looked at herself as at a stranger, seeing her beauty with a curious detachment, and admiring it without personal vanity or egoism, or any small, triumphant feeling. Yet it was not her beauty which fascinated her eyes, but an imaginative look in them and in the whole face. For the first time she fully realised why she had a curious, an evocative, influence on certain people, why she called the hidden children of the secret places of their souls, why those children heard, and stretched out their hands, and lifted their eyes and opened their lips.

There was a summoning, and yet a distant expression in her eyes. She saw it herself. They were like eyes that had looked on magic, that would look on magic again.

A maid came to help her. In a moment she had picked up her bouquet of roses and her music-case, and was back in the green drawing-room.

There were more people in it now. Fritz was still hovering about looking remarkably out of place and strangely ill at ease. To-day his usual imperturbable self-confidence had certainly deserted him. He spoke to people but his eyes were on the door. Lady Holme knew that he was waiting for Miss Schley. She felt a sort of vague pity for his uneasiness. It was time for the concert to begin, but the Princesses had not yet arrived. A murmur of many voices came from the hidden room beyond the screen where the audience was assembled. Several of the performers began to look rather strung up. They smiled and talked with slightly more vivacity than was quite natural in them. One or two of the singers glanced over their songs, and pointed out certain effects they meant to make to the principal accompanist, an abnormally thin boy with thick dark hair and flushed cheeks. He expressed comprehension, emphasising it by finger-taps on the music and a continual, "I see! I see!" Two or three of the members of the committee looked at their watches, and the murmur of conversation in the hidden concert-room rose into a dull roar.

Lady Holme sat down on a sofa. Sometimes when she was going to sing she felt nervous. There are very few really accomplished artists who do not.

But to-day she was not at all nervous. She knew she was going to do well—as well as when she sang to Lady Cardington, even better. She felt almost as if she were made of music, as if music were part of her, ran in her veins like blood, shone in her eyes like light, beat in her heart like the pulse of life. But she felt also as if she were still at a window, looking down a road, and listening to the sound of an approach.

"Did you see him?"

A lady near her was speaking to a friend.

"Yes. Doesn't he look shocking? Such an alteration!"

"Poor fellow! I wonder he cares to go about."

"And he's so clever. He helped me in a concert once—the Gordon boys, you know—and I assure you—"

She did not catch anything more, but she felt a conviction that they were speaking of Rupert Carey, and that he must be in the concert-room. Poor Carey! She thought of the Arkell House ball, but only for a moment. Then someone spoke to her. A moment later Miss Schley came slowly into the room, accompanied by a very small, wiry-looking old woman, dreadfully dressed, and by Leo Ulford, who was carrying a bouquet of red carnations. The kind care of Mr. Ongrin had provided a bouquet for each lady who was performing.

As Leo came in he looked round swiftly, furtively. He saw Fritz, and a flush went over his face. Then Lady Holme saw him look at her with a scowl, exactly like the scowl of an evil-tempered schoolboy. She bowed to him slightly. He ignored the recognition, and spoke to Miss Schley with a heavy assumption of ignominious devotion and intimacy. Lady Holme could scarcely help smiling. She read the little story very plainly—the little common story of Leo's desire to take a revenge for his thrashing fitting in with some similar desire of Miss Schley's; on her part probably a wish to punish Fritz for having ventured to say something about her impudent mimicry of his wife. Easy to read it was, common-minded, common-hearted humanity in full sail to petty triumph, petty revenge. But all this was taking place in the room behind Lady Holme, and she was leaning from the window watching the white road. But Fritz? She glanced round the drawing-room and saw that he was moved by the story as they had meant him to be moved. The angry jealousy of the primitive, sensual man was aflame, His possessive sense, one of the strongest, if not the strongest, of such a man's senses, was outraged. And he showed it.

He was standing with a middle-aged lady, one of the committee, but he had ceased from talking to her, and was staring at Miss Schley and Leo with the peculiar inflated look on his face that was characteristic of him when his passions were fully roused. Every feature seemed to swell and become bloated, as if under the influence of a disease or physical seizure. The middle-aged lady looked at him with obvious astonishment, then turned away and spoke to the French actor.

Miss Schley moved slowly into the middle of the room. She did not seem to see Fritz. Two or three people came to speak to her. She smiled but did not say much. The little wiry-looking old lady, her mother from Susanville, stood by her in an effaced manner, and Leo, holding the bouquet, remained close beside her, standing over her in his impudent fashion like a privileged guardian and lover.

Lady Holme was watching Fritz. The necessary suppression of his anger at such a moment, and in such surroundings, suppression of any demonstration of it at least, was evidently torturing him. Someone—a man—spoke to him. His wife saw that he seemed to choke something down before he could get out a word in reply. Directly he had answered he moved away from the man towards Miss Schley, but he did not go up to her. He did not trust himself to do that. He stood still again, staring. Leo bent protectively over the American. She smiled at him demurely beneath lowered eyelids. The little old lady shook out her rusty black dress and assumed an absurd air of social sprightliness, making a mouth bunched up like an old-fashioned purse sharply drawn together by a string.

There was a sudden lull in the roar of conversation from the concert-room, succeeded by a wide rustling noise. The Princesses had at length arrived, and the audience was standing up as they came in and took their seats. After a brief silence the rustling noise was renewed as the audience sat down again. Then the pianist hurried up to a grave-looking girl who was tenderly holding a violin, took her hand and led her away behind the screen. A moment later the opening bars of a duet were audible.

The people in the artists' room began to sit down with a slight air of resignation. The French actor looked at the very pointed toes of his varnished boots and composed his india-rubber features into a solemn, almost priestly, expression. Lady Holme went over to a sofa near the screen and listened attentively to the duet, but from time to time she glanced towards the middle of the room where Miss Schley was still calmly standing up with Leo holding the bouquet. The mother from Susanville had subsided on a small chair with gilt legs, spread out her meagre gown, and assumed the aspect of a roosting bird at twilight. Fritz stood up with his back against the wall, staring at Miss Schley. His face still looked bloated. Presently Miss Schley glanced at him, as if by accident, looked surprised at seeing him there, and nodded demurely. He made a movement forward from the wall, but she immediately began to whisper to Leo Ulford, and after remaining for a moment in an attitude of angry hesitation he moved backward again. His face flushed scarlet.

Lady Holme realised that he was making a fool of himself. She saw several pairs of eyes turned towards him, slight smiles appearing on several faces. The French actor had begun to watch him with an expression of close criticism, as a stage manager watches an actor at rehearsal. But she did not feel as if she cared what Fritz was doing. The sound of the violin had emphasised her odd sensation of having nothing to do with what was going on in the room. Just for one hour Fritz's conduct could not affect her.

Very soon people began to whisper round her. Artists find it very difficult to listen to other artists on these occasions. In a minute or two almost everybody was speaking with an air of mystery. Miss Schley put her lips to Leo Ulford's ear. Evidently she had a great deal to say to him. He began to pout his lips in smiles. They both looked across at Lord Holme. Then Miss Schley went on murmuring words into Leo's ear and Leo began to shake with silent laughter. Lord Holme clenched his hands at his sides. The French actor, still watching him closely, put up a fat forefinger and meditatively traced the outline of his own profile, pushing out his large flexible lips when the finger was drawing near to them. The whole room was full of the tickling noise of half-whispered conversation.

Presently the music stopped. Instantly the tickling noise stopped too. There was languid applause—the applause of smart people on a summer afternoon—from beyond the screen. Then the grave girl reappeared, looking graver and hot. Those who had been busily talking while she was playing gathered round her to express their delight in her kind accompaniment. The pianist hurried up to a stout man with a low, turned-down collar and a white satin tie, whose double chin, and general air of rather fatuous prosperity, proclaimed him the possessor of a tenor voice, and Miss Schley walked quietly, but with determination, up to where Lady Holme was sitting and took a seat beside her.

"Glad to meet you again," she drawled.

She called Leo Ulford with a sharp nod. He hesitated, and began to look supremely uncomfortable, twisting the bouquet of carnations round and round in nervous hands.

"I've been simply expiring all season to hear you sing," Miss Schley continued.

"How sweet of you!"

"That is so. Mr. Ulford, please bring my flowers."

Leo had no alternative but to obey. He came slowly towards the sofa, while the tenor and the pianist vanished behind the screen. That he was sufficiently sensitive to be conscious of the awkwardness of the situation Miss Schley had pleasantly contrived was very apparent. He glowered upon Lady Holme, forcing his boyish face to assume a coarsely-determined and indifferent expression. But somehow the body, which she knew her husband had thrashed, looked all the time as if it were being thrashed again.

The voice of the hidden tenor rose in "*Celeste Aida!*" and Lady Holme listened with an air of definite attention, taking no notice of Leo. The music gave her a perfect excuse for ignoring him. But Miss Schley did not intend to be interfered with by anything so easily trampled upon as an art. Speaking in her most clear and choir-boyish tones, she said to Leo Ulford:

"Sit down, Mr. Ulford. You fidget me standing."

Then turning again to Lady Holme she continued:

"Mr. Ulford's been so lovely and kind. He came up all the way from Hertfordshire just to take care of marmar and me to-day. Marmar's fair and crazy about him. She says he's the most lovely feller in Europe."

Leo twisted the bouquet. He was sitting now on the edge of a chair, and shooting furtive glances in the direction of Lord Holme, who had begun to look extremely stupid, overwhelmed by the cool impudence of the American.

"Your husband looks as if he were perched around on a keg of rattlesnakes," continued Miss Schley, her clear voice mingling with the passionate tenor cry, "*Celeste Aida!*" "Ain't he feeling well to-day?"

"I believe he is perfectly well," said Lady Holme, in a very low voice.

It was odd, perhaps, but she did not feel at all angry, embarrassed, or even slightly annoyed, by Miss Schley's very deliberate attempt to distress her. Of course she understood perfectly what had happened and was happening. Fritz had spoken to the actress about her mimicry of his wife, had probably spoken blunderingly, angrily. Miss Schley was secretly furious at his having found out what she had been doing, still more furious at his having dared to criticise any proceeding of hers. To revenge herself at one stroke on both Lord and Lady Holme she had turned to Leo Ulford, whose destiny it evidently was to be used as a weapon against others. Long ago Lady Holme had distracted Leo's wandering glances from the American and fixed them on herself. With the instinct to be common of an utterly common nature Miss Schley had resolved to awake a double jealousy—of husband and wife—by exhibiting Leo Ulford as her *ami intime,* perhaps as the latest victim to her fascination. It was the vulgar action of a vulgar woman, but it failed of its effect in one direction. Lord Holme was stirred, but Lady Holme was utterly indifferent. Miss Schley's quick instinct told her so and she was puzzled. She did not understand Lady Holme. That was scarcely strange, for to-day Lady Holme did not understand herself. The curious mental detachment of which she had been conscious for some time had increased until it began surely to link itself with something physical, something sympathetic in the body that replied to it. She asked herself whether the angel were spreading her wings at last. All the small, sordid details of which lives lived in society, lives such as hers, are full, details which assume often an extraordinary importance, a significance like that of molecules seen through a magnifying glass, had suddenly become to her as nothing. A profound indifference had softly invaded her towards the petty side of life. Miss Schley, Leo Ulford, even Fritz in his suppressed rage and jealousy of a male animal openly trampled upon, had nothing to do with her, could have no effect on her at this moment. She remembered that she had once sighed for release. Well, it seemed to her as if release were at hand.

The tenor finished his romance. Again the muffled applause sounded. As the singer came from behind the screen, wiping beads of perspiration from his self-satisfied face, Lady Holme got up and congratulated him. Then she crossed over to her husband.

"Why don't you go into the concert-room, Fritz? You're missing everything, and you're only in the way here."

She did not speak unkindly. He said nothing, only cleared his throat.

"Go in," she said. "I should like to have you there while I am singing."

He cleared his throat again.

"Right you are."

He stared into her eyes with a sort of savage admiration.

"Cut her out," he said. "Cut her out! You can, and—damn her!—she deserves it."

Then he turned and went out.

Lady Holme felt rather sick for a moment. She knew she was going to sing well, she wished to sing well—but not in order to punish Miss Schley for having punished Fritz. Was everything she did to accomplish some sordid result? Was even her singing—the one thing in which Robin Pierce and some other divined a hidden truth that was beautiful—was even that to play its contemptible part in the social drama in which she was so inextricably entangled? Those gossamer threads were iron strands indeed.

Someone else was singing—her friend with the contralto voice.

She sat down alone in a corner. Presently the French actor began to give one of his famous monologues. She heard his wonderfully varied elocution, his voice—intelligence made audible and dashed with flying lights of humour rising and falling subtly, yet always with a curious sound of inevitable simplicity. She heard gentle titterings from the concealed audience, then a definite laugh, then a peal of laughter quite gloriously indiscreet. The people were waking up. And she felt as if they were being prepared for her. But why had Fritz looked like that, spoken like that? It seemed to spoil everything. To-day she felt too far away from—too far beyond, that was the truth—Miss Schley to want to enter into any rivalry with her. She wished very much that she had been placed first on the programme. Then there could have been no question of her cutting out the American.

As she was thinking this Miss Schley slowly crossed the room and came up to her.

"Lady Holme," she said, "I come next."

"Do you?"

"I do. And then you follow after."

"Well?"

"Say, would you mind changing it? It don't do to have two recitations one after the other. There ought to be something different in between."

Lady Holme looked at her quite eagerly, almost with gratitude.

"I'll sing next," she said quickly.

"Much obliged to you, I'm sure. You're perfectly sweet."

Lady Holme saw again a faint look of surprise on the American's white face, succeeded instantly by an expression of satisfaction. She realised that Miss Schley had some hidden disagreeable reason for her request. She even guessed what it was. But she only felt glad that, whatever happened, no one could accuse her of trying to efface any effect made by Miss Schley upon the audience. As she sang before the "imitations," if any effect were to be effaced it must be her own. The voice of the French actor ceased, almost drowned in a ripple of laughter, a burst of quite warm applause. He reappeared looking calm and magisterial. The applause continued, and he had to go back and bow his thanks. The tenor, who had not been recalled, looked cross and made a movement of his double chin that suggested bridling.

"Now, Miss Schley!" said the pianist. "You come now!"

"Lady Holme has very kindly consented to go first," she replied.

Then she turned to the French actor and, in atrocious but very self-possessed French, began to congratulate him on his performance.

"Oh, well—" the pianist hurried up to Lady Holme. "You have really—very well then—these are the songs! Which do you sing first? Very hot, isn't it?"

He wiped his long fingers with a silk pocket-handkerchief and took the music she offered to him.

"The Princesses seem very pleased," he added. "Marteau—charming composer, yes—very pleased indeed. Which one? 'C'est toi'? Certainly, certainly."

He wiped his hands again and held out one to lead Lady Holme to the platform. But she ignored it gently and went on alone. He followed, carrying the music and perspiring. As they disappeared Miss Schley got up and moved to a chair close by the screen that hid the platform. She beckoned to Leo Ulford and he followed her.

As Lady Holme stepped on to the low platform, edged with a bank of flowers, it seemed to her as if with one glance she saw everyone in the crowded room, and felt at least something swiftly of each one's feeling.

The two Princesses sat together looking kind and serious. As she curtseyed to them they bowed to her and smiled. Behind them she saw a compact mass of acquaintances: Lady Cardington sitting with Sir Donald and looking terribly sad, even self-conscious, yet eager; Mrs. Wolfstein with Mr. Laycock; Mr. Bry, his eyeglass fixed, a white carnation in his coat; Lady Manby laughing with a fat old man who wore a fez, and many others. At the back she saw Fritz, standing up and staring at her with eyes that seemed almost to cry, "Cut her out!" And in the fourth row she saw a dreary, even a horrible, sight—Rupert Carey's face, disfigured by the vice which was surely destroying him, red, bloated, dreadfully coarsened, spotted. From the midst of the wreckage of the flesh his strange eyes looked out with a vivid expression of hopelessness. Yet in them burned fires, and in fire there is an essence of fierce purity. The soul in those eyes seemed longing to burn up the corruption of his body, longing to destroy the ruined temple, longing to speak and say, "I am in prison, but do not judge of the prisoner by examining the filthiness of his cell."

As Lady Holme took in the audience with a glance there was a rustle of paper. Almost everyone was looking to see if the programme had been altered. Lady Holme saw that suddenly Fritz had realised the change that had been made, and what it meant. An expression of anger came into his face.

She felt that she saw more swiftly, and saw into more profoundly to-day than ever before in her life; that she had a strangely clear vision of minds as well as of faces, that she was vivid, penetrating. And she had time, before she began to sing, for an odd thought of the person drowning who flashes back over the ways of his past, who is, as it were, allowed one instant of exceptional life before he is handed over to death. This thought was clear, clean cut in her mind for a moment, and she put herself in the sounding arms of the sea.

Then the pianist began his prelude, and she moved a step forward to the flowers and opened her lips to sing.

She sang by heart the little story drawn from the writing of Jalalu'd dinu'r Rumi. The poet who had taken it had made a charming poem of it, delicate, fragile, and yet dramatic and touched with fervour, porcelain with firelight gleaming on it here and there. Lady Holme had usually a power of identifying herself thoroughly with what she was singing, of concentrating herself with ease upon it, and so compelling her hearers to be concentrated upon her subject and upon her. To-day she was deeper down in words and music, in the little drama of them, than ever before. She was the man who knocked at the door, the loved one who cried from within the house. She gave the reply, "*C'est moi!*" with the eagerness of that most eager of all things—Hope. Then, as she sang gravely, with tender rebuke, "This house cannot shelter us both together," she was in the heart of love, that place of understanding. Afterwards, as one carried by Fate through the sky, she was the man set down in a desert place, fasting, praying, educating himself to be more worthy of love. Then came the return, the question, "*Qui est la?*" the reply;—reply of the solitary place, the denied desire, the longing to mount, the educated heart—"*C'est toi!*" the swiftly-opening door, the rush of feet that were welcome, of outstretched arms for which waited a great possession.

Something within her lived the song very fully and completely. For once she did not think at all of what effect she was making. She was not unconscious of the audience. She was acutely conscious of the presence of people, and of individuals whom she knew; of Fritz, of Lady Cardington, Sir Donald, even of poor, horrible Rupert Carey. But with the unusual consciousness was linked a strange indifference, a sense of complete detachment. And this enabled her to live simultaneously two lives—Lady Holme's and another's. Who was the other? She did not ask, but she felt as if in that moment a prisoner within her was released. And yet, directly the song was over and the eager applause broke out, a bitterness came into her heart. Her sense, banished for the moment, of her own personality and circumstances returned upon her, and that "*C'est toi!*" of the educated heart seemed suddenly an irony as she looked at Fritz's face. Had any lover gone into the desert for her, fasted and prayed for her, learned for her sake the right answer to the ceaseless question that echoes in every woman's heart?

The pianist modulated, struck the chord of a new key, paused, then broke into a languid, honey-sweet prelude. Lady Holme sang the Italian song which had made Lady Cardington cry.

Afterwards, she often thought of her singing of that particular song on that particular occasion as people think of the frail bridges that span the gulfs between one fate and another. And it seemed to her that while she was crossing this bridge, that was a song, she had a faint premonition of the land that lay before her on the far side of the gulf. She did not see clearly any features of the landscape, but surely she saw that it was different from all that she had known. Perhaps she deceived herself. Perhaps she fancied that she had divined something that was in reality hidden from her. One thing, however, is certain—that she made a very exceptional effect upon her audience. Many of them, when later they heard of an incident that occurred within a very short time, felt almost awestricken for a moment. It seemed to them that they had been visited by one of the messengers—the forerunners of destiny—that they had heard a whispering voice say, "Listen well! This is the voice of the Future singing."

Many people in London on the following day said, "We felt in her singing that something extraordinary must be going to happen to her." And some of them at any rate, probably spoke the exact truth.

Lady Holme herself, while she sang her second song, really felt this sensation—that it was her swan song. If once we touch perfection we feel the black everlasting curtain being drawn round us. We have done what we were meant to do and can do no more. Let the race of men continue. Our course is run out. To strive beyond the goal is to offer oneself up to the derision of the gods. In her song, Lady Holme felt that suddenly, and with great ease, she touched the perfection that it was possible for her to reach. She felt that, and she saw what she had done—in the eyes of Lady Cardington that wept, in Sir Donald's eyes, which had become young as the eyes of Spring, and in the eyes of that poor prisoner who was the real Rupert Carey. When she sang the first refrain she knew.

"Torna in fior di giovinezza

Isaotta Blanzesmano,

Dice: Tutto al mondo e vano:

Nell'amore ogni dolcezza."

She understood while she sang—she had never understood before, nor could conceive why she understood now—what love had been to the world, was being, would be so long as there was a world. The sweetness of love did not merely present itself to her imagination, but penetrated her soul. And that penetration, while it carried with it and infused through her whole being a delicate radiance, that was as the radiance of light in the midst of surrounding blackness—beams of the moon in a forest—carried with it also into her heart a frightful sense of individual isolation, of having missed the figure of Truth in the jostling crowd of shams.

Fritz stood there against the wall. Yes—Fritz. And he was savagely rejoicing in the effect she was making upon the audience, because he thought, hoped, that it would lessen the triumph of the woman who was punishing him.

She had missed the figure of Truth. That was very certain. And as she sang the refrain for the last time she seemed to herself to be searching for the form that must surely be very wonderful, searching for it in the many eyes that were fixed upon her. She looked at Sir Donald:

"Dice: Tutto al mondo e vano:"

She looked at Rupert Carey:

"Nell'amore ogni dolcezza."

She still looked at Carey, and the hideous wreckage of the flesh was no longer visible to her. She saw only his burning eyes.

Directly she had finished singing she asked for her motor cloak. While they were fetching it she had to go back twice to the platform to bow to the applause.

Miss Schley, who was looking angry, said to her:

"You're not going away before my show?"

"I want to go to the concert room, where I can hear better, and see," she replied.

Miss Schley looked at her doubtfully, but had to go to the platform. As she slowly disappeared behind the screen Lady Holme drew the cloak round her, pulled down her veil and went quickly away.

She wanted—more, she required—to be alone.

At the hall door she sent a footman to find the motor car. When it came up she said to the chauffeur:

"Take me home quickly and then come back for his lordship."

She got in.

As the car went off swiftly she noticed that the streets were shining with wet.

"Has it been raining?" she asked.

"Raining hard, my lady."

CHAPTER XVI

ON the following morning the newspapers contained an account of the concert at Manchester House. They contained also an account of a motor accident which had occurred the same afternoon between Hyde Park Corner and Knightsbridge.

On the wet pavement Lord Holme's new car, which was taking Lady Holme to Cadogan Square at a rapid pace, skidded and overturned, pinning Lady Holme beneath it. While she was on the ground a hansom cab ran into the car.

At their breakfasts her friends, her acquaintances, her enemies and the general public read of her beautiful singing at the concert, and read also the following paragraph, which closed the description of the accident:

> "We deeply regret to learn that Lady Holme was severely injured in the face by the accident. Full particulars have not reached us, but we understand that an immediate operation is necessary and will be performed to-day by Mr. Bernard Crispin the famous surgeon. Her ladyship is suffering great pain, and it is feared that she will be permanently disfigured."

The fierce change which Lady Holme had longed for was a reality. One life, the life of the siren, had come to an end. But the eyes of the woman must still see light. The heart of the woman must still beat on.

Death stretched out a hand in the darkness and found the hand of Birth.

CHAPTER XVII

ON a warm but overcast day, at the end of the following September, a woman, whose face was completely hidden by a thick black veil, drove up to the boat landing of the town of Como in a hired victoria. She was alone, but behind her followed a second carriage containing an Italian maid and a large quantity of luggage. When the victoria stopped at the water's edge the woman got out slowly, and stood for a moment, apparently looking for something. There were many boats ranged along the quay, their white awnings thrown back, their oars resting on the painted seats. Beside one, which was larger than the others, soberly decorated in brown with touches of gold, and furnished with broad seats not unlike small armchairs, stood two bold-looking Italian lads dressed in white sailors' suits. One of them, after staring for a brief instant at the veiled woman, went up to her and said in Italian:

"Is the signora for Casa Felice?"

"Yes."

The boy took off his round hat with a gallant gesture.

"The boat is here, signora."

He led the way to the brown-and-gold craft, and helped the lady to get into it. She sat down on one of the big seats.

"That is the luggage," she said, speaking Italian in a low voice, and pointing to the second carriage from which the maid was stepping. The two boatmen hastened towards it. In a few minutes maid and luggage were installed in a big black gondola, oared by two men standing up, and the brown boat, with the two lads in white and the veiled woman, glided out on the calm water.

The day was a grey dream, mystical in its colourless silence. Blue Italy was shrouded as the woman's face was shrouded. The speechlessness of Nature environed her speechlessness. She was an enigma set in an enigma, and the two rowers looked at her and at the sunless sky, and bent to their oars gravely. A melancholy stole into their sensitive dark faces. This new *padrona* had already cast a shadow upon their buoyant temperaments.

She noticed it and clasped her hands together in her lap. She was not accustomed yet to her new *role* in life.

The boat stole on. Como was left behind. The thickly-wooded shores of the lake, dotted with many villas, the tall green mountains covered with chestnut trees, framed the long, winding riband of water which was the way to Casa Felice. There were not many other boats out. The steamer had already started for Bellagio, and was far away near the point where Torno nestles around its sheltered harbour. The black gondola was quickly left behind. Its load of luggage weighed it down. The brown boat was alone in the grey dream of the sunless autumn day.

Behind her veil Lady Holme was watching the two Italian boys, whose lithe bodies bent to their oars, whose dark eyes were often turned upon her with a staring scrutiny, with the morose and almost violent expression that is the child of frustrated curiosity.

Was it true? Was she in real life, or sitting there, watching, thinking, striving to endure, in a dream? Since the accident which had for ever changed her life she had felt many sensations, a torrent of sensations, but never one exactly like this, never one so full of emptiness, chaos, grey vacancy, eternal stillness, unreal oppression and almost magical solitude as this. She had thought she had suffered all things that she could suffer. She had not yet suffered this. Someone, the Governing Power, had held this in reserve. Now it was being sent forth by decree. Now it was coming upon her. Now it was enveloping her. Now it was rolling round her and billowing away on every side to unimaginably remote horizons.

Another and a new emotion of horror was to be hers. Would the attack of the hidden one upon her never end? Was that quiver of poisoned arrows inexhaustible?

She leaned back against the cushions without feeling them. She wanted to sink back as the mortally wounded sink, to sink down, far down, into the gulf where surely the dying go to find, with their freezing lips, the frozen lips of Death. She shut her eyes.

Presently, with the faint splash of the oars in the water, there mingled a low sound of music. The rower nearest to her was singing in an under voice to keep his boy's heart from succumbing to the spell of melancholy. She listened, still wrapped in this dreadful chaos that was dreamlike. At first the music was a murmur. But presently it grew louder. She could distinguish words now and then. Once she heard *carissima*, a moment afterwards *amore*. Then the poison in which the tip of this last arrow had been curiously steeped began its work in her. The quivering creature hidden within her cowered, shrank, put up trembling hands, cried out, "I cannot endure this thing. I do not know how to. I have never learnt the way. This is impossible for me. This is a demand I have not the capacity to fulfil!" And, even while it cowered and cried out, knew, "This I must endure. This demand I shall be made to fulfil. Nothing will serve me; no outstretched hands, no wailings of despair, no prayers, no curses even will save me. For I am the soul in the hands of the vivisector."

Along the lake, past the old home of La Taglioni, past the Villa Pasta with its long garden, past little Torno with its great round oleanders and its houses crowding to the shore, the boatman sang. Gathering courage as his own voice dispersed his melancholy, and the warm hopes of his youth spread their wings once more, roused by the words of love his lips were uttering, he fearlessly sent out his song. Love in the South was in it, love in the sun, embraces in warm scented nights, longings in moonlight, attainment in darkness. The boy had forgotten the veiled lady, whose shrouded face and whose silence had for a moment saddened him. His hot, bold nature reasserted itself, the fire of his youth blazed up again. He sang as if only the other boatman had been there and they had seen the girls they loved among the trees upon the shore.

And the soul writhed, like an animal stretched and strapped upon the board, to whom no anaesthetic, had been given.

Never before would it have been possible to Lady Holme to believe that the mere sound of a word could inflict such torment upon a heart as the sound of the word *amore*, coming from the boatman's lips, now inflicted upon hers. Each time it came, with its soft beauty, its languor of sweetness— like a word reclining—it flayed her soul alive, and showed her red, raw bareness.

Yet she did not ask the man to stop singing. Few people in the hands of Fate ask Fate for favours. Instinct speaks in the soul and says, "Be silent."

The boat rounded the point of Torno and came at once into a lonelier region of the lake. Autumn was more definite here. Its sadness spoke more plainly. Habitations on the shores were fewer. The mountains were more grim, though grander. And their greyness surely closed in a little upon the boat, the rowers, the veiled woman who was being taken to Casa Felice.

Perhaps to combat the gathering gloom of Nature the boatman sang more loudly, with the full force of his voice. But suddenly he seemed to be struck by the singular contrast opposed to his expansive energy by the silent figure opposite to him. A conscious look came into his face. His voice died away abruptly. After a pause he said,

"Perhaps the signora is not fond of music?"

Lady Holme wanted to speak, but she could not. She and this bright-eyed boy were not in the same world. That was what she felt. He did not know it, but she knew it. And one world cannot speak through infinite space with another.

She said nothing. The boy looked over his shoulder at his companion. Then, in silence, they both rowed on.

And now that the song had ceased she was again in the grey chaos of the dream, in the irrevocable emptiness, the intense, the enormous solitude that was like the solitude of an unpeopled eternity in which man had no lot.

Presently, with a stroke of his right oar, the boy who had sung turned the boat's prow toward the shore, and Lady Holme saw a large, lonely house confronting them on the nearer bank of the lake. It stood apart. For a long distance on either side of it there was no other habitation. The flat, yellow facade rose out of the water. Behind was a dim tangle of densely-growing trees rising up on the steep mountain side towards the grey sky. Lady Holme could not yet see details. The boat was still too far out upon the lake. Nor would she have been able to note details if she had seen them. Only a sort of heavy impression that this house had a pale, haunted aspect forced itself dully upon her.

"Ecco Casa Felice, signora!" said the foremost rower, half timidly, pointing with his brown hand.

She made an intense effort and uttered some reply. The boy was encouraged and began to tell her about the beauties of the house, the gardens, the chasm behind the piazza down which the waterfall rushed, to dive beneath the house and lose itself in the lake. She tried to listen, but she could not. The strangeness of her being alone, hidden behind a dense veil, of her coming to such a retired house in the autumn to remain there in utter solitude, with no object except that of being safe from the intrusion of anyone who knew her, of being hidden from all watching eyes that had ever looked upon her—the strangeness of it obsessed her, was both powerful and unreal. That she should be one of those lonely women of whom the world speaks with a lightly-contemptuous pity seemed incredible to her. Yet what woman was lonelier than she?

The boat drew in toward the shore and she began to see the house more plainly. It was large, and the flat facade was broken in the middle by an open piazza with round arches and slender columns. This piazza divided the house in two. The villa was in fact composed of two square buildings connected together by it. From the boat, looking up, Lady Holme saw a fierce mountain gorge rising abruptly behind the house. Huge cypresses grew on its sides, towering above the slate roof, and she heard the loud noise of falling water. It seemed to add to the weight of her desolation.

The boat stopped at a flight of worn stone steps. One of the boys sprang out and rang a bell, and presently an Italian man-servant opened a tall iron gate set in a crumbling stone arch, and showed more stone steps leading upward between walls covered with dripping lichen. The boat boy came to help Lady Holme out.

For a moment she did not move. The dreamlike feeling had come upon her with such force that her limbs refused to obey her will. The sound of the falling water in the mountain gorge had sent her farther adrift into the grey, unpeopled eternity, into the vague chaos. But the boy held out his hand, took hers. The strong clasp recalled her. She got up. The Italian man-servant preceded her up the steps into a long garden built up high above the lake on a creeper-covered wall. To the left was the house door. She stood still for an instant looking out over the wide expanse of unruffled grey water. Then, putting her hand up to her veil as if to keep it more closely over her face, she slowly went into the house.

CHAPTER XVIII

DESPAIR had driven Lady Holme to Casa Felice. When she had found that the accident had disfigured her frightfully, and that the disfigurement would be permanent, she had at first thought of killing herself. But then she had been afraid. Life had abruptly become a horror to her. She felt that it must be a horror to her always. Yet she dared not leave it then, in her home in London, in the midst of the sights and sounds connected with her former happiness. After the operation, and the verdict of the doctors, that no more could be done than had been done, she had had an access of almost crazy misery, in which all the secret violence of her nature had rushed to the surface from the depths. Shut up alone in her room, she had passed a day and a night without food. She had lain upon the floor. She had torn her clothes into fragments. The animal that surely dwells at the door of the soul of each human being had had its way in her, had ravaged her, humiliated her, turned her to savagery. Then at last she had slept, still lying upon the floor. And she had waked feeling worn out but calm, desperately calm. She defied the doctors. What did they know of women, of what women can do to regain a vanished beauty? She would call in specialists, beauty doctors, quacks, the people who fill the papers with their advertisements.

Then began a strange defile of rag-tag humanity to the Cadogan Square door—women, men, of all nationalities and pretensions. But the evil was beyond their power. At last an American specialist, who had won renown by turning a famous woman of sixty into the semblance of a woman of six-and-thirty—for a short time—was called in. Lady Holme knew that his verdict must be final. If he could do nothing to restore her vanished loveliness nothing could be done. After being closeted with her for a long time he came out of her room. There were tears in his eyes. To the footman who opened the hall door, and who stared in surprise, he explained his emotion thus.

"Poor lady," he said. "It's a hopeless case."

"Ah!" said the man, who was the pale footman Lady Holme had sent with the latch-key to Leo Ulford.

"Hopeless. It's a hard thing to have to tell a lady she'll always be—be—"

"What, sir?" said the footman.

"Well—what people won't enjoy looking at."

He winked his eyes. He was a little bald man, with a hatchet face that did not suggest emotion.

"And judging by part of the left side of the face, I guess she must have been almost a beauty once," he added, stepping into the square.

That was Lady Holme now. She had to realise herself as a woman whom people would rather not look at.

All this time she had not seen Fritz. He had asked to see her. He had even tried to insist on seeing her, but so long as there was any hope in her of recovering her lost beauty she had refused to let him come near her. The thought of his eyes staring upon the tragic change in her face sent cold creeping through her veins. But when the American had gone she realised that there was nothing to wait for, that if she were ever to let Fritz see her again it had better be now. The bandages in which her face had been swathed had been removed. She went to a mirror and, setting her teeth and clenching her hands, looked into it steadily.

She did not recognise herself. As she stood there she felt as if a dreadful stranger had come into the room and was confronting her.

The accident, and the surgical treatment that had followed upon it, had greatly altered the face. The nose, once fine and delicate, was now coarse and misshapen. A wound had permanently distorted the mouth, producing a strange, sneering expression. The whole of the right side of the face was puffy and heavy-looking, and drawn down towards the chin. It was also at present discoloured. For as Lady Holme lay under the car she had been badly burnt. The raw, red tinge would no doubt fade away with time, but the face must always remain unsightly, even a little grotesque, must always show to the casual passer-by a woman who had been the victim of a dreadful accident.

Lady Holme stared at this woman for a long time. There were no tears in her eyes. Then she went to the dressing-table and began to make up her face. Slowly, deliberately, with a despairing carefulness, she covered it with pigments till she looked like a woman in Regent Street. Her face became a frightful mask, and even then the fact that she was disfigured was not concealed. The application of the pigments began to cause her pain. The right side of her face throbbed. She looked dreadfully old, too, with this mass of paint and powder upon her—like a hag, she thought. And it was obvious that she was trying to hide something. Anyone, man or woman, looking upon her, would divine that so much art could only be used for the concealment of a dreadful disability. People, seeing this mask, would suppose—what might they not suppose? The pain in her face became horrible. Suddenly, with a cry, she began to undo what she had done. When she had finished she rang the bell. Her maid knocked at the door. Without opening it she called out:

"Is his lordship in the house?"

"Yes, my lady. His lordship has just come in."

"Go and ask him to come up and see me."

"Yes, my lady."

Lady Holme sat down on the sofa at the foot of the bed. She was trembling violently. She sat looking on the ground and trying to control her limbs. A sort of dreadful humbleness surged through her, as if she were a guilty creature about to cringe before a judge. She trembled till the sofa on which she was sitting shook. She caught hold of the cushions and made a strong effort to sit still. The handle of the door turned.

"Don't come in!" she cried out sharply.

But the door opened and her husband appeared on the threshold. As he did so she turned swiftly so that only part of the left side of her face was towards him.

"Vi!" he said. "Poor old girl, I—"

He was coming forward when she called out again "Stay there, Fritz!"

He stopped.

"Why?" he asked.

"I—I—wait a minute. Shut the door."

He shut the door. She was still looking away from him.

"Do you understand?" she said, still in a sharp voice.

"Understand what?"

"That I'm altered, that the accident's altered me—very much?"

"I know. The doctor said something. But you look all right."

"From there."

The trembling seized her again.

"Well, but—it can't be so bad—"

"It is. Don't move! Fritz—"

"Well?"

"You—do you care for me?"

"Of course I do, old girl. Why, you know—"

Suddenly she turned round, stood up and faced him desperately.

"Do you care for me, Fritz?" she said.

There was a dead silence. It seemed to last for a long while. At length it was broken by a woman's voice crying:

"Fritz,—Fritz—it isn't my fault! It isn't my fault!"

"Good God!" Lord Holme said slowly.

"It isn't my fault, Fritz! It isn't my fault!"

"Good God! but—the doctor didn't—Oh—wait a minute—"

A door opened and shut. He was gone. Lady Holme fell down on the sofa. She was alone, but she kept on sobbing:

"It isn't my fault, Fritz! It isn't my fault, Fritz!"

And while she sobbed the words she knew that her life with Fritz Holme had come to an end. The chapter was closed.

From that day she had only one desire—to hide herself. The season was over. London was empty. She could travel. She resolved to disappear. Fritz had stayed on in the house, but she would not see him again, and he did not press her to. She knew why. He dreaded to look at her. She would see no one. At first there had been streams of callers, but now almost everybody had left town. Only Sir Donald came to the door each day and inquired after her health. One afternoon a note was brought to her. It was from Fritz, saying that he had been "feeling a bit chippy," and the doctor advised him to run over to Homburg. But he wished to know what she meant to do. Would she go down to her father?—her mother, Lady St. Loo, was dead, and her father was an old man—or what? Would she come to Homburg too?

When she read those words she laughed out loud. Then she sent for the *New York Herald* and looked for the Homburg notes. She found Miss Pimpernel Schley's name among the list of the newest arrivals. That evening she wrote to her husband:

> "*Do not bother about me. Go to Homburg. I need rest and I want to be alone. Perhaps I may go to some quiet place in Switzerland with my maid. I'll let you know if I leave town. Good-bye.*
>
> "*VIOLA HOLME.*"

At first she had put only Viola. Then she added the second word. Viola alone suggested an intimacy which no longer existed between her and the man she had married.

The next day Lord Holme crossed the Channel. She was left with the servants.

Till then she had not been out of the house, but two days afterwards, swathed in a thick veil, she went for a drive in the Park, and on returning from it found Sir Donald on the door-step. He looked frailer than ever and very old. Lady Holme would have preferred to avoid him. Since that interview with her husband the idea of meeting anyone she knew terrified her. But he came at once to help her out of the carriage. Her face was invisible, but he knew her, and he greeted her in a rather shaky voice. She could see that he was deeply moved, and thanked him for his many inquiries.

"But why are you still in London?" she said.

"You are still in London," he replied.

She was about to say good-bye on the door-step; but he kept her hand in his and said:

"Let me come in and speak to you for a moment."

"Very well," she said.

When they were in the drawing-room she still kept the veil over her face, and remained standing.

"Sir Donald," she said, "you cared for me, I know; you were fond of me."

"Were?" he answered.

"Yes—were. I am no longer the woman you—other people—cared for."

"If there is any change—" he began.

"I know. You are going to say it is not in the woman, the real woman. But I say it is. The change is in what, to men, is the real woman. This change has destroyed any feeling my husband may have had for me."

"It could never destroy mine," Sir Donald said quietly.

"Yes, it could—yours especially, because you are a worshipper of beauty, and Fritz never worshipped anything except himself. I am going to let you say good-bye to me without seeing me. Remember me as I was."

"But—what do you mean? You speak as if you would no longer go into the world."

"I go into the world! You haven't seen me, Sir Donald."

She saw an expression of nervous apprehension come into his face as he glanced at her veil.

"What are you going to do, then?" he said.

"I don't know. I—I want a hiding-place."

She saw tears come into his old, faded eyes.

"Hush!" he said. "Don't-"

"A hiding-place. I want to travel a long way off and be quite alone, and think, and see how I can go on, if I can go on."

Her voice was quite steady.

"If I could do something—anything for you!" he murmured.

"You fancy you are still speaking to the woman who sang, Sir Donald."

"Would you—" Suddenly he spoke with some eagerness. "You want to go away, to be alone?"

"Yes, I must."

"Let me lend you Casa Felice!"

"Casa Felice!"

She laughed.

"To be sure; I was to baptise it, wasn't I?"

"Ah, that—will you have it for a while?"

"But you are going there!"

"I will not go. It is all ready. The servants are engaged. You will be perfectly looked after, perfectly comfortable. Let me feel I can do something for you. Try it. You will find beauty there—peace. And I—I shall be on the lake, not far off."

"I must be alone," she said wearily.

"You shall be. I will never come unless you send for me."

"I should never send for you or for anyone."

She did not say then what she would do, but three days later she accepted Sir Donald's offer.

And now she was alone in Casa Felice. She had not even brought her French maid, but had engaged an Italian. She was resolved to isolate herself with people who had never seen her as a beautiful woman.

CHAPTER XIX

LADY HOLME never forgot that first evening at Casa Felice. The strangeness of it was greater than the strangeness of any nightmare. When she was shut up in her bedroom in London she had thought she realised all the meaning of the word loneliness. Now she knew that then she had not begun to realise it. For she had been in her own house, in the city which contained a troop of her friends, in the city where she had reigned. And although she knew that she would reign no more, she had not grasped the exact meaning of that knowledge in London. She had known a fact but not fully felt it. She had known what she now was but not fully felt what she now was. Even when Fritz, muttering almost terrified exclamations, had stumbled out of the bedroom, she had not heard the dull clamour of finality as she heard it now.

She was an exile. She was an outcast among women. She was no longer a beautiful woman, she was not even a plain woman—she was a dreadful-looking human being.

The Italian servants by whom she was surrounded suddenly educated her in the lore of exact knowledge of herself and her present situation.

Italians are the most charming of the nations, but Italians of the lower classes are often very unreserved in the display of their most fugitive sensations, their most passing moods. The men, especially when they are young, are highly susceptible to beauty in women. They are also—and the second emotion springs naturally enough from the first—almost childishly averse from female ugliness. It is a common thing in Italy to hear of men of the lower classes speak of a woman's plainness with brutality, with a manner almost of personal offence. They often shrink from personal ugliness as Englishmen seldom do, like children shrinking from something abnormal—a frightening dwarf, a spectre.

Now that Lady Holme had reached the "hiding-place" for which she had longed, she resolved to be brutal with herself. Till now she had almost perpetually concealed her disfigured face. Even her servants had not seen it. But in this lonely house, among these strangers, she knew that the inevitable moment was come when she must begin the new life, the terrible life that was henceforth to be hers. In her bedroom she took off her hat and veil, and without glancing into the glass she came downstairs. In the hall she met the butler. She saw him start.

"Can I have tea?" she said, looking at him steadily.

"Yes, signora," he answered, looking down.

"In the piazza, please."

She went out through the open door into the piazza. The boy who had sung in the boat was there, watering some geraniums in pots. As she came out he glanced up curiously, at the same time pulling off his hat. When he saw her his mouth gaped, and an expression of pitiless repulsion came into his eyes. It died out almost instantaneously, and he smiled and began to speak about the flowers. But Lady Holme had received her education. She knew what she was to youth that instinctively loves beauty.

She sat down in a cane chair. It seemed to her as if people were scourging her with thongs of steel, as if she were bleeding from the strokes.

She looked out across the lake.

The butler brought tea and put it beside her. She did not hear him come or go. Behind her the waterfall roared down between the cypresses. Before her the lake spread out its grey, unruffled surface. And this was the baptism of Casa Felice, her baptism into a new life. Her agony was the more intense because she had never been an intellectual woman, had never lived the inner life. Always she had depended on outward things. Always she had been accustomed to bustle, movement, excitement, perpetual intercourse with people who paid her homage. Always she had lived for the world, and worshipped, because she had seen those around her worshipping, the body.

And now all was taken from her. Without warning, without a moment for preparation, she was cast down into Hell. Even her youth was made useless to her.

When she thought of that she began to cry, sitting there by the stone balustrade of the piazza, to cry convulsively. She remembered her pity for old age, for the monstrous loss it cannot cease from advertising. And now she, in her youth, had passed it on the road to the pit. Lady Cardington was a beautiful woman. She pitied herself bitterly because she was morbid, as many beautiful women are when they approach old age. But she was beautiful. She would always be beautiful. She might not think it, but she was still a power, could still inspire love. In her blanched face framed in white hair there was in truth a wonderful attraction.

Whiteness—Lady Holme shuddered when she thought of whiteness, remembering what the glass had shown her.

Fritz—his animal passion for her—his horror of her now—Miss Schley—their petty, concealed strife—Rupert Carey's love—Leo Ulford's desire of conquest—his father's strange, pathetic devotion—Winter falling at the feet of Spring—figures and events from the panorama of her life now ended flickered through her almost numbed mind, while the tears still ran down her face.

And Robin Pierce?

As she thought of him more life quickened in her mind.

Since her accident he had written to her several times, ardent, tender letters, recalling all he had said to her, recounting again his adoration of her for her nature, her soul, the essence of her, the woman in her, telling her that this terror which had come upon her only made her dearer to him, that—as she knew—he had impiously dared almost to long for it, as for an order of release that would take effect in the liberation of her true self.

These letters she had read, but they had not stirred her. She had told herself that Robin did not know, that he was a self-deceiver, that he did not understand his own nature, which was allied to the nature of every living man. But now, seeking some, even the smallest solace in the intense agony of desolation that was upon her, she caught—in her bleeding woman's heart—at this hand stretched out from Rome. She got up, went to her bedroom, unlocked her despatch-box, took out these letters of Robin's. They had not stirred her, yet she had kept them. Now she came down once more to the piazza, sat by the tea-table, opened them, read them, re-read them, whispered them over again and again. Something she must have; some hand she must catch at. She could not die in this freezing cold which she had never known, this cold that came out of the Inferno, at whose cavern mouth she stood. And Robin said he was there—Robin said he was there.

She did not love Robin. It seemed to her now that it would be grotesque for her to love any man. Her face was not meant for love. But as she read these ardent, romantic letters, written since the tragedy that had overtaken her, she began to ask herself, with a fierce anxiety, whether what Robin affirmed could be the truth? Was he unlike other men? Was his nature capable of a devotion of the soul to another soul, of a devotion to which any physical ugliness, even any physical horror, would count as nothing?

After that last scene with Fritz she felt as if he were no longer her husband, as if he were only a man who had fled from her in fear. She did not think any more of his rights, her duties. He had abandoned his rights. What duties could she have towards a man who was frightened when he looked at her? And indeed all the social and moral questions to which the average woman of the world pays—because she must pay—attention had suddenly ceased to exist for Lady Holme. She was no longer a woman of the world. All worldly matters had sunk down beneath her feet with her lost beauty. She had wanted to be free. Well, now she was surely free. Who would care what she did in the future?

Robin said he was there.

She thought that, unless she could feel that in world there was one man who wanted to take care of her, she must destroy herself. The thought grew in her as she sat there, till she said to herself, "If it is true what he says, perhaps I shall be able to live. If it is not true—" She looked over the stone balustrade at the grey waters of the lake. Twilight was darkening over them.

Late that evening, when she was sitting in the big drawing-room staring at the floor, the butler came in with a telegram. She opened it and read:

> "Sir Donald has told me you are at Casa Felice; arrive to-morrow from Rome—ROBIN."

"No answer," she said.

So he was coming—to-morrow. The awful sense of desolation lifted slightly from her. A human being was travelling to her, was wanting to see her. To see her! She shuddered. Then fiercely she asked herself why she was afraid. She would not be afraid. She would trust in Robin. He was unlike other men. There had always been in him something that set him apart, a strangeness, a romance, a love of hidden things, a subtlety. If only he would still care for her, still feel towards her as he had felt, she could face the future, she thought. They might be apart. That did not matter. She had no thought of a close connection, of frequent intercourse even. She only wanted desperately, frantically, to know that someone who had loved her could love her still in spite of what had happened. If she could retain one deep affection she felt that she could live.

The morrow would convince her.

That night she did not sleep. She lay in bed and heard the water falling in the gorge, and when the dawn began to break she did a thing she had not done for a long time.

She got out of bed, knelt down and prayed—prayed to Him who had dealt terribly with her that He would be merciful when Robin came.

When it was daylight and the Italian maid knocked at her door she told her to get out a plain, dark dress. She did her hair herself with the utmost simplicity. That at least was still beautiful. Then she went down and walked in the high garden above the lake. The greyness had lifted and the sky was blue. The mellowness rather than the sadness of autumn was apparent, throned on the tall mountains whose woods were bathed in sunshine. All along the great old wall, that soared forty feet from the water, roses were climbing. Scarlet and white geraniums bloomed in discoloured ancient vases. Clumps of oleanders showed pink showers of blossoms. Tall bamboos reared their thin heads towards the tufted summits of palms that suggested Africa. Monstrous cypresses aspired, with a sort of haughty resignation, above their brother trees. The bees went to and fro. Flies circled and settled. Lizards glided across the warm stones and rustled into hiding among the ruddy fallen leaves. And always the white water sang in the gorge as it rushed towards the piazza of Casa Felice.

And Lady Holme tried to hope.

Yet, as she walked slowly to and fro amid the almost rank luxuriance of the garden, she was gnawed by a terrible anxiety. The dreadful humbleness, the shrinking cowardice of the unsightly human being invaded her. She strove to put them from her. She strove to call Robin's own arguments and assertions to her aid. What she had been she still was in all essentials. Her self was unharmed, existed, could love, hate, be tender, be passionate as before. Viola was there still within her, the living spirit to which a name had been given when she was a little child. The talent was there which had spoken, which could still speak, through her voice. The beating heart was there which could still speak through her actions. The mysteries of the soul still pursued their secret courses within her, like far-off subterranean streams. The essential part of her remained as it had been. Only a little outside bit of a framework had been twisted awry. Could that matter very much? Had she not perhaps been morbid in her despair?

She determined to take courage. She told herself that if she allowed this dreadful, invading humbleness way in her she would lose all power to dominate another by showing that she had ceased to dominate herself. If she met Robin in fear and trembling she would actually teach him to despise her. If she showed that she thought herself changed, horrible, he would inevitably catch her thought and turn it to her own destruction. Men despise those who despise themselves. She knew that, and she argued with herself, fought with herself. If Robin loved the angel; surely he could still love. For if there were an angel within her it had not been harmed. And she leaned on the stone wall and prayed again while the roses touched her altered face.

It seemed to her then that courage was sent to her. She felt less terrified of what was before her, as if something had risen up within her upon which she could lean, as if her soul began to support the trembling, craven thing that would betray her, began to teach it how to be still.

She did not feel happy, but she felt less desperately miserable than she had felt since the accident.

After *dejeuner* she walked again in the garden. As the time drew near for Robin to arrive, the dreadful feverish anxiety of the early morning awoke again within her. She had not conquered herself. Again the thought of suicide came upon her, and she felt that her life or death were in the hands of this man whom yet she did not love. They were in his hands because he was a human being and she was one. There are straits in which the child of life, whom the invisible hand that is extended in a religion has not yet found, must find in the darkness a human hand stretched out to it or sink down in utter terror and perhaps perish. Lady Holme was in such a strait. She knew it. She said to herself quite plainly that if Robin failed to stretch out his hand to her she could not go on living. It was clear to her that her life or death depended upon whether he remained true to what he had said was his ideal, or whether he proved false to it and showed himself such a man as Fritz, as a thousand others.

She sickened with anxiety as the moments passed.

Now, leaning upon the wall, she began to scan the lake. Presently she saw the steamer approaching the landing-stage of Carate on the opposite bank. The train from Rome had arrived. But Robin would doubtless come by boat. There was at least another hour to wait. She left the wall and walked quickly up and down, moving her hands and her lips. Now she almost wished he were not coming. She recalled the whole story of her acquaintance with Robin — his adoration of her when she was a girl, his wish to marry her, his melancholy when she refused him, his persistent affection for her after she had married Fritz, his persistent belief that there was that within her which Fritz did not understand and could never satisfy, his persistent obstinacy in asserting that he had the capacity to understand and content this hidden want. Was that true?

Fritz had cared for nothing but the body, yet she had loved Fritz. She did not love Robin. Yet there was a feeling in her that if he proved true to his ideal now she might love him in the end. If only he would love her — after he knew.

She heard a sound of oars. The blood rushed to her face. She drew back from the wall and hurried into her house. All the morning she had been making up her mind to go to meet Robin at once in the sunlight, to let him know all at once. But now, in terror, she went to her room. With trembling hands she pinned on a hat; she took out of a drawer the thick veil she wore when travelling and tied it tightly over her face. Panic seized her.

There was a knock at the door, the announcement that a signore was waiting in the drawing-room for the signora.

Lady Holme felt an almost ungovernable sensation of physical nausea. She went to her dressing-case and drank one or two burning drops of eau de Cologne. Then she pulled down the veil under her chin and stood in the middle of the room for several minutes without moving. Then she went downstairs quickly and went quickly into the drawing-room.

Robin was there, standing by the window. He looked excited, with an excitement of happiness, and this gave to him an aspect of almost boyish youth. His long black eyes shone with eagerness when she came into the room. But when he saw the veil his face changed.

"You don't trust me!" he said, without any greeting.

She went up to him and put out her hand.

"Robin!" she said.

"You don't trust me," he repeated.

He took her hand. His was hot.

"Robin—I'm a coward," she said.

Her voice quivered.

"Oh, my dearest!" he exclaimed, melted in a moment.

He took her other hand, and she felt his hands throbbing. His clasp was so ardent that it startled her into forgetting everything for one instant, everything that except these clasping hands loved her hands, loved her. That instant was exquisitely sweet to her. There was a stinging sweetness in it, a mystery of sweetness, as if their four hands were four souls longing to be lost in one another.

"Now you'll trust me," he said.

She released her hands and immediately her terror of doubt returned.

"Let us go into the garden," she answered.

He followed her to the path beside the wall.

"I looked for you from here," she said.

"I did not see you."

"No. When I heard the boat I—Robin, I'm afraid—I'm afraid."

"Of me, Viola?"

He laughed joyously.

"Take off your veil," he said.

"No, no—not yet. I want to tell you first—"

"To tell me what?"

"That my—that my—Robin, I'm not beautiful now."

Her voice quivered again.

"You tell me so," he answered.

"It's true."

"I don't believe it."

"But," she began, almost desperately, "it's true, Robin, oh, it's true! When Fritz—"

She stopped. She was choking.

"Oh—Fritz!" he said with scathing contempt.

"No, no, listen! You've got to listen." She put her hand on his arm. "When Fritz saw me—afterwards he—he was afraid of me. He couldn't speak to me. He just looked and said—and said—"

Tears were running down behind the veil. He put up his hand to hers, which still touched his arm.

"Don't tell me what he said. What do I care? Viola, you know I've almost longed for this—no, not that, but—can't you understand that when one loves a woman one loves something hidden, something mystical? It's so much more than a face that one loves. One doesn't want to live in a house merely because it's got a nice front door."

He laughed again as if he were half ashamed of his own feeling.

"Is that true, Robin?"

The sound of her voice told him that he need not be afraid to be passionate.

"Sit down here," he said.

They had reached an old stone bench at the end of the garden where the woods began. Two cypresses towered behind it, sad-looking sentinels. There was a gap in the wall here through which the lake could be seen as one sat upon the bench.

"I want to make you understand, to make you trust me."

She sat down without speaking, and he sat beside her.

"Viola," he said, "there are many men who love only what they can see, and never think of the spirit behind it. They care only for a woman's body. For them the woman's body is the woman. I put it rather brutally. What they can touch, what they can kiss, what they can hold in their arms is all to them. They are unconscious of the distant, untameable woman, the lawless woman who may be free in the body that is captive, who may be unknown in the body that is familiar, who may even be pure in the body that is defiled as she is immortal though her body is mortal. These men love the flesh only. But there are at least some men who love the spirit. They love the flesh, too, because it manifests the spirit, but to them the spirit is the real thing. They are always stretching out their arms to that. The hearth can't satisfy them. They demand the fire. The fire, the fire!" he repeated, as if the word warmed him. "I've so often thought of this, imagined this. It's as if I'd actually foreseen it."

He spoke with gathering excitement.

"What?" she murmured.

"That some day the woman men—those men I've spoken of—loved would be struck down, and the real woman, the woman of the true beauty, the mystic, the spirit woman, would be set free. If this had not happened you could perhaps never have known who was the man that really loved you—that loved the real you, the you that lies so far beyond the flesh, the you that has sung and suffered—"

"Ah, suffered!" she said.

But there was a note of something that was not sorrow in her voice.

"If you want to know the man I mean," Robin said, "lift up your veil, Viola."

She sat quite still for a moment, a moment that seemed very long. Then she put up both hands to her head, untied the veil and let it fall into her lap. He looked at her, and there was silence. They heard the bees humming. There were many among the roses on the wall. She had turned her face fully towards him, but she kept her eyes on the veil that lay in her lap. It was covered with little raised black spots. She began to count them. As the number mounted she felt her body turning gradually cold.

"Fifteen—sixteen-seventeen"—she formed the words with her lips, striving to concentrate her whole soul upon this useless triviality—"eighteen—nineteen—twenty."

Little drops of moisture came out upon her temples. Still the silence continued. She knew that all this time Robin was looking into her face. She felt his eyes like two knives piercing her face.

"Twenty-one—twenty-two—"

"Viola!"

He spoke at last and his voice was extraordinary. It was husky, and sounded desperate and guilty.

"Well?" she said, still looking at the spots.

"Now you know the man I spoke of."

Yes, it was a desperate voice and hard in its desperation.

"You mean that you are the man?"

Still she did not look up. After a pause she heard him say:

"Yes, that I am the man."

Then she looked up. His face was scarlet, like a face flushed with guilt. His eyes met hers with a staring glance, yet they were furtive. His hands were clenched on his knees. When she looked at him he began to smile.

"Viola," he said, "Viola."

He unclenched his hands and put them out towards her, as if to take her hands. She did not move.

"Poor Robin!" she said.

"Poor—but—what do you mean?" he stammered.

He never turned his eyes from her face.

"Poor Robin!—but it isn't your fault."

Then she put out her hand and touched his gently.

"My fault?

"That it was all a fancy, all a weaving of words. You want to be what you thought you were, but you can't be."

"You're wrong, Viola, you're utterly wrong—"

"Hush, Robin! That woman you spoke of—that woman knows."

He cleared his throat, got up, went over to the wall, leaned his arms upon it and hid his face on them. There were tears in his eyes. At that moment he was suffering more than she was. His soul was rent by an abject sense of loss, an abject sense of guilty impotence and shame. It was frightful that he could not be what he wished to be, what he had thought he was. He longed to comfort her and could not do anything but plunge a sword into her heart. He longed to surround her with tenderness—yes, he was sure he longed—but he could only hold up to her in the sun her loneliness. And he had lost—what had he not lost? A dream of years, an imagination that had been his inseparable and dearest companion. His loneliness was intense in that moment as was hers. The tears seemed to scald his eyes. In his heart he cursed God for not permitting him to be what he longed to be, to feel what he longed to feel. It seemed to him monstrous, intolerable, that even our emotions are arranged for us as are arranged the events of our lives. He felt like a doll, a horrible puppet.

"Poor old Robin!"

She was standing beside him, and in her voice there was, just for a moment, the sound that sometimes comes into a mother's voice when she speaks to her little child in the dark.

At the moment when he knew he did not love the white angel she stood beside him.

And she thought that she was only a wretched woman.

CHAPTER XX

ROBIN had gone. He had gone, still protesting that Lady Holme was deceiving herself, protesting desperately, with the mistaken chivalry of one who was not only a gentleman to his finger-tips but who was also an almost fanatical lover of his own romance. After recovering from the first shock of his disillusion, and her strange reception of it, so different from anything he could have imagined possible in her, or indeed in any woman who had lived as she had, he had said everything that was passionate, everything that fitted in with his old protestations when she was beautiful. He had spoken, perhaps, even more to recall himself than to convince her, but he had not succeeded in either effort, and a strange, mingled sense of tragic sadness and immense relief invaded him as the width of waterway grew steadily larger between his boat and Casa Felice. He could have wept for her and for himself. He could even have wept for humanity. Yet he felt the comfort of one from whom an almost intolerable strain has just been removed. To a man of his calibre, sensitive, almost feminine in his subtlety, the situation had been exquisitely painful. He had felt what Viola was feeling as well as what he was feeling. He had struggled like a creature taken in a net. And how useless it had all been! He found himself horribly inferior to her. Her behaviour at this critical moment had proved to him that in his almost fantastic conception of her he had shown real insight. Then why had his heart betrayed his intellect? Why had his imagination proved true metal, his affection false? He asked himself these questions. He searched his own nature, as many a man has done in moments when he has found himself unworthy. And he was met by mystery, by the "It was impossible for me!" which stings the soul that would be strong. He remembered Carey's words that night in Half Moon Street when Sir Donald had accompanied him home after the dinner in Cadogan Square. Sir Donald had gone. He and Carey were alone, and he had said that if one loves, one loves the kernel not the shell. And Carey had said, "I think if the shell is a beautiful shell, and becomes suddenly broken, it makes a devil of a lot of difference in what most people think of the kernel." And when he—Robin— had replied, "It wouldn't to me," Carey had abruptly exclaimed, "I think it would." After Carey had gone Robin remembered very well saying to himself that it was strange no man will believe you if you hint at the truth of your true self. That night he had not known his true self and Carey had known it. But then, had he loved the shell only? He could not believe it. He felt bewildered. Even now, as the boat crept onward through the falling darkness, he felt that he loved Viola, but as someone who had disappeared or who was dead. This woman whom he had just left was not Viola. And yet she was. When he was not looking at her and she spoke to him, the past seemed to take the form of the present. When she had worn the veil and had touched him all his pulses had leaped. But when she had touched him with those same hands after the veil had fallen, there had been frost in his veins. Nothing in his body had responded. The independence of the flesh appalled him. It had a mind of its own then. It chose and acted quite apart from the spirit which dwelt in it. It even defied that spirit. And the eyes? They had become almost a terror to him. He thought of them as a slave thinks of a cruel master. Were they to coerce his soul? Were they to force his heart from its allegiance? He had always been accustomed to think that the spirit was essentially the governing thing in man, that indestructible, fierce, beautiful flame which surely outlives death and time. But now he found himself thinking of the flesh, the corruptible part of man that mingles its dust with the earth, as dominant over the spirit. For the first time, and because of his impotence to force his body to feel as his spirit wished it to feel, he doubted if there were a future for the soul, if there were such a condition as immortality. He reached Villa d'Este in a condition of profound depression, almost bordering on despair.

Meanwhile Viola, standing by the garden wall, had watched the boat that carried Robin disappear on the water. Till it was only a speck she watched. It vanished. Evening came on. Still she stood there. She did not feel very sad. The strange, dreamlike sensation of the preceding day had returned to her, but with a larger vagueness that robbed it of some of its former poignancy. It seemed to her that she felt as a spirit might feel— detached. She remembered once seeing a man, who called himself an "illusionist," displaying a woman's figure suspended apparently in mid-air. He took a wand and passed it over, under, around the woman to show that she was unattached to anything, that she did not rest upon anything. Viola thought that she was like that woman. She was not embittered. She was not even crushed. Her impulse of pity, when she understood what Robin was feeling, had been absolutely genuine. It had rushed upon her. It remained with her. But now it was far less definite, and embraced not only Robin but surely other men whom she had never known or even seen. They could not help themselves. It was not their fault. They were made in a certain way.

They were governed. It seemed to her that she looked out vaguely over a world of slaves, the serfs of God who have never been emancipated. She had no hope. But just then she had no fear. The past did not ebb from her, nor did the future steal towards her. The tides were stilled. The pulses of life were stopped. Everything was wrapped in a cold, grey calm. She had never been a very thoughtful woman. She had not had much time for thought. That is what she herself would probably have said. Seldom had she puzzled her head over the mysteries of existence. Even now, when she confronted the great mystery of her own, she did not think very definitely. Before Robin came her mind had been in a fever. Now that he was gone the fever had gone with him. Would it ever return? She did not ask or wonder.

The night fell and the servant came to summon her to dinner. She shook her head.

"The signora will not eat anything?"

"No, thank you."

She took her arms from the wall and looked at the man.

"Could I have the boat?"

"The signora wishes to go on the lake?"

"Yes."

"I will tell Paolo."

Two or three minutes later the boy who had sung came to say that the boat was ready.

Lady Holme fetched a cloak, and went down the dark stone staircase between the lichen-covered walls to the tall iron gate. The boat was lying by the outer steps. She got in and Paolo took the oars.

"Where does the signora wish to go?"

"Anywhere out on the lake."

He pushed off. Soon the noise of the waterfall behind Casa Felice died away, the spectral facade faded and only the plash of the oars and the tinkle of fishermen's bells above the nets, floating here and there in the lake, were audible. The distant lights of mountain villages gleamed along the shores, and the lights of the stars gleamed in the clear sky.

Now that she was away from the land Lady Holme became more conscious of herself and of life. The gentle movement of the boat promoted an echoing mental movement in her. Thoughts glided through the shadows of her soul as the boat glided through the shadows of the night. Her mind was like a pilgrim, wandering in the darkness cast by the soul.

She felt, first, immensely ignorant. She had scarcely ever, perhaps never, consciously felt immensely ignorant before. She felt also very poor, very small and very dingy, like a woman very badly dressed. She felt, finally, that she was the most insignificant of all the living things under the stars to the stars and all they watched, but that, to herself, she was of a burning, a flaming significance.

There seemed to be bells everywhere in the lake. The water was full of their small, persistent voices.

So had her former life been full of small, persistent voices, but now, abruptly, they were all struck into silence, and she was left listening—for what? For some far-off but larger voice beyond?

"What am I to do? What am I to do?"

Now she began to say this within herself. The grey calm was floating away from her spirit, and she began to realise what had happened that afternoon. She remembered that just before Robin came she had made up her mind that, though she did not love him, he held the matter of her life or death in his power. Well, if that were so, he had decided. The dice had been thrown and death had come up. No hand had been stretched out in the darkness to the child.

She looked round her. On every side she saw smooth water, a still surface which hid depths. At the prow of the boat shone a small lantern, which cast before the boat an arrow of light. And as the boat moved this arrow perpetually attacked the darkness in front. It was like the curiosity of man attacking the impenetrable mysteries of God. It seemed to penetrate, but always new darkness disclosed itself beyond, new darkness flowed silently around.

Was the darkness the larger voice?

She did not say this to herself. Her mind was not of the definite species that frames such silent questions often. But, like all human beings plunged in the strangeness of a terror that is absolutely new, and left to struggle in it quite alone, she thought a thousand things that she did not even know she thought, her mind touched many verges of which she was not aware. There were within her tremendous activities of which she was scarcely conscious. She was like a woman who wakes at night without knowing why, and hears afterwards that there was a tumult in the city where she dwelt.

Gradually, along devious ways, she came to the thought that life had done with her. It seemed to her that life said to her, "Woman, what have I to do with thee?" The man who had sworn to protect her could not endure to look at her. The man who had vowed that he loved her soul shrank before her face. She had never been a friend to women. Why should they wish to be her friends now? They would not wish it. And if they did she felt their friendship would be useless to her, more—horrible. She would rather have shown her shattered face to a thousand men than to ten women. She had never "bothered" much about religion. No God seemed near her now. She had no sense of being chastened because she was loved. On the other hand, she did feel as if she had been caught by a torturer who did not mean to let her go.

It became obvious to her that there was no place for her in life, and presently she returned to the conclusion that, totally unloved, she could not continue to exist.

She began definitely to contemplate self-destruction.

She looked at the little arrow of light beyond the boat's prow. Like that little arrow she must go out into the darkness. When? Could she go to-night? If not, probably she could never go at all by her own will and act. It should be done to-night then, abruptly, without much thought. For thought is dangerous and often paralysing.

She spoke to the boat boy. He answered. They fell into conversation. She asked him about his family, his life, whether he would have to be a soldier; whether he had a sweetheart. She forced herself to listen attentively to his replies. He was a responsive boy and soon began to talk volubly, letting the oars trail idly in the water. With energy he paraded his joyous youth before her. Even in his touches of melancholy there was hope. His happiness confirmed her in her resolution. She put herself in contrast with this boy, and her heart sank below the sources of tears into a dry place, like the valley of bones.

"Will you turn towards Casa Feli—towards the house now," she said presently.

The boat swung round, and instantly the boy began to sing.

"Yes, I can do it to-night," she thought.

His happy singing entered like iron into her soul.

When the pale facade of Casa Felice was visible once more, detaching itself from the surrounding darkness, she said to the boy carelessly:

"Where do you put the boat at night?"

"The signora has not seen?"

"No."

"Under the house. There is deep water there. One can swim for five minutes without coming out into the open."

"I should like to see that place. Can I get out of the boat there?"

"Si, signora. There is a staircase leading into the piazza by the waterfall."

"Then row in."

"Si, signora."

He was beginning to sing again, but suddenly he stopped, looked over his shoulder and listened.

"What is it?" she asked quickly.

"There is a boat, signora."

"Where."

She looked into the darkness but saw nothing.

"Close to the house, signora."

"But how do you know?"

"I heard the oars. The man in the boat was not rowing, but just as I began to sing he began to row. When I stopped singing he stopped rowing."

"You didn't see the boat?"

"No, signora. It carries no light."

He looked at her mysteriously.

"*It may be the contrabbandieri.*"

"Smugglers?"

"Yes."

He turned his head over his shoulder and whistled, in a peculiar way. There was no reply. Then he bent down over the gunwale of the boat till his ear nearly touched the water, and listened.

"The boat has stopped. It must be near us."

His whole body seemed quivering with attentive life, like a terrier's when it stands to be unchained.

"Might it not be a fisherman?" asked Lady Holme.

He shook his head.

"This is not the hour."

"Some tourists, perhaps, making an excursion?"

"It is too far. They never come here at night."

His eyes stared, his attitude was so intensely alert and his manner so mysterious that, despite her desperate preoccupation, Lady Holme found herself distracted for a moment. Her mind was detached from herself, and fixed upon this hidden boat and its occupant or occupants.

"You think it is *contrabbandieri*?" she whispered. He nodded.

"I have been one, signora."

"You!"

"Yes, when I was a boy, in the winter. Once, when we were running for the shore, on a December night, the *carabinieri* fired on us and killed Gaetano Cremona."

"Your companion?"

"Yes. He was sixteen and he died. The boat was full of his blood."

She shuddered.

"Row in," she said. "That boat must have gone."

"Non, signora. It has not. It is close by and the oars are out of the water."

He spoke with certainty, as if he saw the boat. Then, reluctantly, he dipped his oars in the lake, and rowed towards the house, keeping his head half turned and staring into the darkness with eyes that were still full of mystery and profound attention.

Lady Holme looked over the water too, but she saw nothing upon its calm surface.

"Go into the boat-house," she said.

Paolo nodded without speaking. His lips were parted.

"Chi e la?" she heard him whisper to himself.

They were close to the house now. Its high, pale front, full of shuttered windows, loomed over them, and the roar of the waterfall was loud in their ears. Paolo turned the boat towards his right, and, almost directly, Lady Holme saw a dark opening in the solid stone blocks on which the house was built. The boat glided through it into cover, and the arrow of light at the prow pierced ebon blackness, while the plash of the oars made a curious sound, full of sudden desolation and weariness. A bat flitted over the arrow of light and vanished, and the head of a swimming rat was visible for a moment, pursued by a wrinkle on the water.

"How dark it is here," Lady Holme said in a low voice. "And what strange noises there are."

There was terror in the sound of the waterfall heard under this curving roof of stone. It sounded like a quantity of disputing voices, quarrelling in the blackness of the night. The arrow of light lay on a step, and the boat's prow grated gently against a large ring of rusty iron.

"And you tie up the boat here at night?" she asked as she got up.

"Si, signora."

While she stood on the step, close to the black water, he passed the rope through the ring, and tied it deftly in a loose knot that any backward movement of the boat would tighten. She watched with profound attention his hands moving quickly in the faint light cast by the lantern.

"How well you tie it," she said.

He smiled.

"Si, signora."

"Is it easy to untie?"

"Si, signora."

"Show me, will you? It—it holds so well that I should have thought it would be difficult."

He looked up at her with a flash of surprise. Something in her voice had caught his young attention sharply. She smiled at him when she saw the keen inquiry in his large eyes.

"I'm interested in all these little things you do so well," she said.

He flushed with pride, and immediately untied the knot, carefully, showing her exactly how he did it.

"Thank you. I see. It's very ingenious."

"Si, signora. I can do many things like that."

"You are a clever boy, Paolo."

He tied the knot again, unhooked the lantern; jumped out of the boat, and lighted her up the staircase to a heavy wooden door. In another moment she stood on the piazza close to the waterfall. The cold spray from it fell on her face. He pushed the door to, but did not lock it.

"You leave it like that at night?" she asked.

"Non, signora. Before I go to bed I lock it."

"I see."

She saw a key sticking out from the door.

"*A rivederci*, Paolo."

"*A rivederci*, signora."

He took off his hat and went swiftly away. The light of the lantern danced on the pavement of the piazza, and, for one instant, on the white foam of the water falling between the cypresses.

When Viola was alone on the piazza she went to the stone balustrade and looked over it at the lake. Was there a boat close by? She could not see it. The chiming bells of the fishermen came up to her, mingling with the noise of the cascade. She took out her watch and held it up close to her eyes. The hour was half-past nine. She wondered what time Italian servants went to bed.

The butler came out and begged to know if she would not eat something. He seemed so distressed at her having missed dinner, that she went into the house, sat down at the dining table and made a pretence of eating. A clock struck ten as she finished.

"It is so warm that I am going to sit out in the piazza," she said.

"Will the signora take coffee?"

"No—yes, bring me some there. And tell my maid—tell the servants they needn't sit up. I may stay out quite late. If I do, I'll lock the door on to the piazza when I go in."

"Si, signora."

When she reached the piazza she saw a shining red spark just above the balustrade. Paolo was there smoking a black cigar and leaning over sideways.

"What are you looking for?" she asked.

"That boat, signora. It has not gone."

"How do you know? It may have gone when we were in the boat-house."

He shook his head.

"You could not have heard the oars through the noise of the waterfall."

"Si, signora. It has not gone. Shall I take the boat and—"

"No, no," she interrupted quickly. "What does it matter? Go and have supper."

"I have had it, signora."

"Then, when you have finished smoking, you'd better go to bed."

She forced herself to smile lightly.

"Boys like you need plenty of sleep."

"Four hours is enough, signora."

"No, no. You should go to bed early."

She saw an odd expression come into his face. He looked over at the water, then at her, with a curious dawning significance, that would almost have been impudent if it had not been immensely young and full of a kind of gnomish sympathy.

"I'll go to bed, signora!" he said.

Then he looked at her again and there were doubt and wonder in his eyes.

She turned away, with a sickness at her heart. She knew exactly what he had thought, was thinking. The suspicion had crossed his mind that she knew why the hidden boat was there, that she wished no one else to suspect why it was there. And then had followed the thought, "Ma—per questa signora—non e possibile."

At certain crises of feeling, a tiny incident will often determine some vital act. So it was now. The fleeting glance in a carelessly expressive boy's eyes at this moment gave to Lady Holme's mind the last touch it needed to acquire the impetus which would carry it over the edge of the precipice into the abyss. The look in Paolo's eyes said to her, "Life has done with you. Throw it away." And she knew that though she had thought she had already decided to throw it away that night, she had really not decided. Secretly she had been hesitating. Now there was no more hesitation in her. She drank her coffee and had the cup taken away, and ordered the lights in the drawing-room to be put out.

"When I come in I shall go straight up to bed," she said. "Leave me a candle in the hall."

The lights went out behind the windows. Blank darkness replaced the yellow gleam that had shone upon them. The two houses on either side of the piazza were wrapped in silence. Presently there was a soft noise of feet crossing the pavement. It was Paolo going to lock the door leading to the boathouse. Lady Holme moved round sharply in her chair to watch him. He bent down. With a swift turn of his brown wrists he secured the door and pulled the key out of the lock. She opened her lips to call out something to him, but when she saw him look at the key doubtfully, then towards her, she said nothing. And he put it back into the keyhole. When he did that she sighed. Perhaps a doubt had again come into his young mind. But, if so, it had come too late. He slipped away smiling, half ironically, to himself.

Lady Holme sat still. She had wrapped a white cloth cloak round her. She put up her hand to the disfigured side of her face, and touched it, trying to see its disfigurement as the blind see, by feeling. She kept her hand there, and her hand recognized ugliness vividly. After two or three minutes she took her hand away, got up and walked to and fro in the piazza, very near to the balustrade.

Now she was thinking fiercely.

She thought of Fritz. What would he feel when he knew? Shocked for a moment, no doubt. After all, they had been very close to each other, in body at least, if not in soul. And the memory of the body would surely cause him to suffer a little, to think, "I held it often, and now it is sodden and cold." At least he must think something like that, and his body must shudder in sympathy with the catastrophe that had overtaken its old companion. She felt a painful yearning to see Fritz again. Yet she did not say to herself that she loved him any more. Even before the accident she had begun to realise that she had not found in Fritz the face of truth among the crowd of shams which all women seek, ignorantly or not. And since the accident—there are things that kill even a woman's love abruptly. And for a dead love there is no resurrection.

Yet to-night she felt infinitely tender over Fritz, as if she stood by him again and saw the bandage darkened by the red stain.

Then she thought of the song she had sung to Lady Cardington, the song which had surely opened the eyes of her own drowsy, if not actually sleeping, heart:

"*Tutto al mondo e vano:*

Nell'amore ogni dolcezza."

It was horribly true to her to-night. She could imagine now, in her utter desolation, that for love a woman could easily sacrifice the world. But she had had the world—all she called the world—ruthlessly taken from her, and nothing had been given to her to fill its place. Possibly before the accident she might have recoiled from the idea of giving up the world for love. But now, as she walked to and fro, it seemed to her as if a woman isolated from everything with love possessed the world and all that is therein. Vaguely she remembered the story she had heard about this very house, Casa Felice. There had been a romance connected with it. Two lovers had fled here, had lived here for a long time. She imagined them now, sitting together at night in this piazza, hearing the waterfall together, looking at the calm lake together, watching the stars together. The sound of the water was terrible to her. To them how beautiful it must have been, how beautiful the light of the stars, and the lonely gardens stretching along the lake, and the dim paths between the cypresses, and the great silence that floated over the lake to listen to the waterfall. And all these things were terrible to her—all. Not one was beautiful. Each one seemed to threaten her, to say to her, "Leave us, we are not for such as you." Well, she would obey these voices. She would go. She wrapped the cloak more closely round her, went to the balustrade and leaned over it looking at the water.

It seemed to her as if her life had been very trivial. She thought now that she had never really enjoyed anything. She looked upon her life as if it were down there in the water just beneath her, and she saw it as a broken thing, a thing in many fragments. And the fragments, however carefully and deftly arranged, could surely never have been fitted together and become a complete whole. Everything in her life had been awry as her face was now awry, and she had not realised it. Her love for Fritz, and his— what he had called his, at least—for her, had seemed to her once to be a round and beautiful thing, a circle of passion without a flaw. How distorted, misshapen, absurd it had really been. Nothing in her life had been carried through to a definite end. Even her petty struggle with Miss Schley had been left unfinished. Those who had loved her had been like spectres, and now, like spectres, had faded away. And all through their spectral love she had clung to Fritz. She had clasped the sand like a mad-woman, and never felt the treacherous grains shifting between her arms at the touch of every wind.

A sudden passionate fury of longing woke in her to have one week, one day, one hour of life, one hour of life now that her eyes were open, one moment only—even one moment. She felt that she had had nothing, that every other human being must have known the *dolcezza*, the ineffable, the mysterious ecstasy, the one and only thing worth the having, that she alone had been excluded, when she was beautiful, from the participation in joy that was her right, and that now, in her ugliness, she was irrevocably cast out from it.

It was unjust. Suddenly she faced a God without justice in His heart, all-powerful and not just. She faced such a God and she knew Hell.

Swiftly she turned from the balustrade, went to the door by the waterfall, unlocked it and descended the stone staircase. It was very dark. She had to feel her way. When she reached the last step she could just see the boat lying against it in the black water. She put out her hand and felt for the ring through which the rope was slipped. The rope was wet. It took her some minutes to undo it. Then she got into the boat. Her eyes were more accustomed to the darkness now, and she could see the arched opening which gave access to the lake. She found the oars, pushed them into the rowlocks, and pulled gently to the opening. The boat struck against the wall and grated along it. She stood up and thrust one hand against the stone, leaning over to the side. The boat went away swiftly, and she nearly fell into the water, but managed to save herself by a rapid movement. She sank down, feeling horribly afraid. Yet, a moment after, she asked herself why she had not let herself go. It was too dark there under the house. Out in the open air it would be different, it would be easier. She wanted the stars above her. She did not know why she wanted them, why she wanted anything now.

The boat slipped out from the low archway into the open water.

It was a pale and delicate night, one of those autumn nights that are full of a white mystery. A thin mist lay about the water, floated among the lower woods. Higher up, the mountains rose out of it. Their green sides looked black and soft in the starlight, their summits strangely remote and inaccessible. Through the mist, here and there, shone faintly the lights of the scattered villages. The bells in the water were still ringing languidly, and their voices emphasised the pervading silence, a silence full of the pensive melancholy of Nature in decline.

Viola rowed slowly out towards the middle of the lake. Awe had come upon her. There seemed a mystical presence in the night, something far away but attentive, a mind concentrated upon the night, upon Nature, upon herself. She was very conscious of it, and it seemed to her not as if eyes, but as if a soul were watching her and everything about her; the stars and the mountains, the white mist, even the movement of the boat. This concentrated, mystical attention oppressed her. It was like a soft, impalpable weight laid upon her. She rowed faster.

But now it seemed to her as if she were being followed. Casa Felice had already disappeared. The shore was hidden in the darkness. She could only see vaguely the mountain-tops. She paused, then dipped the oars again, but again—after two or three strokes—she had the sensation that she was being followed. She recalled Paolo's action when they were returning to Casa Felice in the evening, leaned over the boat's side and put her ear close to the water.

When she did so she heard the plash of oars—rhythmical, steady, and surely very near. For a moment she listened. Then a sort of panic seized her. She remembered the incident of the evening, the hidden boat, Paolo's assertion that it was waiting near the house, that it had not gone. He had said, too, that the unseen rower had begun to row when he began to sing, had stopped rowing when he stopped singing. A conviction came to her that this same rower as now following her. But why? Who was it? She knew nobody on the lake, except Robin. And he—no, it could not be Robin.

The ash of the oars became more distinct. Her unreasoning fear increased. With the mystical attention of the great and hidden mind was now blent a crude human attention. She began to feel really terrified, and, seizing her oars, she pulled frantically towards the middle of the lake.

"Viola!"

Out of the darkness it came.

"Viola!"

She stopped and began to tremble. Who—what—could be calling her by name, here, in the night? She heard the sound of oars plainly now. Then she saw a thing like a black shadow. It was the prow of an advancing boat. She sat quite still, with her hands on the oars. The boat came on till she could see the figure of one man in it, standing up, and rowing, as the Italian boatmen do when they are alone, with his face set towards the prow. A few strong strokes and it was beside her, and she was looking into Rupert Carey's eyes.

CHAPTER XXI

SHE sat still without saying anything. It seemed to her as if she were on the platform at Manchester House singing the Italian song. Then the disfigured face of Carey—disfigured by vice as hers now by the accident—had become as nothing to her. She had seen only his eyes. She saw only his eyes now. He remained standing up in the faint light with the oars in his hands looking at her. Round about them tinkled the bells above the nets.

"You heard me call?" he said at last, almost roughly.

She nodded.

"How did you—?" she began, and stopped.

"I was there this evening when you came in. I heard your boy singing. I was under the shadow of the woods."

"Why?"

All this time she was gazing into Carey's eyes, and had not seen in them that he was looking, for the first time, at her altered face. She did not realise this. She did not remember that her face was altered. The expression in his eyes made her forget it.

"I wanted something of you."

"What?"

He let the oars go, and sat down on the little seat. They were close to each other now. The sides of the boats touched. He did not answer her question.

"I know I've no business to speak to you," he said. "No business to come after you. I know that. But I was always a selfish, violent, headlong brute, and it seems I can't change."

"But what do you want with me?"

Suddenly she remembered—put her hands up to her face with a swift gesture, then dropped them again. What did it matter now? He was the last man who would look upon her in life. And now that she remembered her own condition she saw his. She saw the terror of his life in his marred features, aged, brutalised by excess. She saw, and was glad for a moment, as if she met someone unexpectedly on her side of the stream of fate. Let him look upon her. She was looking upon him.

"What do you want?" she repeated.

"I want a saviour," he said, staring always straight at her, and speaking without tenderness.

"A saviour!"

For a moment she thought of the Bible, of religion; then of her sensation that she had been caught by a torturer who would not let her go.

"Have you come to me because you think I can tell you of saviour?" she said.

And she began to laugh.

"But don't you see me?" she exclaimed. "Don't you see what I am now?"

Suddenly she felt angry with him because his eyes did not seem to see the dreadful change in her appearance.

"Don't you think I want a saviour too?" she exclaimed.

"I don't think about you," he said with a sort of deliberate brutality. "I think about myself. Men generally do when they come to women."

"Or go away from them," she said.

She was thinking of Robin then, and Fritz.

"Did you know Robin Pierce was here to-day?" she asked.

"Yes. I saw him leave you."

"You saw—but how long have you been watching?"

"A long time."

"Where do you come from?"

He pointed towards the distant lights behind her and before him.

"Opposite. I was to have stayed with Ulford in Casa Felice. I'm staying with him over there."

"With Sir Donald?"

"Yes. He's ill. He wants somebody."

"Sir Donald's afraid of me now," she said, watching him closely. "I told him to live with his memory of me. Will he do that?"

"I think he will. Poor old chap! he's had hard knocks. They've made him afraid of life."

"Why didn't you keep your memory of me?" she said, with sudden nervous anger. "You too? If you hadn't come to-night it would never have been destroyed."

Her extreme tension of the nerves impelled her to an exhibition of fierce bitterness which she could not control. She remembered how he had loved her, with what violence and almost crazy frankness. Why had he come? He might have remembered her as she was.

"I hate you for coming," she said, almost under her breath.

"I don't care. I had to come."

"Why? Why?"

"I told you. I want a saviour. I'm down in the pit. I can't get out. You can see that for yourself."

"Yes," she answered, "I can see that."

"Give me a hand, Viola, and—you'll make me do something I've never done, never been able to do."

"What?" she half whispered.

"Believe there's a God—who cares."

She drew in her breath sharply. Something warm surged through her. It was not like fire. It was more like the warmth that comes from a warm hand laid on a cold one. It surged through her and went away like a travelling flood.

"What are you saying?" she said in a low voice. "You are mad to come here to-night, to say this to me to-night."

"No. It's just to-night it had to be said."

Suddenly she resolved to tell him. He was in the pit. So was she. Well, the condemned can be frank with one another though all the free have to practise subterfuge.

"You don't know," she said, and her voice was quiet now. "You don't know why it was mad of you to come to-night. I'll tell you. I've come out here and I'm not going back again."

He kept his eyes on hers, but did not speak.

"I'm going to stay out here," she said.

And she let her hand fall over the side of the boat till her fingers touched the water.

"No," he said. "You can't do that."

"Yes. I shall do it. I want to hide my face in the water."

"Give me a hand first, Viola."

Again the warmth went through her.

"Nobody else can."

"And you've looked at me!" she said.

There was a profound amazement in her voice.

"It's only when I look at you," he said, "that I know there are stars somewhere beyond the pit's mouth."

"When you look at me—now?"

"Yes."

"But you are blind then?" she said.

"Or are the others blind?" he asked.

Instinctively, really without knowing what she did, she put up her hand to her face, touched it, and no longer felt that it was ugly. For a moment it seemed to her that her beauty was restored.

"What do you see?" she asked. "But—but it's so dark here."

"Not too dark to see a helping hand—if there is one," he answered.

And he stretched out his arm into her boat and took her right hand from the oar it was holding.

"And there is one," he added.

She felt a hand that loved her hand, and there was no veil over her face. How strange that was. How utterly impossible it seemed. Yet it was so. No woman can be deceived in the touch of a hand on hers. If it loves—she knows.

"What are you going to do, Viola?"

"I don't know."

There was a sound almost of shame, a humble sound, in her voice.

"I can't do anything," she murmured. "You would know that to-morrow, in sunlight."

"To-morrow I'll come in sunlight."

"No, no. I shall not be there."

"I shall come."

"Oh!—good-night," she said.

She began to feel extraordinarily, terribly excited. She could not tell whether it was an excitement of horror, of joy—what it was. But it mounted to her brain and rushed into her heart. It was in her veins like an intoxicant, and in her eyes like fire, and thrilled in her nerves and beat in her arteries. And it seemed to be an excitement full of passionate contradictions. She was at the same time like a woman on a throne and a woman in the dust— radiant as one worshipped, bowed as one beaten.

"Good-night, good-night," she repeated, scarcely knowing what she said.

Her hand struggled in his hand.

"Viola, if you destroy yourself you destroy two people."

She scarcely heard him speaking.

"D'you understand?"

"No, no. Not to-night. I can't understand anything to-night."

"Then to-morrow."

"Yes, to-morrow-to-morrow."

He would not let go her hand, and now his was arbitrary, the hand of a master rather than of a lover.

"You won't dare to murder me," he said.

"Murder—what do you mean?"

He had used the word to arrest her attention, which was wandering almost as the attention of a madwoman wanders.

"If you hide your face in the water I shall never see those stars above the pit's mouth."

"I can't help it—I can't help anything. It's not my fault, it's not my fault."

"It will be your fault. It will be your crime."

"Your hand is driving me mad," she gasped.

She meant it, felt that it was so. He let her go instantly. She began to row back towards Casa Felice. And now that mystical attention of which she had been conscious, that soul watching the night, her in the night, was surely profounder, watched with more intensity as a spectator bending down to see a struggle. Never before had she felt as if beyond human life there was life compared with which human life was as death. And now she told herself that she was mad, that this shock of human passion coming suddenly upon her loneliness had harmed her brain, that this cry for salvation addressed to one who looked upon herself as destroyed had deafened reason within her.

His boat kept up with hers. She did not look at him. Casa Felice came in sight. She pulled harder, like a mad creature. Her boat shot under the archway into the darkness. Somehow—how, she did not know—she guided it to the steps, left it, rushed up the staircase in the dark and came out on to the piazza. There she stopped where the waterfall could cast its spray upon her face. She stayed till her hair and cheeks and hands were wet. Then she went to the balustrade. His boat was below and he was looking up. She saw the tragic mask of his face down in the thin mist that floated about the water, and now she imagined him in the pit, gazing up and seeking those stars in which he still believed though he could not see them.

"Go away," she said, not knowing why she said it or if she wished him to go, only knowing that she had lost the faculty of self-control and might say, do, be anything in that moment.

"I can't bear it."

She did not know what she meant she could not bear.

He made a strange answer. He said:

"If you will go into the house, open the windows and sing to me—the last song I heard you sing—I'll go. But to-morrow I'll come and touch my helping hand, and after to-morrow, and every day."

"Sing—?" she said vacantly. "To-night!"

"Go into the house. Open the window. I shall hear you."

He spoke almost sternly.

She crossed the piazza slowly. A candle was burning in the hall. She took it up and went into the drawing-room, which was in black darkness. There was a piano in it, close to a tall window which looked on to the lake. She set the candle down on the piano, went to the window, unbarred the shutters and threw the window open. Instantly she heard the sound of oars as Carey sent his boat towards the water beneath the window. She drew back, went again to the piano, sat down, opened it, put her hands on the keys. How could she sing? But she must make him go away. While he was there she could not think, could not grip herself, could not—She struck a chord. The sound of music, the doing of a familiar action, had a strange effect upon her. She felt as if she recovered clear consciousness after an anaesthetic. She struck another chord. What did he want? The concert—that song. Her fingers found the prelude, her lips the poetry, her voice the music. And then suddenly her heart found the meaning, more than the meaning, the eternal meanings of the things unutterable, the things that lie beyond the world in the deep souls of the women who are the saviours of men.

When she had finished she went to the window. He was still standing in the boat and looking up, with the whiteness of the mist about him.

"When you sing I can see those stars," he said. "Do you understand?"

She bent down.

"I don't know—I don't think I understand anything," she whispered. "But—I'll try—I'll try to live."

Her voice was so faint, such an inward voice, that it seemed impossible he could have heard it. But he struck the oars at once into the water and sent the boat out into the shadows of the night.

And she stood there looking into the white silence, which was broken only by the faint voices of the fishermen's bells, and said to herself again and again, like a wondering child:

"There must be a God, there must be; a God who cares!"

EPILOGUE

IN London during the ensuing winter people warmly discussed, and many of them warmly condemned, a certain Italian episode, in which a woman and a man, once well-known and, in their very different ways, widely popular in Society, were the actors.

In the deep autumn Sir Donald Ulford had died rather suddenly, and it was found in his will that he had left his newly-acquired property, Casa Felice, to Lady Holme, who—as everybody had long ago discovered—was already living there in strict retirement, while her husband was amusing himself in various Continental towns. This legacy was considered by a great number of persons to be "a very strange one;" but it was not this which caused the gossip now flitting from boudoir to boudoir and from club to club.

It had become known that Rupert Carey, whose unfortunate vice had been common talk ever since the Arkell House ball, was a perpetual visitor to Casa Felice, and presently it was whispered that he was actually living there with Lady Holme, and that Lord Holme was going to apply to the Courts for a divorce. Thereupon many successful ladies began to wag bitter tongues. It seemed to be generally agreed that the affair was rendered peculiarly disgraceful by the fact that Lady Holme was no longer a beautiful woman. If she had still been lovely they could have understood it! The wildest rumours as to the terrible result of the accident upon her had been afloat, and already she had become almost a legend. It was stated that when poor Lord Holme had first seen her, after the operation, the shock had nearly turned his brain. And now it was argued that the only decent thing for a woman in such a plight to do was to preserve at least her dignity, and to retire modestly from the fray in which she could no longer hope to hold her own. That she had indeed retired, but apparently with a man, roused much pious scorn and pinched regret in those whose lives were passed amid the crash of broken commandments.

One day, at a tea, a certain lady, animadverted strongly upon Lady Holme's conduct, and finally remarked:

"It's grotesque! A woman who is disfigured, and a man who is, or at any rate was, a drunkard! Really it's the most disgusting thing I ever heard of!"

Lady Cardington happened to be in the room and she suddenly flushed.

"I don't think we know very much about it," she said, and her voice was rather louder than usual.

"But Lord Holme is going to—" began the lady who had been speaking.

"He may be, and he may succeed. But my sympathies are not with him. He left his wife when she needed him."

"But what could he have done for her?"

"He could have loved her," said Lady Cardington.

The flush glowed hotter in the face that was generally as white as ivory.

There was a moment of silence in the room. Then Lady Cardington, getting up to go, added:

"Whatever happens, I shall admire Mr. Carey as long as I live, and I wish there were many more men like him in the world."

She went out, leaving a tense astonishment behind her.

Her romantic heart, still young and ardent, though often aching with sorrow, and always yearning for the ideal love that it had never found, had divined the truth these chattering women had not imagination enough to conceive of, soul enough to appreciate if they had conceived of it.

In that Italian winter, far away from London, a very beautiful drama of human life was being enacted, not the less but the more beautiful because the man and woman who took part in it had been scourged by fate, had suffered cruel losses, were in the eyes of many who had known them well pariahs—Rupert Carey through his fault, Lady Holme through her misfortune.

Long ago, at the Arkell House ball, Lady Holme had said to Robin Pierce that if Rupert Carey had the chance she could imagine him doing something great. The chance was given him now of doing one of the greatest things a human being can do—of winning a soul that is in despair back to hope, of winning a heart that is sceptical of love back to belief in love. It was a great thing to do, and Carey set about doing it in a strange way. He cast himself down in his degradation at the feet of this woman whom he was resolved to help, and he said, "Help me!" He came to this woman who was on the brink of self-destruction and he said, "Teach me to live!"

It was a strange way he took, but perhaps he was right—perhaps it was the only way. The words he spoke at midnight on the lake were as nothing. His eyes, his acts in sunlight the next day, and day after day, were everything. He forced Viola to realise that she was indeed the only woman who could save him from the vice he had become the slave of, lift him up out of that pit in which he could not see the stars. At first she could not believe it, or could believe it only in moments of exaltation. Lord Holme and Robin Pierce had rendered her terrified of life and of herself in life. She was inclined to cringe before all humanity like a beaten dog. There were moments, many moments at first, when she cringed before Rupert Carey. But his eyes always told her the same story. They never saw the marred face, but always the white angel. The soul in them clung to that, asked to be protected by that. And so, at last, the white angel—one hides somewhere surely in every woman—was released.

There were sad, horrible moments in this drama of the Italian winter. The lonely house in the woods was a witness to painful, even tragic, scenes. Viola's love for Rupert Carey was reluctant in its dawning and he could not rise at once, or easily, out of the pit into the full starlight to which he aspired. After the death of Sir Donald, when the winter set in, he asked her to let him live in the house on the opposite side of the piazza from the house in which she dwelt. They were people of the world, and knew what the world might say, but they were also human beings in distress, and they felt as if they had passed into a region in which the meaning of the world's voices was lost, as the cry of an angry child is lost in the vastness of the desert. She agreed to his request, and they lived thus, innocently, till the winter was over and the spring came to bring to Italy its radiance once more.

Even the spring was not an idyll. Rupert Carey had struggled upward, but Viola, too, had much to forget and very much to learn. The egoist, spoken of by Carey himself one night in Half Moon Street, was slow to fade in the growing radiance that played about the angel's feet. But it knew, and

Carey knew also, that it was no longer fine enough in its brilliant selfishness to stand quite alone. With the death of the physical beauty there came a modesty of heart. With the understanding, bitter and terrible as it was, that the great, conquering outward thing was destroyed, came the desire, the imperious need, to find and to develop if possible the inner things which, perhaps, conquer less easily, but which retain their conquests to the end. There was growth in Casa Felice, slow but stubborn, growth in the secret places of the soul, till there came a time when not merely the white angel, but the whole woman, angel and that which had perhaps been devil too, was able to accept the yoke laid upon her with patience, was able to say, "I can endure it bravely."

Lord Holme presently took his case to the Courts. It was undefended and he won it. Not long ago Viola Holme became Viola Carey.

When Robin Pierce heard of it in Rome he sat for a long time in deep thought. Even now, even after all that had passed, he felt a thrill of pain that was like the pain of jealousy. He wished for the impossible, he wished that he had been born with his friend's nature; that, instead of the man who could only talk of being, he were the man who could be. And yet, in the past, he had sometimes surely defended Viola against Carey's seeming condemnation! He had defended and not loved—but Carey had judged and loved.

Carey had judged and loved, yet Carey had said he did not believe in a God. Robin wondered if he believed now.

Robin was in Rome, and could not hear the words of a man and a woman who were sitting one night, after the marriage, upon a piazza above the Lake of Como.

The man said:

"Do you remember Robin's '*Danseuse de Tunisie*'?"

"The woman with the fan?"

"Yes. I see her now without the fan. With it she was a siren, perhaps, but without it she is—"

"What is she without it?"

"Eternal woman. Ah, how much better than the siren!"

There was a silence filled only by the voice of the waterfall between the cypresses. Then the woman spoke, rather softly.

"You taught her what she could be without the fan. You have done the great thing."

"And do you know what you have done?"

"I?"

"Yes. You have taught me to see the stars and to feel the soul beyond the stars."

"No, it was not I."

Again there was a silence. Then the man said:

"No, thank God—it was not you."